The Scorpion

Gerri Hill

Bella
BOOKS

2009

Bella Books, Inc.
P.O. Box 10543
Tallahassee, FL 32302

Printed in the United States of America on acid-free paper

First Edition Bella Books 2009

Cover Design: Stephanie Solomon-Lopez
Editor: Medora MacDougall

ISBN-10: 1-59493-162-3
ISBN-13: 978-1-59493-162-8

About the Author

Gerri Hill has sixteen published works, including 2009
GCLS winner *Partners* and 2007 GCLS winners *Behind the Pine
Curtain* and *The Killing Room*, as well as GCLS finalist *Hunter's
Way* and Lambda finalist *In the Name of the Father*. She began
writing lesbian romance as a way to amuse herself while snowed
in one winter in the mountains of Colorado and hasn't looked
back. Her first published work came in 2000 with *One Summer
Night*. Hill's love of nature and of being outdoors usually makes
its way into her stories as her characters often find themselves
in beautiful natural settings. When she isn't writing, Hill and
her longtime partner, Diane, can be found at their home in East
Texas, where their vegetable garden, orchard and five acres of
piney woods keep them busy. They share their lives with two
Australian shepherds and an assortment of furry felines. For
more, see her Web site: www.gerrihill.com.

CHAPTER ONE

Bailey sat in her car, trying to shake the profound sadness that always gripped her when she visited her mother. She clenched her jaw. No, not her mother. Only the shell of her mother. Her mother had slipped away months ago when Alzheimer's claimed her at a relatively young age.

She allowed her thoughts to drift back over happier times, snapshots of her life flashing through her mind—her high school graduation and them arguing over the dress her mother insisted she wear, her brief two years in college and them arguing over her acceptance into the police academy, the smiles and tight hugs from her mother and dad when she graduated, her brother's wedding day and another argument over the dress. She laughed quietly as she remembered the tuxedo she'd rented only to have her mother put a firm foot down and issue a warning, "over my dead body." So they compromised. The god-awful flowery dress her mother had picked out was replaced with a sleek black pantsuit, one that her mother conceded looked "very attractive" on her. Turned out it didn't matter. Kevin's marriage lasted all of six months, and the four of them ended up going to the beach house to celebrate the divorce. But the happy times waned as the disease took over, leaving less and less of her mother behind. It had been nearly ten months since her mother even recognized her. Six months since she'd spoken a word. And now, as the doctor said, there was nothing to do but wait.

She took a deep breath, then started the car, glancing once over her shoulder to the care facility her mother had been in for the last year, ever since Bailey could no longer care for her herself. As always when she left here, she had to fight the guilt that tried to settle on her heart. She'd done the best she could: she knew that. But still...

CHAPTER TWO

Marty smoothed her slacks as she waited. She was ten minutes early for her appointment with the city attorney, James Garza, and she glanced at her reflection in the mirror, wishing she'd chosen the more businesslike skirt in her luggage instead of the beige slacks she'd slipped on that morning. She always tried to blend in, wearing something conservative and neutral, nothing to call attention to herself. She'd learned long ago to melt into her surroundings. And here in Brownsville, in the Rio Grande Valley at the tip of Texas, she suspected professional women were still the minority.

"Miss Edwards? He'll see you now."

Marty smiled and nodded, following the receptionist down a carpeted hallway. She was motioned inside a large office, the drapes pulled wide to allow in the morning sun. The city attorney was much younger than she would have imagined, and she stuck her hand out in greeting, flashing what she hoped was a charming smile.

"Mr. Garza, thank you so much for seeing me."

"Of course, Mrs. Edwards. Please have a seat."

"Miss Edwards," she corrected, "but please call me Marty." She settled in the plush visitor's chair and crossed her legs, again wishing she'd worn a skirt, albeit, for a completely different reason. He wasn't wearing a wedding ring, and she was not afraid to flirt shamelessly to get what she wanted. "And I won't take up too much of your time. I know you must be extremely busy."

He nodded politely. "I understand you are a writer," he said.

She shook her head. "Journalist. Big difference," she said with a grin. "I found that out the hard way."

"I apologize. I have not had the pleasure of reading your book."

"Oh, please don't apologize. True crime stories don't normally make the top of the bestsellers list. Mine certainly didn't." She leaned forward slightly, pleased when his eyes found her cleavage. "Some police departments are extremely wary when a civilian wants a look at a cold case. Especially when that civilian is a journalist." She tucked her blond hair behind her ears and met his eyes. "I've found it best to get permission first." She smiled again. "That's why I'm here."

"You're doing another book on cold cases?"

"Eventually, yes. Only five cases made it into the first book. Five of probably twenty I researched."

"What brings you down to Brownsville? You're from Atlanta, correct?"

"I've been in Atlanta since college, but my research takes me all over." She handed him a piece of paper. "The case I'm interested in is a decade old. Carlos Romero. I was contacted by his sister. She read in my book where another ten-year-old case was reopened. With success. She thought I might want to include her brother's story in my next book."

James Garza folded his hands together and watched her. "I don't have a problem with granting access to old case files, Miss

Edwards—Marty," he said. "Especially one that is ten years old. I actually came here from Phoenix a couple of years ago, and it was quite common for cold cases to be revisited there. Although here in Brownsville, as small as we are, I can't imagine there being many unsolved murders."

"Phoenix? What a coincidence. I'm heading there next," she lied. "Perhaps you have a contact I could get in touch with?"

"Of course." He reached for his business card and flipped it over, jotting down the information for her. "Ray Conaway is who you need to see," he said as he handed her the card. "He'll take care of you."

"Mr. Garza, I appreciate that. I hope you don't mind if I tell him you sent me."

"Please, by all means. And call me James."

"Excellent," she said, feeling that her face would break from the constant smiling she was doing. "Now, I've taken up enough of your time. What can I give to the police department to access the file?"

"In Phoenix, we had an actual authorization form." He reached for the phone, asking his secretary to join them. "My guess is, we have no such thing here. I'll have Lucila draft one up for you."

She stood and again reached her hand out. "You've been very accommodating, James. Thank you so much."

"It's my pleasure to meet you, Marty." He paused. "If you're going to be in town long, perhaps you would allow me to take you to dinner one night."

"Absolutely." As always, she hated this part of the game. But again, she smiled brightly, as if she couldn't wait for them to meet up for dinner. "If you'll allow me to get settled," she said, glancing at his card, "I'll call you later in the week."

"I look forward to it."

Ten minutes later, with her authorization letter tucked into her laptop bag, she walked down the steps of City Hall, the bright sunshine warm on this April day. Her normal routine was to head

5

over to the police station immediately, and she didn't plan to veer from that today, despite the enticing smells coming from the many local restaurants lining Market Square. She took a deep breath, inhaling the aroma of fresh Mexican food, knowing she didn't have the luxury of lunch. She was anxious to get started.

CHAPTER THREE

"A ten-year-old cold case?" He shook his head. "Waste of time, ma'am."

Marty followed the uniformed police officer down the corridor to the old file room. He flipped on the light, the dusty fluorescent bulbs casting a yellowish glow over the rows and rows of neatly stacked boxes, all containing the physical evidence of thousands of cases.

"Well, I have a lot of time to waste," she said, glancing at the boxes as they walked past. "How many years do you keep in here?"

"A lot," he said absently as he slowed, his hands pointing at each box as if counting. "Here we are. Let's see... Case file #389044. Carlos Romero." He looked up quickly. "That's one of Lieutenant Marsh's cases. Have you cleared this with him?"

She shook her head and held up the letter from James Garza. "The city attorney, Mr. Garza, has given me permission.

Remember?"

"Yeah, I know that, but I think we should still run it by the lieutenant."

"Fine," she said curtly, watching as he moved away and pulled out his cell phone. She thought it odd that he wasn't using the radio clipped to his belt, but she'd found that all police departments did things differently. She shifted slightly, feigning interest in other file boxes, trying unsuccessfully to listen to his muted conversation.

"He wants to see you first."

Marty let out a heavy sigh. "And he'll be right over?"

"No, ma'am. You're to report to him."

"Look, Officer, is this really necessary? It's a ten-year-old case," she said, pointing to it. "Look at the evidence marker. It hasn't been opened since," she looked closer, "two months after his murder. What's the big deal?"

"Not my call, ma'am. Head upstairs, third floor. Ask for Lieutenant Marsh."

"Fine," she said again, her tone anything but fine. Police departments, as a rule, were usually very accommodating to her. But there were always those few, apparently like Lieutenant Marsh, who were possessive and overprotective of their files, even those cases that were ten years old. Just the fact that the evidence box hadn't been opened since two months after the murder told her that no one in the department had given the case a thought since. Which also led her to believe Kesara Romero, the victim's sister, when she said the police hardly questioned or interviewed anyone; they had simply closed the case and called it a gang killing.

She stepped off the elevator on the third floor, finding herself in a narrow hallway facing swinging double doors. She heard papers being rustled and glanced to her right, finding someone who she guessed was a receptionist. The older Hispanic woman smiled warmly at her.

"May I help you?"

"I'm looking for Lieutenant Marsh," she said. She walked closer and returned her smile. "I'm Marty Edwards. I was supposed to ask for him here."

The woman nodded and picked up the phone, announcing her. The call ended quickly. "Go into the squad room. Turn left. His office is the second one."

"Thank you."

The squad room was relatively quiet, only a handful of people, mostly men, talked in hushed tones. Again, it seemed odd, but she reminded herself that this wasn't a large bustling city. Brownsville was home to less than two hundred thousand souls.

She knocked lightly on the closed door, watching as the two men inside ended their animated conversation and motioned to her to enter. She had a feeling her charm and wit wouldn't get her as far with these two as they had with James Garza. But she put on her game face anyway, smiling brightly in what she hoped was a non-threatening, friendly way.

"I'm Marty Edwards," she said quickly, holding her hand out to the man standing just inside the room.

"Captain Diaz," he said with a slight nod.

"Pleasure to meet you, Captain." She turned to the man still sitting behind the desk, his face showing his annoyance. She ignored the blatant look of displeasure and held her hand out to him anyway. "You must be Lieutenant Marsh then," she said.

He snubbed her outstretched hand and motioned to the chair instead. "I'm curious as to why you're interested in this particular case."

She didn't acknowledge his rudeness and said evenly, "Nice to meet you, Lieutenant." She sat down, glancing at Captain Diaz as he did the same. "I'm a journalist by trade. From Atlanta," she added. "I'm interested in cold cases. I've researched them all across the country."

"And wrote a book about them, I understand."

"More and more police departments are actively working

their cold cases," she said. "Several actually have Web sites dedicated to them, asking for help from the public to solve them." She hesitated, wondering how much of the information the sister gave her she should divulge to him. She decided none. Her instincts told her this man didn't want her near his case files. "I ran across this case while researching another gang-related killing," she lied. "Gang-related killings are the hardest to prosecute, I'm told." He seemed to relax a bit, and she was glad she hadn't mentioned Kesara Romero.

"So your next book is about gang killings then?" he asked.

"Yes," she said immediately. "Not to say that I'll even use this particular case in the book. In my first book, only five cases made the cut after I started with well over twenty." Again, she offered a charming smile, hoping he couldn't tell she was lying through her teeth.

"Even so, the captain and I are quite disappointed that Mr. Garza would agree to this without consulting the police. But then, he is new here," he said dismissively.

"Oh? I thought he told me he'd been here a couple of years."

"Exactly my point," he said, the quick smile he flashed not reaching his eyes.

"I guess I don't understand your qualms about allowing me access to the file, Lieutenant. It's ten years old. It wasn't classified as a sensitive case and sealed by a judge. I don't imagine there was controversy surrounding it, was there?" She laughed quietly. "But I doubt you would remember that. It's been so long ago."

"You're right. The case doesn't ring a bell." He looked at Captain Diaz, who had been quiet during the exchange. "Are you okay with allowing her access, Captain?"

"I don't see a problem with it, if you're agreeable," he said. "With security, of course."

"Security?" she asked.

"I'll have someone assigned to you," Lieutenant Marsh said. "You won't be allowed to photocopy anything, and obviously you won't be allowed to remove anything from the file."

Great. A babysitter. But she wasn't in any position to argue. "That's fine, Lieutenant. I appreciate that. I should be out of your hair in a couple of days." She stood, this time not bothering with a handshake. "May I start today?"

"In the morning," he said. "And you won't have unlimited access. I'll give you one hour each day."

She nodded, wondering why he felt the need to make this as difficult as possible for her. But again, she ignored his condescending attitude and plastered a smile to her face. "Thank you. I'll be by first thing."

She walked out, feeling their eyes on her. She had a feeling her stay in Brownsville was going to be anything but routine.

CHAPTER FOUR

Bailey waited patiently in front of Lieutenant Marsh's desk as he totally ignored her. She hated when he did this—summoning her to his office only to make her wait while he finished whatever task he was on. It was his way of reminding her she was his subordinate, as if she needed reminding. She kept the same bored expression on her face that she'd sported for the last two years, knowing it pissed him off.

"I have an assignment for you," he finally said without looking up.

Yes, something else she hated. She was given assignments, not cases. Her face was expressionless when he glanced up at her.

"We've got a nosy reporter hanging around. I need you to monitor her, Bailey. She's going to be looking at an old case, doing a little snooping, I imagine. Sit with her in the interrogation room, make sure she doesn't do anything improper. I've given her access to the files for one hour each day. Got it?"

"Isn't this something a desk jockey could do, Lieutenant? Instead of a detective?"

"*Detective*?" His laugh was cold. "No, *Detective* Bailey, I want you to do it. Is there a problem with that?"

"It's the same problem I always have. You give me *assignments*. Menial tasks. I'm a detective, yet I'm not allowed to do my job. That's my problem."

He stood up and faced her, his stare piercing, but she refused to blink, refused to take a step back.

"You want to know why? Because you're not one of us, Bailey. You're an outsider from Houston. You've got to earn your stripes here," he said. "I don't care what you did in Houston. I don't care how many commendations or medals you got. I don't care if your captain down there is friends with the chief here. I don't care that they pulled some strings and moved you in as detective when a lot of good men were passed over. I don't care about those things, Bailey." He paused. "You want to know why I don't care? Because I don't know you. And I don't like you. Therefore, I don't trust you." He sat down again. "My concern right now is this damn reporter nosing into a cold case. And that goddamn city attorney giving her written permission without consulting me—*that* concerns me as well."

Bailey wasn't in a position to question his concerns, and frankly, she didn't care. But reporters looking at cold cases... well, that happened all the time in Houston. Anything that helped shed light on the case was helpful, because in the end, it was all about solving the crime. But she kept her mouth shut, waiting to be dismissed.

"She'll be here this morning. I've arranged for her to be in the interrogation room. Please make sure the evidence box is sealed again properly after she's done."

Bailey nodded, taking that as her dismissal. He stopped her before she walked out.

"Oh, and Bailey, if there's anything suspicious about her, if she starts asking a lot of questions, you'll let me know, right?"

"Of course."

She left him, feeling as frustrated today as she had two years ago when she'd first transferred to Brownsville. *Yep, Lieutenant, you'll be the first one I tell if she's asking questions.* "You can count on me," she murmured to herself.

"Detective Bailey?"

Bailey turned, seeing Mrs. Jimenez coming toward her. "Good morning, Rosaline."

"*Buenos dias*, Kristen," she said. "The lieutenant said to let you know when the reporter got here."

Bailey nodded. "What about the evidence box?"

"Yes, I sent word down to Officer Reyes. He'll bring it up."

"Thank you. Lieutenant Marsh said to put it in the interrogation room."

"*Sí.* I take her there now, yes?"

"Yes, please. I'll be there in a minute."

Bailey stopped by her desk—her extremely clean and tidy desk—and picked up her coffee mug.

"What's up, Bailey? Saw you in the lieutenant's office."

Bailey glanced at Marcos, her so-called partner. "Oh, just more exciting detective work for me," she said. "I'm keeping a reporter company."

He nodded. "I heard. Some cold case, right?"

"Yeah. How did you know? He didn't tell me much about it."

"Oh, you know. Word spreads," he said.

She filled her coffee cup, ignoring the others in the squad room. They all treated her the same way. As an outsider. Marcos treated her a little better than the rest, if only because technically, they were partners. It wasn't like they worked cases together. At least not in the field. Her job was usually phone work while he did the *real* police work. At first, she thought it was because she was a woman and they weren't used to working with women. But after a few months, she realized it was because she wasn't from there, she wasn't a native, and she didn't work her way up through the system. She was an outsider with connections. And so they didn't trust her, and they weren't going to let her inside their

14

little team. Even after two years. It didn't matter that she put her time in at Houston P.D. It didn't matter that she had a bullet wound to prove it. It didn't matter how many commendations she came with. They weren't going to let her in. After a while, her response was to ignore them and go about her business, knowing she was just biding her time until she could leave here. Maybe go back to Houston. She missed the challenges there, she missed the camaraderie of the guys. They were a tight unit. They were a team. A good team. And they would welcome her back, she knew.

"How long have you been here, Marcos?"

"A long time, Bailey. Why?"

"I'm wondering how long I have to be here before you guys start treating me like a cop," she said.

"I think that's a beef to take up with Marsh. Everyone sees how he treats you and just follows his lead."

"What are you? In your forties? Why are you still a detective?"

Marcos laughed. "I like it. I don't aspire to be a sergeant or a lieutenant. Too much bullshit."

"You were military, right?"

"Army, yeah. Just four years. When I got out, I joined the force. I was twenty-three and tough as they come." He laughed. "Or so I thought." The smile left his face. "Stick with it, Bailey. Marsh can't ride your ass forever."

She blew out a heavy sigh and nodded, then made her way down the hall to the interrogation room. Reyes was just bringing the evidence box up on a cart, and she held the door open for him.

"Call me when you're done and I'll come back for it."

Bailey nodded and followed him inside. The reporter was younger than she'd expected, blond hair layered around her face framing her expressive hazel eyes. She returned the smile of the other woman and shook her hand.

* * *

15

"I'm Marty Edwards," she said, offering her hand and flashing her practiced smile.

"Detective Bailey."

"Oh, my. Your lieutenant must *really* be concerned with me if he's pulling a detective in to babysit," she teased, hoping the detective had a sense of humor. The smile faded from her face at Marty's words.

"My babysitting duties have little to do with you and everything to do with me." She pointed at the box. "Shall we?"

Ah. So the detective was in the doghouse for something. Not wanting to question her statement, she nodded. "Yes, let's get started. I assume you'll want to break the evidence seal?"

Marty pulled out her legal-sized notepad and the mechanical pencil she hardly ever used. She glanced up as the detective sliced open the seal with the small paper cutter the officer had left. All of the notes she'd made were on her laptop and she wished she'd had the foresight to print them out. At least the questions she'd come up with. Because there was only one reason she was in the interrogation room. She was being monitored. Anything she said would be recorded, and she had no doubt that the cameras would zoom in on her laptop screen should she open it. She thought it ironic at how paranoid she was being just because she thought Lieutenant Marsh was paranoid enough to bug the room in the first place.

"Here you are."

"Thank you, Detective Bailey. I'm sorry you have to sit in here with me. I'm sure it'll be terribly boring for you."

"I'll try to stay out of your way." The detective pulled out a chair at the other end of the table. "Do you want any coffee or anything?"

"No, thanks," Marty said, holding up her water bottle. "I learned long ago that coffee in squad rooms was brutal."

"That's true." She pointed beside the box. "There's a pair of latex gloves there, if you plan to handle the evidence."

Marty nodded. She knew the routine. She pulled the

16

evidence box closer and peered inside. There wasn't a whole lot to it. Two folders. One, the medical examiner's report. The other contained the reports and witness questionnaires from the police. She set them aside for now and slipped on the gloves before taking out the plastic bag. Inside were bloody clothes, the ones Carlos was wearing when they found him. They appeared to be a newer pair of jeans and a button-down blue shirt. Not something she would imagine a gang member wearing. Another bag contained personal items—a watch, a wallet and a chain with a religious medallion on it. All three were coated with dried blood. She carefully opened up the wallet, seeing a handsome young man smiling back at her. His driver's license. There were a few bills—nineteen dollars in all—and a creased family photo. She recognized Carlos and assumed the younger girl beside him was his sister, Kesara Romero. The others most likely were his parents and older siblings. Again, nothing about the wallet screamed "gang member." The only other item in the box was in a separate bag—a glass paperweight with a scorpion encased inside it. She turned it around in her hands, noting that the felt fabric on the back of it was soaked in blood, now long dried.

She put everything back into the box and took her gloves off, wanting to make notes of all she found before reading through the reports. She held the pad protectively in front of her, using some of the shorthand she'd developed years ago. If her suspicions were true and she was being taped, she doubted the camera would be able to pick up her scribble. Her handwriting was atrocious, and even she had a hard time deciphering it.

"A reporter who uses a legal pad instead of a laptop. I didn't think those existed any longer."

Marty looked over at the detective. "I prefer the old-fashioned way," she said. Then she followed the detective's gaze to her bag, which, it was blatantly obvious, held a laptop. She met the woman's eyes, wondering if she would say anything. She didn't.

After making notes of everything in the evidence bags, she picked up the medical examiner's file and flipped through it, glancing over the medical jargon. She would read it more thoroughly tomorrow. Today, she just wanted to get a feel for things and her hour limit was fast approaching. She jotted down some medical terms she wanted to clarify, then slowed her reading when she found the passage she was looking for. As Kesara had said, her brother had been mutilated. His eyes had been gouged out, his tongue removed, and his abdomen split open the length of his torso. His skull had been smashed. No wonder everything was soaked in blood. Cause of death—"blunt force trauma." A nice way of saying he'd been butchered, Marty thought. The eyes and tongue were removed antemortem.

"Jesus," she whispered. She glanced at the detective, finding her watching. She closed the file quickly and picked up the police reports. They were very generic, almost as if the detectives were going through the motions. And most likely they were. Gang killings, especially when the police thought both victim and perpetrator were involved, seldom got a thorough investigation.

She wrote down the names of the persons interviewed, already knowing who they were from Kesara. The police had spoken to the mother, the sister, a high school teacher and a supposed friend. She read through the brief account of what the mother, sister and teacher had said. Each was very similar. Good kid, good grades. Never involved with a gang. The friend—or "alleged" friend, since Kesara had told her none of the family had ever heard of this boy before—is the one who said Carlos was a gang member and that he was on his way to meet them that night. A rival gang had intercepted him. She stared at the writing at the end of the file: "No witnesses. No suspects. Gang-related." And stamped across that in bold letters, "UNSOLVED." She flipped through the pages again, surprised that there were no photos of the crime scene. She picked up the medical examiner's file, but there were no photos there either.

That's odd.

She started copying, word for word, the statement of Javier Torres, the alleged friend. Nowhere in the file could she find an address for him or any other identification, such as a Social Security number or driver's license information. She glanced again at the detective and again found her watching. Did she dare ask what their normal procedure was here regarding informants? Detective Bailey looked friendly enough. There was nothing about her that Marty found threatening, and she assumed the detective would happily answer her questions. But again, the sense that she was being filmed and recorded caused her to keep her questions to herself.

Turned out it didn't matter. There was a quick knock on the door before it opened. The receptionist stuck her head inside.

"Excuse me, Detective, but the lieutenant said to remind you the hour was up."

"Thank you, Rosaline."

Marty sat back, her annoyance showing on her face, she was sure. Her watch told her she'd been in here for fifty-two minutes. And at least five of those minutes had been spent waiting for the evidence box to arrive.

"I'm sorry, Miss Edwards, but we'll have to call it a day."

Marty stared at her, noting that the apology was sincere. "No problem," she said as she began gathering her things. "And please call me Marty. I'll be back in the morning. Will that suit you?"

"I'm at your disposal." The detective reached into her pocket and pulled out a card. "If you're going to be later or if you want to schedule a particular time, just call me. I'll have the evidence box waiting for you."

"Thank you," she said, almost in a whisper. Detective Bailey nodded, and Marty knew her suspicions were correct. The room was indeed bugged.

* * *

The reporter had barely made it down the hall before Lieutenant Marsh walked into the room. Bailey ignored him as she resealed the evidence box.

19

"So how did it go?"

Bailey shrugged. "She didn't ask any questions." Bailey knew full well he had watched the whole thing. She didn't doubt that he'd recorded it as well. She also knew the reporter most likely suspected the same.

"And she's coming back tomorrow?"

"Yes."

He came closer, elbowing her out of the way as he spun the box around, looking at the label. "I vaguely remember this case. Gang killing, yes." He looked at her. "These are nearly impossible to solve. Those bastards disappear into thin air when they want to."

"That's what I've been told."

Lieutenant Marsh tapped the top of the box while he stared at her. "So, Bailey, this reporter, you think she's going to interview people again or what?"

"She didn't say."

"What does your *gut* tell you, Bailey?"

Her gut told her that Marsh was awfully worried about this reporter snooping in a ten-year-old cold case, that's what. But she kept the bored expression on her face, telling him what he wanted to hear. "Reporters ask questions. I would imagine she's going to try to interview again, yes."

"Then perhaps we should offer our services. What do you think?"

"So you want me to what? Follow her?"

"Nothing quite so obvious, Bailey. I thought perhaps we could offer to escort her around town. Take her to the crime scene area, that type of thing. After all, she doesn't know her way around Brownsville. I would hate to have her on the wrong side of town. You know, wrong time-wrong place. Pretty blond thing like that. Anything could happen."

Bailey was stunned by the underlying threat in his words and the coldness of his eyes. Marty Edwards was definitely snooping into something she shouldn't. "Sure, if that's what you want. It's not like I'm loaded down with cases or anything."

"Good, Bailey. Because if you play your cards right, this might just be the ticket to get you a little more involved, shall we say."

She forced a smile to her face, hoping she appeared eager. "Yes, sir. That would be great. What do you want me to do?"

"Just be as accommodating as possible. Take her where she wants to go. Gain her confidence, Bailey. I want to know what she's up to. I want to know why this case," he said as he tapped the box again. "It could be, as she said, she's writing a book. If so, all the better. Just find out what you can. Keep me informed, Bailey."

"Yes, sir, I will."

"Good girl. There might be a future for you here after all."

Bailey strove to keep her face expressionless, knowing the cameras were still live. *Good girl, my ass.*

CHAPTER FIVE

Marty leaned back against the pillows on the bed, juggling her laptop and her scribbled notes as she finished transcribing them. She read through the notes she'd loaded days earlier, the account the sister gave her, her own impressions after speaking with Kesara. And by no stretch of the imagination could she pencil Carlos Romero into a gang. He just didn't fit the profile. Yet the police, based upon a statement by Javier Torres, had concluded that Carlos was not only a gang member, but that he was killed by an unknown assailant from a rival gang. Case closed.

Marty ran a hand through her hair, pushing it off her forehead as she scanned the statement from Torres again. According to him, Carlos had near daily involvement with the *Los Rebeldes*, a small gang that was trying to gain a foothold on the southeast side of Brownsville. Marty shook her head. If you believed his teacher's statement, Carlos went to school every day. He was responsible and studious. He was involved in athletics. He had an after-school job, according to his sister. None of that pointed to "daily involvement" in a gang.

Looking at it from the outside, ten years later, it almost appeared as if the police were looking for any excuse to close the case without investigating it. And labeling it gang-related was the easiest way. Which led to another question. Why?

Marty slid the laptop onto the bed and brought her legs up and crossed them, her mind racing over the many questions she wanted to ask. She wondered if the two investigating officers were still on the force. And if so, whether Lieutenant Marsh would allow her to question them.

"I'm going to guess no," she said to her empty hotel room.

Perhaps Detective Bailey would be willing to shed some light on the case. She seemed friendly enough. But she didn't dare ask her questions while in the interrogation room. Marty's gaze moved across the room to the small desk, lighting on the business card the detective had given her. She could call her, but that seemed a bit brash. Maybe after their hour session tomorrow she could get her alone long enough to ask a few questions. Or better yet, invite her on a lunch date.

Marty was used to flirting with men to get answers. She saw no reason she couldn't do the same with Detective Bailey. Of course, her stereotyping could be way off, but she didn't think so. It wasn't that Bailey exuded a masculine presence. She didn't. Her dark hair was longer than Marty's, touching her shoulders. And even though her face had a natural attractiveness, Marty had noted the woman wore just the barest touch of makeup. But lesbian police officers who were out had a certain air about them, she had discovered last year while researching a piece she was writing on discrimination in the workplace. So she would turn on her charm and try to get Bailey to join her for lunch. Maybe she would wear a skirt tomorrow after all.

CHAPTER SIX

Bailey picked up her phone without looking at it, her eyes still focused on the online newspaper she was reading.

"Good morning, Detective Bailey. It's Marty Edwards."

Bailey pulled her attention from the computer. "Good morning, Miss Edwards."

"Please call me Marty. I hope I'm not interrupting anything."

Bailey looked around at the near-empty squad room. "No, of course not. I'm at your beck and call, remember?"

"Well, I'm going to stop at the Starbucks down here on the corner," she said. "Can I get you something?"

Bailey eyed the putrid coffee in her cup and smiled. "Bribing me with real coffee?"

"Yes," Marty said with a laugh. "But I'm stopping anyway. I thought it was the least I could do since you've been assigned as my babysitter."

"Then thank you. I accept."

"What's your favorite?"

"I like too many of them to have a favorite. How about a white chocolate mocha?"

"Coming right up. I'll be there in a few."

She disconnected before Bailey could say anything else. Bailey tossed out the rest of her squad room coffee and placed a call to Reyes to bring the evidence box up. She was already seated in the interrogation room when Rosaline escorted the reporter inside. Marty Edwards knew they were being filmed and recorded again, Bailey suspected, and was trying to temper her smile. Nevertheless, she met Bailey's gaze and gave her a slight wink before handing over the mocha.

"Thank you," Bailey said with a subtle nod. She found it amazing that they could communicate without saying anything. She pointed to the evidence box. "Ready?"

"Please."

Bailey turned the box to face her, hesitating slightly as she noticed the seal she'd placed on it yesterday had been cut and resealed. Someone had opened the evidence box. She sliced through the tape, pretending not to notice, then slid the box closer to the reporter. Without a word, she took her seat at the end of the table, keeping her gaze even as she watched Marty Edwards open the box. Today the reporter ignored the evidence bags and took out the two files instead. No doubt she suspected her time would be cut short again and she wanted a closer look at the files. Bailey watched as she scribbled quickly on the legal pad, looking back occasionally at the file before writing down more. After nearly twenty minutes of this, she put her pen down and stretched her back, tossing a quick glance Bailey's way. Their eyes met for just a second before the reporter looked away.

Bailey quietly sipped her mocha, trying to keep the same bored expression on her face as yesterday. Truth was, she was curious about the case. She knew nothing of it, and no one had shared the details with her. The reporter was obviously intrigued by it, and Lieutenant Marsh was being so protective of the evidence box that you'd think it held state secrets or something. That was the real reason she was curious. She trusted Marsh even less than he trusted her.

She placed the empty cup on the table, watching with fascination as the reporter pulled on the latex gloves. There was a slight pause and a quick frown as she pulled out the bag with the victim's personal effects. She went through them again much as she'd done the previous day, opening the wallet and looking at what Bailey assumed was a photo, then again counting the bills left inside. She put it all back quickly, took off the gloves and scribbled some more on her notepad.

The reporter finally sat back and put her pen down, her sigh quite loud in the empty room. It was time, Bailey knew, to offer her services as the lieutenant had suggested. But she didn't want Marty Edwards to talk and ask questions in here, where the lieutenant was taping them. For some reason, Bailey felt the need to protect her.

"I guess I'm done for the day," Marty said. She looked at her watch. "Forty-five minutes today."

Bailey nodded. She stood and moved closer, pulling the evidence box down the table toward her. "I was thinking, if you're planning on interviewing anyone, or if you wanted to see the crime scene area, then you should probably have an escort around town." Bailey met her eyes, hoping she would be careful with her answer.

"I thought I might visit the mother," Marty said. "And perhaps the street where the body was found." She didn't look away from Bailey's stare. "There's not much evidence. No wonder it's a cold case. There wasn't anything for the police to go on."

"Yes. Sometimes cases are like that." Bailey picked up the tape. "I'll be happy to take you around town if you like," she offered.

"That's very accommodating, Detective. I would appreciate that."

Bailey nodded, then sealed the evidence box, scribbling her

name across the tape. "I need to make sure this is secured first, Miss Edwards. If you want to wait outside for me, we can get started now." She paused. "Unless you'd rather do it another time?"

"No, no. The sooner I do it, the sooner I'm out of your hair." She gathered her notepad and shoved it in her bag. "I'll meet you out front, Detective."

* * *

To say that she was shocked by the detective's offer was an understatement. Pleased and shocked. However, Marty had recognized Detective Bailey's shift from friendly on the phone to extremely formal in the interrogation room. The detective was trying to warn her that they were being monitored. Marty had a hundred questions for her, the first being, What the hell had happened to the scorpion paperweight that had been in the evidence box yesterday?

The paperweight was the one thing in the evidence box she had wanted to get more detail on. According to her Internet research the previous night, scorpion idols had been left at crime scenes in the area since the mid-seventies, the signature of a supposed drug cartel. The scorpion paperweight had been found at eight murder scenes in the Rio Grande Valley in the last ten years. Prior to that there had been plastic scorpions, paper scorpions, even the image of a scorpion carved into the victims' abdomens. A person or a drug cartel had never been specifically linked to the idols, so most of the articles simply referred to the person in charge as the Scorpion.

Strikingly, all this information had come from individual Web sites and crime blogs. Marty could find no mention of the Scorpion in any police filings or reports, and she'd searched every city in the Rio Grande Valley, as far east as Corpus Christi and as far west as Laredo.

She heard footsteps behind her and turned, smiling at

Detective Bailey as she walked up to her. "Thank you for getting me out of there, Detective," she said. "I always get the creeps when I'm being watched and recorded."

"Yeah. I hoped you knew that was the case."

Marty tilted her head and stared at her. "Why are you helping me?"

"Because now I'm as curious as you are." The detective started walking and Marty followed. "Besides, I'm supposed to be spying on you and getting information so that I can report back to Lieutenant Marsh."

"Really? Is this standard procedure when anyone looks at a cold case?"

Detective Bailey laughed. "I would bet you are the first to do so." She stopped. "Where's your car?"

"I parked in the public lot across the street."

"Good. Drive back down Elizabeth. There's an Applebee's restaurant about six blocks or so. I'll pick you up there."

Marty frowned. "Or we could just leave my car here and I could ride with you now," she suggested.

"No. I want them to think we're having lunch there."

"Okay, now I'm confused. Someone's going to follow us?"

"Call me paranoid, but I'm guessing they bugged your car. Or at the very least, put a tracking device on it."

"But—"

"We'll talk later."

Detective Bailey walked away and Marty could do nothing except follow her instructions. She suddenly felt like she was in a spy movie. *Tracking device?* Good grief, it was an old, dusty cold case which hadn't been given a thought in ten years. Now, they were taking evidence from the box, monitoring her in the interrogation room and asking one of their detectives to spy on her. And that very same detective was now trying to help her.

Or is she? Maybe she was only pretending to help her to get information.

Information about what? Marty shook her head. It wasn't

28

like she knew any secrets. Not yet. But she felt she could trust Detective Bailey. She'd always been a good judge of people. You could look someone in the eye and find out all sorts of things. Warm eyes or cold eyes? Soft or hard? Truth or lies? Friend or foe? Detective Bailey had dark brown eyes. And they were warm, not cold. So yes, she could trust her. She would have to.

CHAPTER SEVEN

"It's nothing fancy, but at least we'll have privacy."

Marty smiled as she waited for Detective Bailey to pick up their fried seafood baskets. The short drive to Port Isabel had been made in relative silence, Marty content to watch the city of Brownsville disappear as they headed to the bay that separated the mainland from South Padre Island. The outdoor café overlooked the bay, and—after they ordered—Marty had found an empty picnic table where they could talk freely without being overheard.

"Had you come two weeks ago, this place would have been crawling with college students," the detective said as she placed a basket in front of her.

"Spring break never occurred to me," Marty admitted. "Although I never thought I'd be at Padre Island either." After dousing her fries with ketchup, she slid the bottle across the table and took the tarter sauce Detective Bailey handed her.

"I just wanted to get out of town. Unfortunately, I don't trust anyone there. Lieutenant Marsh has always been a bit weird, but I've never seen him like this."

"You don't trust who? The police?"

"Look, no offense, Miss Edwards, but I'm not certain I trust you either. You're a reporter. You've got your own agenda."

"Fair enough, Detective." She smiled. "But the trust issue goes both ways." She picked up a shrimp and bit it in half, swallowing before continuing. "Why do you think they would put a tracking device on my rental car?"

"Because they're curious as to why you're here. They don't know why you chose this particular case. They're worried about something, although I don't know what it is. And they don't trust you." She dipped her fried fish into the tarter sauce and took a bite, then motioned to Marty's basket. "How is it?"

"Good. I don't get seafood often in Atlanta. Certainly not fresh like this."

"This place goes to the marina every morning when the shrimp boats come in."

"Do you live down here?"

"No. I've just spent a lot of time on the island." She wiped her hands on a napkin, then picked up her tea. "Why this case, Miss Edwards?"

Marty grabbed another shrimp with her fingers, then paused. "What's your name, Detective?"

"Excuse me?"

"Your name. I hate this formality. Miss Edwards. Detective Bailey." She bit into her shrimp and smiled. "So?" she asked as she chewed.

"It's Kristen."

"Nice. I think it suits you. So you'll please call me Marty?"

"Okay. But I can't guarantee you I'll answer to Kristen. Most everyone just calls me Bailey."

"I'll try to remember that. I just hate calling people by their last names. It's so impersonal."

Kristen shrugged. "It comes with the job." She took another sip of tea, glancing at Marty over the rim. "So why this case?" she asked again.

Marty pushed the basket aside and leaned her elbows on the table. "Do you know anything about it? This case?"

"No. I've only been here a couple of years."

"Well, let me give you a little background then. Carlos Romero, age eighteen, is the victim. According to his mother, that fateful Friday night in November—ten years ago this year— he left her home to meet his cousins in Matamoras for dinner, something they did nearly every Friday night. I thought it was for underage partying across the border, but Kesara—that's the sister—said it was little more than an outdoor café around the market where they ate and hung out. She said it was a place they could go and not get hassled."

Kristen pointed at Marty's basket. "Are you going to eat that last shrimp?"

"Help yourself." Marty smiled as the detective plopped it in her mouth in one bite. "Anyway, Carlos was late getting home from work so the cousins left without him. His plan was to take the bus to the border crossing and walk across, then catch a ride back with them."

"So I take it he never made it?"

"Right." Marty handed Kristen a napkin. "You've got ketch-up…here," she said, pointing to the corner of her own mouth. She watched as the detective wiped it away, then continued. "So it looks like a random crime against an innocent," she said. "The kid was a straight-A student, a star baseball player. He had an after-school job at a little grocery store in their neighborhood. Just a good kid." She took a swallow of her tea, then cleared her throat. "He was butchered, basically. His eyes were gouged out. His tongue removed. His belly cut open."

She watched Kristen absorb this information with only a twitch of her lips. "The statements in the file are from the mother and her account of Carlos's plans for that night. There

32

is a statement from the sister, Kesara, to the effect that he was a motivated high school senior who wanted nothing more than to go to college and get out of Brownsville. A third statement is from a high school teacher, again he was just a good kid, never in trouble." Marty leaned forward. "Here's where it gets weird. The police come back and ask all three if Carlos was ever involved in a gang. All three said no way. Then there's a fourth statement from a boy named Javier Torres who implicated Carlos as a member of a gang, a 'highly involved' member of a gang."

Kristen nodded. "Okay. And?"

"Kesara says they'd never heard of this Javier person who was supposedly good friends with Carlos. She said the guys Carlos was friends with—and his cousins—had also never heard of Javier Torres. Yet the police took his statement, called it all good and closed the case."

"And that was ten years ago? So where do you come in?"

"What do you mean?"

"How did you find out about the case?"

Marty rested her chin in her palm, wishing she knew for certain she could trust this woman. "The truth? Or what I told your lieutenant and the flirty James Garza?"

Kristen laughed. "Lieutenant Marsh was pissed at Garza for giving you authorization."

"Do you know him?"

She shook her head. "Not well, no. But I'm aware of his flirty nature firsthand."

"He asked you out? Surely he knows you're gay." At Kristen's startled look, Marty wanted to take the words back. "I'm sorry. I'm being terribly presumptuous." She lowered her voice. "Or are you closeted?" She was relieved when the other woman grinned.

"Closeted? Hardly."

Marty laughed. "But he asked you out?"

"Yes. I assumed everyone knew I was gay." Kristen leaned her elbows on the table. "Truthfully, no one has ever bothered to ask."

"It's not like I would just assume you were gay. I mean, you don't fit the stereotype," Marty said. No, not from looks alone would she assume Kristen Bailey was a lesbian. Her hair was not cut drastically short. She wasn't wearing men's clothing. At the same time, she wouldn't call her overly feminine. She wore dark slacks and loafers. Her watch was not gold or silver, but an understated leather band. She wore no jewelry, not even earrings. And again today, she had on just the barest hint of makeup.

"I did an article a while back, on discrimination issues, and I interviewed quite a few female cops and such," Marty explained. "I found there was a distinct difference in the way straight cops and gay cops carried themselves. I hope I didn't offend you."

"Not at all."

"But what do you mean no one has ever asked? Surely it's come up."

"I'm an outsider. I'm not a local. I'm from Houston and I got this job by my captain pulling some strings." She shrugged. "So I'm not really involved in anything here. Or with anyone, my squad included." She smiled. "I get assigned little projects like this. Keeping an eye on nosy reporters."

Now Marty's curiosity was piqued. And she did what she always did when that happened. She asked questions. "Why are you here instead of Houston?" She thought the detective wasn't going to answer her, but after a few seconds of silence, she did.

"There was an illness in my family. I was needed here."

"What—"

"It's nothing very exciting. Now tell me what you told my lieutenant."

Marty quelled her instinct to ask more questions, deciding to save them for another day. She brought her mind back to the case, remembering the lie she'd told Lieutenant Marsh. "I was contacted by Kesara Romero, the sister. She read my book and thought—"

"What book?"

Marty waved her hand dismissively. "Nothing much, really. I

34

just picked out a handful of cold cases I'd had success with and did this true crime book. It was successful enough in its genre, but certainly nothing mainstream. I think the only reason Kesara read it was because of the subject. It made it more personal for her."

"She's here in Brownsville?"

"No, she's in San Antonio now. We've had three or four phone conversations. To this day, she emphatically denies her brother had anything to do with a gang. She's convinced the police took the easy way out and used the gang angle as an excuse to close the case."

"But you told my lieutenant what?"

"I didn't mention the sister, that's for sure. I could tell he wasn't happy about me being here, so I was trying to be as non-threatening as possible. I told him I was doing a book on gang-related killings and that I'd come upon this case while researching others. I also told him the chances of it making the cut to be in the book were slim."

"So are you really doing another book?"

Marty shook her head. "No. I may do another one someday, but right now, no. I am gathering material only. It's just that after talking to the sister and hearing how certain she was that her brother's killing was not gang-related, well, it got my interest. And now, after reading the file, I'm convinced the crime was barely investigated. No offense to you or your police department, but this case shows incompetence and neglect at the very least," she said, "and a cover-up at the very most." She was a little surprised that Kristen didn't protest. In fact, the detective nodded, as if agreeing with her.

"The evidence box was tampered with," Kristen said after a moment's silence. At Marty's lack of surprise, she raised her eyebrows. "You knew?"

"I assumed," she said. "There was something missing from the box today."

"The seal that I put on there yesterday had been cut and

resealed."

"There was a piece, a glass paperweight thing with a scorpion encased inside—an idol—that was found at the scene. I researched it last night. It's either a death signature of a drug lord or a myth, a hoax." She stared at her. "It was missing from the box this morning."

"What do you mean, a myth?"

"There are references dating back thirty years or more to the symbol of a scorpion being left at murder scenes. The glass paperweight, though, only dates back the last ten, eleven years. Prior to that, there were plastic scorpions, paper scorpions, that sort of thing. The myth part is this—I could not find a single mention of a scorpion idol in *any* police report, and I researched all the departments in the Valley, all the way to Laredo. No mention of it at all."

Kristen wadded up her napkin and tossed it on the table. "What do you make of the murder?"

"What do you mean?"

"Well, the way you described it—the eyes, the tongue—that sounds more like a mafia hit than a gang killing. The eyes, he saw something he shouldn't have. The tongue, so he can't talk."

Marty nodded. She had thought that very thing. "Yes. Which lends credence to the drug lord theory." She leaned closer. "What do you know about the gangs down here?"

"Like I said, I'm pretty much out of the loop when it comes to police business. They have a minor problem with gangs. Probably no more or no less than any other city of Brownsville's economic status."

"Meaning?"

"It's a relatively poor city. And even though there is a university here, the education level is not high. There are very, very few high-paying technical jobs, and unemployment is much higher than the national average."

"A ripe environment for disenchanted youths looking for a way to prosper."

"Yes."

"Drugs?"

"You mean drug trafficking?"

"That too."

Kristen nodded. "We have our share." She reached over and took Marty's basket and placed it inside her own. "And without reading the file myself, it's hard to form an opinion on whether this is a cover-up or not."

"I understand. But let me ask you something. If your lieutenant asked you to keep an eye on me, I doubt he had in mind us discussing the case like this. Are you disobeying his order, or are you fishing for information in a more subtle way?"

"Whatever his agenda is for wanting to know your every move, your every thought about this case, I don't share it. A cold case is a cold case, and any help the police can get in solving it should be a blessing, not a curse. So no, I'm not spying on you. I'm satisfying my own curiosity."

"And when he asks you what you learned?"

"I'll tell him you don't talk much. Of course, I'm to escort you to any interviews you do."

"What if I refuse the police escort?"

"But you won't. You're just as curious as to what the lieutenant is hiding. If you ditch me, you won't have any police contact."

Marty smiled. "You don't trust him, do you?"

"Not in the least."

"Then why are you still here?" Her question was met with silence and a blank stare. Marty's gaze didn't waver. It was the detective who sighed and looked away. The silence was broken by a group of sea gulls that descended on the outdoor café looking for handouts. Marty glanced at one that landed just beyond their picnic table. "I haven't been around coastal areas much," she said. "It's pleasant here."

"Yes. Warm. Hot and muggy in the summer, though. Not even the gulf breeze helps much."

Marty met Kristen's eyes again. "I'm sorry," she said. "I'm

a reporter. I ask questions. I didn't mean to pry into something that is not my business."

The detective simply shrugged and got up, tossing their lunch baskets in the trash.

"You ready to head back?"

Marty followed her, getting back to the topic at hand. "I really wanted to talk to the mother today. Do you think that's possible?"

"Have you called her?"

"No. But Kesara said she didn't work. She should be home."

CHAPTER EIGHT

Bailey drove down Highway 48, back to Brownsville. Although Marty Edwards had given her no reason not to trust her, Bailey kept her thoughts to herself. But from everything the reporter described about the case, from the broken evidence seal and the missing scorpion idol, it reeked of a cover-up. It just seemed like such an insignificant case. Why would it merit a cover-up?

"You seriously think there was a tracking device on my car?" Marty asked.

Bailey glanced at her quickly, then back to the road. "It would be a strange assumption that a local police department would want to track the movements of a reporter, yes. However, based on how Lieutenant Marsh wants me to spy on you, and now everything you've said about the case, then yes, I'd assume that." She put her blinker on, taking a side road to Southmost, where the mother lived. "And it's not that I'm overly paranoid," she said.

"I just have firsthand knowledge, so I know how they operate."

"What do you mean?"

"When I first started here, I knew they were annoyed about how I got the job. I just had no idea they were so pissed. I kept having the feeling that I was being watched, and I had this nagging suspicion that they knew everything I did, everywhere I went. Like not only where I had dinner, but what I had, things like that. After about six weeks, I bought this sweep kit. It'll detect any kind of electronic surveillance device. Phone bugs, room bugs, even body bugs. Wiretaps, video taps. Very James Bondish," she said.

"And what did you find?"

"A tracking device on my car and a handful of bugs inside the house."

"And?"

"And I disabled them."

"Wow. What did your lieutenant say when you called him on it?"

"I never called him on it. But disabling them, of course, told them that I knew. I haven't found anything since then, but we have a bit of a trust issue between us."

"And you don't know why they were doing that?"

"No. Other than they didn't know me, didn't know my work ethic. I thought perhaps they didn't think I was good enough for the job or something. There aren't very many females on the force."

"And what do you think now?"

Bailey shrugged. "I have no idea what they are thinking." Although she now had her suspicions, she just wasn't ready to share them with the reporter.

She turned left onto Southmost Road, taking them down a street that was much more reflective of Mexico than of the U.S. Most of the advertisements were in Spanish, most handwritten. The street was lined with small businesses—auto repairs, sewing, specialty kitchens serving traditional dishes, small grocery stores and meat markets, laundromats and pawn shops. Mixed between the businesses were small, wood-framed homes, the tiny front yards with their chain-link fences ending practically at the edge of the cracked sidewalk.

"I thought maybe everyone was having a yard sale," Marty said. "But the clothes—that's how they dry them, isn't it?"

Bailey nodded. She was used to the sight of clothes hanging on the fences, some on hangers, others not. "Most don't have washers and dryers."

"Used washers and dryers are pretty cheap," Marty said. "So why—?"

"Look at these houses. I doubt any of them are wired for a two-twenty plug, which is what you need for a dryer. Besides, this is what their mothers did, what their grandmothers did. It's just part of laundry day." She slowed as they approached the traffic light. "What street again?"

"Alamosa."

Two blocks later, Bailey turned right onto Alamosa. The houses there were a little larger, although not by much.

"This is it," Marty said, pointing to a neat wood-frame house, the white paint looking fairly new.

Bailey parked along the street and cut the engine. "Do you know Spanish?"

Marty shook her head. "No. Do you?"

"Not enough to carry on a conversation, no."

"It never occurred to me she wouldn't speak English. The daughter did, perfectly. She seemed very educated."

"A lot of the older generations don't speak English." Bailey smiled. "Or they pretend not to." She got out. "Was there anything in the file to suggest they used an interpreter?"

"No."

Marty followed her to the gate, then stopped. "Do we just go in or what? I mean, maybe we should have called first."

"You get better answers if they don't have a chance to prepare," Bailey said. "Or do you take a different approach with cold cases?"

"No, not always." She peered around the yard. "Do you think she has a dog?"

"No. If she did, it would have already alerted her to our presence." Bailey opened the gate and motioned Marty inside. The yard was neat and well-kept, with a couple of religious statues decorating flower beds that looked like they had been freshly planted.

They walked up the two steps to the door, which was open to let in the breeze. An old screen door kept the bugs out. Bailey knocked loudly, her knuckles rapping four times on the wood.

"*Hola. Quien esta alli?*"

Bailey smiled at the dark-skinned woman, her graying hair swept back in a bun. "*Buenas tardes,*" she said. "*Como esta?*"

"*Estoy bien. Como puedo ayudarle?*"

Bailey pointed to Marty. "This is Marty Edwards. A reporter." She turned to Marty. "What's the sister's name again?"

Marty smiled at the woman. "Kesara sent me," she said. "And please say you speak English. Because if you don't, then this will be a very short conversation."

"*Si, si.* I know English. Come in, come in. She call me. You are the reporter she talked to about *mi* Carlos, *si?*"

"Yes, I am."

"And who are you?" she asked as she looked at Bailey.

"She's with the police," Marty said.

The woman frowned and shook her head. "*La policia estupida,*" she spat. "They did nothing. And now a woman? *Que verguenza.*"

"No, no. Detective Bailey is just being kind enough to drive me around Brownsville. She's not really here on official business."

Mrs. Romero eyed her suspiciously, and Bailey thought perhaps she should wait in the car. She was about to offer to do that very thing when the woman pointed at her.

"Do you know of my Carlos?"

"No, ma'am, I'm sorry, but I don't. I've only been in Brownsville a couple of years."

The woman studied her for a moment, then finally nodded. "*Si*. You stay."

"*Gracias*," Bailey said quietly and followed them inside.

"Here is my Carlos," she said, picking up a framed picture from a table that could be described as nothing less than a shrine. "Such a handsome young boy, yes?"

"Oh, yes, ma'am," Marty said. She took the photo and looked at it, then carefully replaced it on the table. "So many trophies," she said pointing to the handful that were proudly displayed.

"He loved his baseball. Since he was a little boy, all he did was play baseball. That was his dream." She sat down in a worn recliner and pointed to an equally worn sofa. "Come. Sit. We talk."

Marty took one end of the sofa, then looked at Bailey. Bailey ignored the silent invitation to sit. She shook her head, instead moving to the table, taking in the various framed photos of the boy, even the clipped newspaper article reporting his murder. It was barely two paragraphs long.

"Kesara tells me that Carlos was going to college, that he had a scholarship," Marty said.

"Yes, he did. The scholarship was for here at *la Universidad*. but he wanted to get out of Brownsville." Mrs. Romero shook her head sadly. "I didn't want my baby leaving, but it was his dream, his life." She shrugged her shoulders. "What could I say?"

"Where did he want to go?"

She smiled. "He wanted to go to the big school in Austin. But of course, we couldn't afford that. We have family in San Antonio. They were going to let him stay with them. So he applied at U.T. there."

"So what was all this business about him being in a gang?" Marty asked. Bailey raised her eyebrows. The reporter certainly got right to the point.

"*Eso es una locura*. My Carlos *nunca*—never—was part of a gang. The police," she said, glancing at Bailey, "would not believe us. Some witness they found." She shook her head. "No one knows this boy. Where did he come from? Why would he tell lies about my Carlos?"

"Forgive me, but are you certain about Carlos? Because you know, children have been known to keep things from their parents," Marty said.

"I'm certain. Not *mi* Carlos. He was a good boy. He study all the time. He go to work. He go to church. He was never once in trouble. Not at school. Not with the police." She shook her head, her eyes staring at Bailey. "No. He was not in a gang. I don't care what the police say."

Marty leaned forward. "Do you have any idea why the police would say that? I mean, they had to have a reason. What do you think?"

"Carlos saw something. Something bad." She glanced at the table, looking at the pictures. "I know how he was killed," she said quietly. "I know about the scorpion that was left. I know what that means."

"Do you know who the Scorpion is?"

"No. But he is a very bad man." Her voice lowered to nearly a whisper. "*El Diablo*. Everyone is scared of him. Including the police."

CHAPTER NINE

"I don't mind saying, I'm a little nervous," Marty said as the detective drove them down the dark street. "Do you think it's safe?"

"Safe? Talking to Quin Mendoza will be safe enough. We're meeting him as Carlos's cousin, not as a gang member. Now, if he feels threatened and *Los Rebeldes* come to his aid, then no, it's not safe. The park we're meeting at is isolated. People don't normally go there after dark. It belongs to the gangs then."

Marty chewed her lower lip, thinking they should reconsider. But Mrs. Romero had told them that Quin Mendoza had joined the gang after Carlos's murder. He wanted to find out who killed him. What he found out was that *Los Rebeldes* knew nothing of Carlos or his murder. Now, according to Mrs. Romero, Quin was deeply involved with the gang, and the family rarely saw him anymore. The little gang that had just been getting a foothold in the city ten years ago was now one of the most powerful. Which made her very nervous.

More nervous than the tracking device they'd found on her rental that afternoon. After visiting with Mrs. Romero, they'd picked up her car and driven to Kristen's duplex. It hadn't taken the detective long to find the device, but they decided not to disable it. They had decided, in fact, to take Marty's rental to meet Quin. "Just in case something happens," the detective had said. Yeah, at least the police would know where to find their bodies.

She pushed that thought away. She was with a police detective. She was perfectly safe.

"Here we go," Kristen said as she turned down another quiet, dark street. "*El Pirata del Parque*. The Pirates Park."

"Great. It couldn't have a nice, non-threatening name, could it?"

Kristen laughed. "Legend has it that pirates used to come up the mouth of the Rio Grande and hide their loot here."

"And I'm guessing none has ever been found?"

"The only loot found around here is drug money," the detective said as she slowed to a crawl. "Dark. Lots of shadows," she said, almost to herself.

Marty swallowed nervously. Yes. Dark and spooky. Which was how the voice on the phone had sounded when she finally had located Quin Mendoza, after five different phone calls, beginning with his mother. She caught her breath as headlights blinked on and off twice. That was their signal.

"Is now a good time to tell you I'm scared?"

"We'll be fine. They have no reason to harm us."

"Do they need a reason?"

Kristen glanced quickly at her as she eased the car forward. "I take it this is your first time interviewing a gang member?"

"Second. Of course, the first one was in jail at the time," Marty admitted.

Kristen pushed her window down as they approached the car. She stopped beside it, and Marty could feel her pulse pounding in her temple. There was no way to see the man's face in the darkness.

"You are the reporter?"

Kristen nodded and pointed at Marty. "Yeah. You're Quin?"

"No. Quin will speak with you. But not here. The park has eyes," he said. "Who knows you are here?"

"No one."

Marty watched as he hesitated, and she imagined him looking around. Finally, he stuck his head out, and Marty was able to see his face. A long red scar was visible across his cheek.

"Go to Sabal Palms. Before the railroad track, there is a road into the palmettos. Park there and wait. Someone will—"

His words were cut off as gunfire exploded around them. Marty screamed as his head was transformed into a mass of tissue and blood, then she was thrown back against the seat as Kristen sped away, the sounds of bullets hitting the rental car echoing in her ears.

"Are you hit?" Kristen yelled as she squealed around the corner, the car fishtailing as the tires lost their traction. "Marty? Are you hit?"

"No. I don't think so, no." Her fingers hurt as she squeezed the dash, watching as the dark street flew by in a blur. Finally, Kristen slowed as she turned onto another street, this one lit by streetlights. "Oh, my God. What the hell just happened?" Marty's mind flashed back to the man's face as it disappeared in the blood. "Oh, my God. Shouldn't we call the police or something? I mean, that man's head was practically blown off." Marty closed her eyes. "Jesus, I can't believe I just saw that." She grabbed Kristen's arm and squeezed tightly. "What should we do? Do you think someone's following us?"

"Just calm down."

"Calm down?" Her voice was loud to her own ears. Loud and shrill, and she took a deep breath. "Calm down?" she asked again. "Someone just tried to kill us."

But Kristen shook her head as she turned again and took

them down a residential street. "No. We weren't the target. If someone was trying to kill us, we'd be as dead as that man." She pulled to a stop. "Stay inside," she said as she got out.

Marty watched Kristen as she walked around the car, studying the damage, she guessed. She couldn't stop her hands from trembling, and she folded them together, her chest still tight, her eyes wide with fear. The closest she'd come to gunfire before this was two years ago when she was digging up witnesses to an old hit-and-run case where two teenagers had been killed. The brother of one of the teens took exception to her questions about alcohol and had grabbed his hunting rifle. But the fear she felt then was nothing like this. She didn't really think he would have shot at her. Now? Despite Kristen saying they weren't the targets, it didn't help her mental state that they'd just been trapped between their contact and automatic weapon fire.

"Doesn't make sense," Kristen said as she got back inside.

"What?"

"It was obviously a hit. Someone knew where we were and what was going down."

"The tracking device?"

"We weren't there long enough for someone to follow us and make the hit. No, this was planned. They don't want us talking to Mendoza."

"Who is *they*?"

"I don't know." Kristen started the car again and pulled away. "I only know we didn't suffer enough damage. That guy was hit dozens of times, his car shot up like it was a gangster hit. Us? A few bullet holes to the frame of the car. That's it. No broken windows, no tires shot out. It's almost as if we are being warned off."

"But not by *Los Rebeldes*. They wouldn't kill one of their own to warn us, would they?"

"No."

"Another gang? Maybe Carlos's death was gang-related. Maybe this other gang doesn't want us snooping around."

48

"First of all, how would they know we're snooping? Secondly, it's a ten-year-old case that wasn't investigated the first time. Why would they care? Even if the police pinpointed a particular gang, it wouldn't matter unless they had the trigger man." She turned onto Highway 77 and sped north, taking the route that they'd taken that afternoon to Kristen's duplex. "I'm going to pick up my car, then follow you to your hotel."

"What about the rental? The damage?"

"Drive it to the station in the morning. The crime lab will want to take a look at it." She glanced at her. "Where are you staying anyway?"

"The Residence Inn, here off of Seventy-seven."

"Okay. Lieutenant Marsh will probably want to talk to you, take a statement."

"Are you sure we shouldn't do it tonight? Shouldn't we call someone?"

"I'll call it in and report it. We can do the paperwork in the morning. It shouldn't be a problem."

CHAPTER TEN

"What the hell were you thinking? A rookie cop knows not to go to *El Pirata del Parque* at night without goddamn backup," Lieutenant Marsh yelled, and Bailey had no doubt half the squad could hear him. "And there was no body. Just a bloody car. Are you sure you saw a man get killed, Bailey?"

"Yes, sir. Half his face was blown off."

"And I guess the reporter saw the same thing?"

"Yes, sir."

Bailey jumped when he slammed a fist down on his desk.

"What were you thinking taking a civilian out like that? She could have been shot. Then what kind of mess would we have on our hands?"

"You told me to be accommodating, Lieutenant. I thought it was better for me to take her out there than for her to venture out alone. That was your intention, wasn't it? To keep an eye on her?"

"My intention was to find out why she is nosing around in this case and then for her to get the hell out of town." He sat down behind his desk and glared at her. "What did you find out?"

"Not much. She went to visit the mother. She gave her the name of this cousin who belongs to *Los Rebeldes*."

"A cousin is a gang banger but not her precious son, huh? Figures." He picked up a gold pen on his desk and twirled it between his fingers. "What else, Bailey?"

"That's it. We didn't get a chance, obviously, to talk to the cousin."

"The cousin was the one shot?"

"No, sir. We were supposed to meet him somewhere else."

"Where were you supposed to meet him?"

"He didn't get a chance to tell us," she lied. Not that she thought she'd find anything out at the railroad tracks at Sabal Palms, but she wanted a chance to look without the lieutenant knowing of the meeting place.

"Well, maybe this little incident will scare the reporter out of town and we can get rid of her." He straightened up. "You may go, Bailey. I want to talk to her when she comes by. I don't need you here."

"Yes, sir."

Bailey closed the door quietly as she left, wondering when the lieutenant had taken the time to read the case file. He seemed much more versed on it now than he had when he'd given her this assignment. She couldn't imagine it was the lieutenant who had broken the evidence seal. But then again…couldn't she?

* * *

After a restless night's sleep—one she attempted with the lights on—Marty finally crawled out of bed at seven and took a hot shower, trying to scrub away the memories of last night. She couldn't close her eyes without seeing that man's face being riddled with bullets. Even now, as she drove to the police station,

51

she could still hear the shots as they peppered her car.

She quickly turned on the stereo, scanning for a radio station, any station, to take her mind off last night. Because frankly, it had spooked her worse than she thought it would. With Detective Bailey, she had put on a brave face. But once Kristen left, once she was alone in her hotel room, the fear and doubts had started creeping in. Maybe she was in over her head with this one. Maybe her knack for solving cold cases had been a fluke. Or perhaps she should just stick with cases of simple, unexplained violence. A single gunshot wound. A clean knife wound. Not a butchered boy with his eyes and tongue cut out, the contents of his abdomen spilled out onto the street as if he were a hog that had been slaughtered.

"Maybe I should just go home," she murmured, chancing a quick glance at herself in the rearview mirror. *Chicken*. She nodded. "Live chicken, dead duck." She laughed quietly, hoping the car wasn't bugged. They'd think she was insane. *So quit talking to yourself!*

Once inside the police station—after the crime lab confiscated her car—she sought out the receptionist, Mrs. Jimenez. But when she asked for Detective Bailey, the receptionist shook her head.

"Lieutenant Marsh wants to see you. Alone."

Marty nodded and smiled politely, wondering if perhaps Kristen were in some sort of trouble because of last night. Before she walked through the double doors, she paused. "Is Detective Bailey in today?"

"Yes. She has already been in with the lieutenant," the receptionist said, her voice low.

Marty gave what she hoped was a sympathetic smile. "Was it bad?" she asked conspiratorially.

The older woman nodded. "Oh, yes. He yelled. I'm glad I wasn't her."

Marty winked. "I hope he doesn't do the same to me." She pushed through the double doors, her eyes finding Kristen's immediately. She looked questioningly at her and was answered with a reassuring—albeit slight—smile.

"Miss Edwards?"

Marty turned, surprised to find Lieutenant Marsh waiting for her. She put on her practiced smile, trying to exude a confidence she didn't feel. "Lieutenant, good morning," she said as she walked toward him.

"Come in, please," he said, not bothering with pleasantries. "Did someone take your car? I left instructions for the crime lab."

"Yes, Lieutenant. An officer met me when I drove up." She slipped her shoulder bag off and clutched it in her arms, as if the familiar presence of her laptop could comfort her.

"So you had a bit of a scare last night."

"Yes. Thankfully Detective Bailey got us out of there quickly."

"I need to apologize for that. You shouldn't have been put in that situation." He sat down and motioned for Marty to do the same. "She should have known better. That park is notorious for gang activity. Apparently, you were at the wrong place at the wrong time."

So the lieutenant didn't think the shooting was related to the cold case. That differed from what Kristin thought. And it certainly differed from how it had felt last night. "We were trying to contact a cousin of Carlos Romero. I'm thankful Detective Bailey was with me. Had I gone alone, I'm not certain the outcome would have been the same."

"I take it you're not one to heed warnings then?"

"Warnings? You just said I was at the wrong place at the wrong time. I wouldn't consider that a warning, Lieutenant."

"I meant *my* warning, Miss Edwards. As a civilian, you have no business attempting to contact a gang member, let alone meet with one. That is very dangerous territory. I'm afraid I won't be able to guarantee your safety if you continue this practice."

Marty smiled, and this time she didn't even bother to try to make it look genuine. "Lieutenant, as a reporter working a cold case, I never assume police protection—or cooperation—although I normally always get the latter. But this case intrigues me," she said, watching his reaction. "I don't believe it was a gang killing," she said, not surprised to see the flicker of annoyance in his eyes.

"Why would you come to that conclusion?"

"The same reason your investigating officers should have come to it ten years ago. Carlos Romero didn't belong to a gang. He was practically an altar boy."

He stood quickly, pointing his finger at her, and she flinched involuntarily. "Do not come in here and accuse my officers of any impropriety," he said loudly. "I read the file. They did their job. There was no evidence. There were no witnesses. Two family members saying he was a saint doesn't hold as much weight as a gang member who says, yeah, the kid was a part of their group. Family members always live in denial." He sat down again, impatiently shuffling papers on his desk. "And this is one reason why I don't like *reporters* digging into police business. Because you don't know what the hell you're doing."

"I apologize if you thought I was accusing your officers of misconduct, Lieutenant. I assure you, I was not. I just don't agree with their conclusion that it was a gang-related killing."

She was surprised by the sneer on his lips. "Well, since you don't consider this gang-related, I suppose you'll be on your way then. That was the reason you were researching this particular case, wasn't it?"

"Yes, I was researching it for a possible segment in my next book. Now, however, I think I may stick with it, just to see if I can shake out who really killed Carlos Romero." She stood, staring at him. "Carlos was the one in the wrong place at the wrong time, Lieutenant. That much is obvious." She turned to go but paused at the door. "I'll understand if you no longer wish for Detective Bailey to assist me, Lieutenant. I'm used to fending for myself."

"No. You don't need to be wandering around Brownsville alone, Miss Edwards. There are parts of this city that can be very dangerous. I think you learned that lesson last night."

She gave a slight nod. "Thank you, Lieutenant. I'll try to keep her out of trouble."

CHAPTER ELEVEN

Bailey pulled out of the police parking lot, again driving her own car as Marty's rental was still with the crime lab. The reporter sat next to her, furiously typing on her laptop.

"You live and breathe by that thing, don't you," Bailey observed.

"Yes. I'd be completely lost if something happened to it."

"Then why the legal pad the other day?"

Marty laughed. "I can barely read my own writing. I figured if the cameras were live in there, they'd have a hell of a time focusing on it." She paused. "Did your lieutenant really yell at you?"

Bailey nodded. "Oh, yeah. I think it was more for show than anything. I doubt he was really that concerned for your safety."

"Well, he wasn't too happy when I hinted his detectives had screwed up the case. But really, cold case or not, there's not much to go on, is there? I mean, there are no witnesses to interview.

And the crime scene," she said, shaking her head. "Have you ever seen a case where there is so little physical evidence? No prints, no strange fibers at the scene, no tire marks. Nothing. It's like—"

"Like the crime lab wasn't even there," Bailey finished for her.

"Exactly. The bloody clothes were logged in by one of the detectives. So was the scorpion idol. There wasn't even a mention that they *attempted* to pull prints from the idol."

"Yeah. But keep in mind, this is a relatively small department in a small city. And ten years ago, who knows what the crime lab was like. It's not like it's cutting edge now. It was probably normal for the detectives to do the legwork at the crime scene."

"I suppose you're right. But based on all this—or the lack of—I don't really see a different outcome to the case. Yeah, we can determine that the police closed it prematurely ten years ago. But so what? Where is there to go?"

"Not your normal cold case?"

"Not the ones I've investigated. There are always witnesses. There are always opinions. There are usually suspects, at least. But this one? Nothing."

"You want me to show you the street where they found him?"

"Do you mind? Just for reference sake." Marty opened a file on her laptop. "How far is it from his house?"

"A good ways. It was down in the old warehouse district. Closer to the border crossing than his home."

"You know, it just occurred to me. His mother said he took the bus to the border crossing, yet there's nothing in the file to suggest they interviewed a bus driver." Marty stared at her. "Wouldn't that be standard procedure? To piece together his route at least?"

"It should have been, yes. But there's nothing about this case to suggest that normal police procedure was followed." Bailey drove down Fourteenth Street before taking a left on Jackson and crossing International Boulevard. She turned again, this time on Van Buren. Most of the warehouses here were vacant and abandoned, the businesses having long moved north to Highway 77. The area was ripe for crime now. The homeless had claimed some of the buildings, gangs others. The dark alleys were where drugs and money exchanged hands on a nightly basis. Now, during the light of day, it didn't look quite so menacing.

"I take it this isn't the hub of activity any longer," Marty said as she looked at the dilapidated buildings.

"No. Ten years ago, I assume a lot of these were still in business. There's a new area to the north, closer to San Benito, where most of these relocated to." Bailey slowed, looking in the rearview mirror at the handful of cars behind them. "The city would be better served if these buildings were condemned and torn down," she said. "You can tell which ones are abandoned and which still have inventory in them."

"How do they keep from getting ripped off?"

"They have a security guard. They have to. But still, this area has a call nearly every night. Shootings, drugs, fights. Always something." She turned right on Ridgely. "The Rio Grande's just over there," she said.

"Where's the border crossing?"

"They would have most likely taken International Boulevard. We turned off of it earlier. About four or five blocks to the north."

"He was found at Ridgely and Twenty-second," Marty said.

Bailey nodded, turning right again.

"Would this have been on his way? This doesn't exactly look like a bus route."

"He lived across the highway on San Rafael. If he caught a bus, he would have most likely caught it on Southmost. Then I would think it would have gone up to Eighteenth, which is International Boulevard. Pretty straight shot."

"So he got off the bus?"

Bailey shrugged. "Bus goes all the way to the border crossing. I'm sure it did ten years ago too."

"Maybe he wasn't familiar with the bus. Maybe he got off too soon."

"Maybe he forgot something. Maybe he wanted to get something to drink. Hell, maybe he had to pee," Bailey suggested. "Gonna be kinda hard to retrace his route." She stopped at the corner of Ridgely and Twenty-second. It was an intersection much like all the others in this area.

"Why weren't there pictures of the crime scene?" Marty asked. "In the file, I mean." She smiled. "Sorry. I know you don't have answers."

"Like we said earlier, there's nothing about this case that is normal." She pointed at Marty's laptop. "Who were the investigating officers?"

Marty scrolled through her notes. "Juan Vargas and Rafael Ortiz." She looked up. "Know them?"

"Ortiz, no," she said. "Never heard of him. But Juan Vargas is still here. He pulls desk duty."

"Do you think Lieutenant Marsh would let me talk to them?"

Bailey shook her head. "No way."

Marty stared at her. "Could you?" she asked quietly.

"Trying to get me in trouble with the boss?"

Marty reached over and squeezed her arm. "No. Sorry."

"Well, maybe I could—"

Her words were cut off as Marty screamed, a loud shrill sound that filled the car. Bailey jerked her head around, following Marty's frightened eyes—and found herself staring into the barrel of a shotgun. Without thinking, she stomped on the gas pedal, tossing them both back against the seat as the car lurched forward. The sound of a shotgun blast was nearly simultaneous with that of the back window being blown out.

"Get down, get *down*," Bailey yelled, holding Marty's head down on the seat as she sped up Ridgely, taking a hard right on Nineteenth, her tires squealing on the pavement. She glanced in the mirror and saw a white car following close behind. She released Marty, turning the wheel quickly and heading left on Harrison. Surely they wouldn't follow them to downtown. They didn't. The white car slowed at the corner of Harrison and

Nineteenth, then sped away.

"Oh, my *God*," Marty whispered as she stared out of the shattered back window.

Bailey drove on, heading back to the police station. "What's with you and us getting shot at?" she asked.

"*Me*? I thought it was you." Marty's hand was shaking as she gripped Bailey's arm. "What the hell is happening?" She loosened her grip. "And don't say it was an attempted carjacking."

"No. That was no carjacking. Something about this case is making someone *very* nervous."

Marty gave a weak smile. "Yeah. That someone is me."

CHAPTER TWELVE

"You want us to do *what*?" Bailey asked, staring at her lieutenant.

"It's not a matter of want, Bailey. You don't have a choice." He turned to Marty. "Miss Edwards, I've sent an officer to your hotel to pack your things."

"But—"

"I'm sorry, Miss Edwards, but this is the only way I can ensure your safety." He flicked his glance to Bailey. "You're marked. Both of you. *Los Demonios Rojos*."

"Marked? How in the hell would they even know that she's—"

"Shut up, Bailey. We're trying to save your sorry ass. You'll do as you're told." He cleared his throat. "Sorry, Miss Edwards. But this is best. Our informants have told us that Los Demonios Rojos has a price on your head. I'm certain that's who shot up your car today. Most likely, they were behind the shooting at the park last night as well."

Marty looked from one to the other, seeing Kristen's barely controlled anger and that of the lieutenant. "So, we're going to where? Like a safe house?"

"Something like that, yes. Just for a few days. Just until we can verify these threats."

"Lieutenant, I must say, this seems highly unusual. I've never—"

"Look, this really isn't up for discussion, Miss Edwards. Unless you're prepared to leave the city and state, this is the only way you'll be safe. Like I said, just for a few days."

She glanced quickly at Kristen, trying to read her, but her face was expressionless, her anger hidden. So she nodded. "Okay, Lieutenant. If you think this is best."

"Good." He stood, walking to the door and holding it open for them. He attempted a smile, one Marty didn't try to return. "Just for a couple of days," he said again.

* * *

Bailey got out of the police cruiser, slinging her backpack over her shoulder, then going around to help Marty as she struggled with her two bags. She took one but didn't say anything. The trip over had been made in silence, and she wanted to keep it that way until they were alone.

"Who owns this?" she asked Officer Alvarez. The beach house was old and appeared to be run down.

"I believe Captain Diaz," he said, handing her a key and a small piece of paper. "He said for you to call this number when you get here."

"So I guess this means you're leaving us here without a vehicle?"

"My orders were to drop you off and head right back."

Bailey glanced at Marty who stood silently by, staring out at the bay, pretending to ignore them. No doubt the reporter was taking in every word. She sighed, nodding at Alvarez, dismissing him. He left without another word, leaving them standing alone by the rickety old front porch.

"Where are we?" Marty asked.

"North of Port Isabel." Bailey pointed to the water. "That's Laguna Madre."

Marty raised an eyebrow.

"The bay that separates the mainland from Padre Island," she clarified.

"Where we had lunch?"

"Yeah. We're about thirty or forty miles north of that." Bailey held up the key. "Shall we?"

"Do you think it's safe to talk in there? Or is it bugged?"

"I think we'll be lucky if it has electricity," she said as she unlocked the door. "But yeah, judging by the appearance, I don't think anyone's been here in a while. I think they just wanted to stick us someplace out of the way." She flipped on a light, glancing around the small living area which was sparsely furnished. A half-wall jutted out to separate the kitchen, and Bailey walked in, turning on the water. "At least we'll have showers," she said.

"Only one bedroom," Marty called from across the room.

"Go for it. I'll take the sofa," she said as she looked out the back window to the bay. Damn, if she'd known this was where they were going to stay, she would have packed more than one pair of shorts.

"Are you sure?"

"No problem," she said as she opened the cabinets in the kitchen. A few dishes, a few pots and pans, not much else. The refrigerator was on but essentially empty—a jar of mustard and three cans of beer. "We're going to starve to death, dear," she called. She jumped as Marty peered over her shoulder.

"I'll say."

Bailey shut the fridge and held up the piece of paper. "Let me call in." She opened the back door and went out, stepping over a board on the deck that was broken. She leaned against the railing, surprised that it was actually Captain Diaz who answered.

She was half-expecting the lieutenant to be giving orders.

"Yes, Bailey, I see you made it."

"Yes, sir."

"Unfortunately, there's not anything there, food-wise. This was spur of the moment, I'm afraid."

"Well, since we're without a car and I don't believe we're within walking distance of anything, do you have a suggestion?" She watched Marty as she joined her, her eyes again going to the water, and Bailey noticed the slight smile on her lips.

"My cousin owns a grocery store not far from there. I've already contacted him. All you have to do is call him and let him know what you need. He'll deliver it out to the house."

"That'll work. Thank you. Do you have any idea how long we'll be here?"

"Marsh thought only two or three days. We should have it resolved by then."

Have what *resolved*? Bailey wondered. *Who's been shooting at us* or *why they're shooting*?

"Also, there's no TV, Bailey. We've found the less we keep there, the less chance we have of getting burglarized."

"We'll manage."

"Good. Here's the number for my cousin."

"One moment. Let me get something to write with." She tugged on Marty's shirt. "Pen?" Marty nodded and went back inside. "Captain, do you really think these shootings have anything to do with the Romero case?"

"Of course, Bailey. Why else?"

Why else? Well, because she didn't really believe the murder was gang-related to begin with. So why would a gang be targeting Marty? She smiled a thank you when Marty handed her a pen. "I've got a pen. Go ahead, sir." She wrote the number on the paper Alvarez had given her, then handed it to Marty. "Thank you. I'll give him a call right now." She slipped the phone back in her pocket and pointed at the paper. "Grocery store. They'll deliver."

"Wonderful. Should I make a list? What would you like?"

"Sure. Chips, dips? Frozen pizza? Stuff like that, I guess."

Marty made a face. "Chips and dips? How about I make the list and surprise you," she suggested.

"You might want to check cookware first. It's pretty bare." Bailey shoved off the railing. "I'd love some more beer, though." She lifted the lid on the rusty barbeque grill, surprised to find that the bottom was still intact. "And a small bag of charcoal and a couple of steaks," she added with a grin. "And you know, stuff for a baked potato maybe?"

"Kris?"

"Hmm?"

"Isn't this all a little odd?" Marty asked. "I mean, we're at a beach house like it's a vacation or something."

"Odd? It's downright weird," she said.

Actually, she hadn't had time to even think about it. Lieutenant Marsh had them whisked off so fast, with only a quick stop at her duplex for clothes, that they hadn't even talked about it. Yeah, it was weird. Since when did the police department harbor nosy reporters in a safe house? Not to mention putting the faithful detective in with her. She doubted seriously that a gang had put a price on them. Of course, there was the matter of the shotgun she'd stared down that morning. She didn't get a good look at the guys in the car, but the car itself, yeah, it was a street car. So, maybe the lieutenant was right. Maybe they were targeted.

CHAPTER THIRTEEN

"So how does one get into cold cases?" Bailey asked. She stretched her legs out, enjoying the warm rays of the sun on her skin. "It's not something you grow up wanting to do, right?"

Marty laughed. "Hardly." She held her beer bottle up. "I don't normally drink beer, but this is pretty good."

Behind her sunglasses, Bailey studied Marty on the chaise lounge, her eyes following the length of her legs. They had changed into shorts and pulled chairs out into the sun. They were relaxing on the deck, but she had dutifully kept her weapon and holster on. The back deck was in relatively good shape if you ignored the handful of broken boards. The same could not be said for the pier out in the bay. The platform was missing more planks than remained, and Bailey didn't want to chance a walk on it, despite the wistfulness in Marty's voice when she mentioned it.

"What do you normally drink?"

"Wine, if anything," Marty said. "I wasn't really around alcohol growing up, so it was a learning experience for me. I've found it best to stick with wine."

Bailey grinned. "College experience?"

"My first party. I was sick for a week afterward. Some spiked punch concoction. To this day I can't drink punch, and I can barely tolerate juice," she said with a smile.

"Tell me about your career," Bailey coaxed.

"Quite by accident, I assure you. My journalism career started off at the college newspaper in Iowa City." She nodded at Bailey's unspoken question. "Yes. University of Iowa. It was nothing exciting, but it was a job and it fit my personality."

"How so?"

Marty flashed a grin. "I'm nosy and I like to ask questions. Anyway, I thought print journalism was going to be my niche, and I'm still floored that I was a TV news anchor for as long as I was."

"Cool. Where?"

"A short stay in Athens, then Atlanta. But God, I hated it."

"Why?"

"A monkey can dress up pretty and read the news. I wanted to be out on the streets getting the story, not smiling and reading a teleprompter as if I didn't have a brain in my head."

Bailey stood and took their empty beer bottles inside. "Where'd you grow up?" she asked as she walked back out and handed Marty a fresh beer. She was surprised by the silence that followed and even more surprised by the distressed look on her face. Bailey sat down and pulled her sunglasses down her nose, meeting Marty's eyes. "Wrong question?"

"I used to think I was as inquisitive as I was because I was interested in other people's lives and wanted to learn about them. Truth was—is—the more questions you ask, the less that get asked of you."

Bailey nodded. "Okay. So you didn't grow up around alcohol. Minister's kid?" she asked. That was met with a smile and a shake of the head. "Okay, no. A monastery?"

Marty laughed. "You think I wouldn't be able to find the communion wine?" She took a deep breath. "Actually, I was a part of the foster care system," she said.

Bailey didn't say anything, waiting for Marty to continue if she chose to.

"My parents and older sister were killed in a car accident when I was two." She pointed at the tiny scar at the edge of her chin. "I required only a few stitches. Obviously my car seat did its job."

"I'm sorry," Bailey said automatically. She'd noticed the scar that first day, but rather than marring Marty's features, it added to her attractiveness, in her opinion.

Marty stared out over the water. "I don't remember them. I have a few pictures, but that's it." She looked back at Bailey, then again to the water. "I was sent to live with my aunt and uncle— my mother's brother—in Iowa. They were simple people, had a farm, struggling to keep up with their own four kids." She turned shadowed eyes to Bailey. "They kept me until I was six. My grandmother took me in, but she wasn't in very good health to begin with. She got really sick, so we went to stay with her younger sister in Minnesota." Marty smiled. "That didn't go well. Back to my aunt and uncle in Iowa."

"What happened that it didn't go well?" Bailey could sense that this whole topic made Marty uncomfortable, but she was curious nonetheless.

"They weren't used to having kids around, for one thing. Then I fell off my bike and broke my arm," she said, pointing to her left one. "Then I got sick. Started with bronchitis, then pneumonia. Spent a couple of weeks in the hospital."

"No insurance?"

"None. I remember missing a bunch of school. It was like they took me there whenever they felt like it, that's all. I was in the second grade. That summer, back to Iowa." She made a face. "Those kids *hated* me," she said quietly. "And I don't know why. I wasn't a bad kid, I wasn't needy. I kept to myself."

She stood then, and Bailey watched her go to the railing and lean on it, her back to the house as she stared out over the water, seemingly transfixed by it. Or perhaps calmed by it.

"When school let out for Christmas, there was a lady at the bus when I tried to get on. She had my old brown suitcase." She turned back around. "Eight years old. It took two weeks to get a foster home. So I missed Christmas that year." She walked back and sat down. "I lost count of how many I lived in. But the last one, I was a sophomore in high school. The Grahams. They were good people. They pushed me to go to college, helped me out as best they could."

Bailey lowered her sunglasses again, searching Marty's eyes, wondering why there wasn't more regret there. She seemed almost at peace. *Maybe that's the only way she can cope.* "Hell of a start to life, huh?"

"Yes. But I guess I didn't really know any different. I changed schools so many times, I think that's where I picked up my habit of asking a hundred questions. New people, new places." She shrugged. "I've probably had a harder time of it as an adult than as a child," she said. "Now I know all the things I didn't back then," she said quietly. "I can't blame my aunt and uncle, really. They didn't ask for a fifth child. But it's a little frightening knowing the only family you had in the world didn't want you." She shielded her eyes but not before Bailey saw the misting of tears. "And now as an adult, it's hell knowing there's no one in my life."

Bailey didn't know what to say, and she certainly didn't want to talk about her own life, but she said the one thing she hoped would matter. "I know…I know what you're feeling," she said.

Marty turned wary eyes on her. "Do you?"

Bailey nodded. "I'm just not there yet."

"You moved to Brownsville because of an illness," Marty stated.

"My mother. I moved here to take care of her. She has Alzheimer's," she explained, surprised at how matter-of-fact she sounded. "My mother left Houston over ten years ago. They had a beach house here on the bay, actually," Bailey said, motioning to the water. "Down in Port Isabel. They'd had it for years and years. My mother was a school teacher so growing up, she'd come up here with me and my brother, and we'd live here during the summer. My dad would come on his days off."

"Is he a cop too?"

Bailey shook her head. "No, fireman. So was his father before him. My brother followed in their shoes, but I wanted something different. It really wasn't until I was in college that I considered the police force." She smiled, remembering the day she told her mother. "My mother and I fought constantly, yet we were as close as you could get. She was my best friend, my confidant and my family."

"They're divorced?"

Bailey looked up. "No. Not divorced." And she wasn't really in the mood to go into all that. "But she's all I have. So I gave up my life in Houston to take care of her. Only I wasn't able to. After about six months it was obvious she couldn't stay by herself while I was at work. She'd wander away, just start walking. One day the neighbors called. She was out in the bay, water up to her waist. She was wearing her robe and slippers. Well, one of them." She smiled, knowing it wasn't funny, but back then, at least her mother was cognizant enough a few days later to talk about it. They'd had a good laugh. Probably the last good laugh they'd had. "She's in an assisted care facility now. They cost a fortune, by the way. I had to sell the beach house to afford it." She held her empty beer bottle tightly. "It's been ten months since she's recognized me. Six months since she's spoken a word."

"I'm sorry," Marty said. "Alzheimer's is a terrible, terrible disease. I can imagine how awful it is to watch a loved one suffer with it."

Bailey peeled the label on her bottle, thinking about the last two years. The last five really. Since the disease was diagnosed. "At first, we managed. We dealt with it. She could still function.

But it just happened so fast. She was only sixty-three when we found out. And now five short years later, she's unresponsive, staring out her window at nothing. All day, every day."

"You go see her often?"

Bailey closed her eyes. "I used to go every day. Now, a couple of times a week. I can't take seeing her like that. I realize she doesn't even know I'm there when I go, but I feel guilty if I don't. I'm all she has. She's all I have."

"What about your brother?"

Bailey shook her head. "No." She met her eyes across the deck. "A story for another time."

"I understand."

Bailey took a deep breath and looked to the sky. "How did we get off on this subject?"

"You asked me how I got started on cold cases," Marty reminded her.

Bailey sat up. "I'm starved. How about you tell me about it over frozen pizza?"

"Judging by your enthusiasm when you saw the steaks, I thought you'd want them tonight."

"We'll save them for tomorrow. Pizza with beer tonight."

"And tomorrow?"

"I snuck a bottle of wine in my backpack."

Marty laughed. "We've been shot at—*twice*—and your lieutenant has ordered protection for a couple of days, and you sneak wine into our safe house?"

Bailey left the kitchen door open to the deck, letting in the breeze off the bay. "I'm not entirely convinced we're in need of a safe house. Are you?"

"Well, granted, this morning could have been a coincidence. We weren't exactly in the best part of town," she said. "But last night, we were in the middle of *something*. We have bullet holes in my rental to prove it." She laughed as she pulled the pizza out of the freezer, "Of course, your car is missing the back window." She looked at the box. "Put the oven on four hundred."

Bailey turned the knob on the ancient stove, then opened the oven door, sticking her hand inside to feel for warmth. "I guess it works." She slammed the door shut and leaned her hip against it. "I've changed my mind about last night. It's almost as if someone didn't want this guy telling us where to meet Quin Mendoza. So they took him out. But at the same time, it's as if they didn't want to hurt us. If you're randomly spraying bullets, chances are both of our cars get hit. Chances are, we get hit. But your car had eight hits. That's it. Think about it. How many shots did we hear? Thirty or forty?"

Marty nodded. "Yeah. At least."

"So, they were either giving us a warning to get the hell out of there or the eight hits were accidental. I think whoever did the hit last night intentionally spared us."

"Who? Why?"

"The million-dollar questions."

"And this morning? You've changed your mind? You think it might have been carjacking?"

Bailey opened the fridge and took out another beer. "My Honda's six years old. You think someone really wanted it that badly that they'd pull a shotgun?"

"I don't know. Do you?"

She twisted the cap on the beer and tossed it in the trash. "How did they know where we were going? I watched. We weren't being followed. So someone was just lying in wait for two helpless females to come by, hoping to steal their car," she said, pausing as she wiggled her eyebrows. "Or we were marked."

"If you're hoping to steal a car and you point a shotgun at those two helpless females," Marty said, "are you really going to shoot the dang thing if they drive off? Talk about calling attention to yourself. What do you hope to accomplish by blowing out the back window?"

"Maybe he was pissed that we didn't stop."

"Or maybe he didn't want your car at all. Maybe he wanted us."

"So tell me how you *really* got into cold cases," Kristen said later as they sat on the floor next to the couch and shared the pizza.

Marty thought back to all the arguments she'd had with her news director, how she'd begged him to let her go out and do a real story. "The news director got tired of me pleading for a story," she said. "I was a journalist. I wanted to be a reporter. I hated the daily ritual of sitting for makeup, looking over a script that someone else had written, smiling on cue and showing just the right amount of sympathy when relaying news of a death." She pointed a slice of pizza at Kristen and donned her most professional expression. "Two bodies were pulled from the wreckage, neither wearing seatbelts. An investigation is still underway, but police believe alcohol and drugs may have been involved." She then flashed a smile and pretended to turn to another camera. "On a lighter note, Boo Boo, the beloved elephant at our local zoo, has finally given birth to a wobbly-kneed three hundred-pound baby boy after a twenty-two month pregnancy." Her eyes widened. "Twenty-two months, ladies. Can you imagine that?" She took a bite out of her pizza and grinned at Kristen. "And that, my friend, is the news," she said as she chewed. "Exciting, isn't it?"

"Very."

"So after begging for a news story, I was given what was supposed to be a fluff piece. It was the tenth anniversary of an unsolved triple murder at a local pizza place. They were doing a memorial. Buzz's Pizza. Doesn't sound very authentic, I know, but they have the best pizza in Atlanta," she said. "Anyway, I was supposed to do a recap on the murders, profile the three girls killed and tell the sad story of how no one was ever convicted. Not only that, but there were never even any suspects. Well, the murders happened well before I hit Atlanta, so I wanted to familiarize myself with the case. The police were extremely accommodating," she said, playfully nudging Kristen's shoulder. "They interviewed a ton of witnesses. Some several times over. One thing that jumped out at me was that the answers seemed almost practiced, you know? So, I went back out and met with some of the witnesses, but I didn't ask questions. I just visited with them and we talked about the case and eventually they began to remember stuff. They weren't answering point blank questions anymore. They were *telling* me the story instead of recounting what happened to a police investigator. Well, I was able to get a better description of the three guys who broke in, this from a woman and her teenaged daughter, who was only six at the time. They were coming home from an aunt's birthday party and it was nearly midnight. They passed by the pizza place as three men were rushing to a car. They couldn't remember if the sports car was blue or black, but the girl could describe them now. At six, she was too scared. In fact, I don't think the police even bothered with her."

"How did you find them? Were they part of the original investigation?"

"Yes. After the news of the murders broke, the woman came forward, just to say she'd seen three men leaving Buzz's after hours. She didn't really have a description of them at the time. And really, when I interviewed her again, she still didn't. But the girl did. Anyway, I just kept digging and found someone who remembered the car—it was dark blue—an older model Trans Am. This from a car buff who was never asked that question by the police. They asked standard questions. The more you got right, the more they asked. They started with him, and he didn't see the guys, didn't know anything, really. So that's all they asked. When I found him, I went deeper. Yeah, he'd seen the car speeding away, but the police didn't ask him about it so he assumed they already knew about the car." She tossed her napkin down and leaned back with a satisfied sigh. "That was pretty good pizza for frozen."

Kristen nodded. "So you got to do your news story?"

"Yes. And I was so excited to put it all together. When it aired and with this new information, well, all of a sudden people started calling the station wanting to give their take on it. They started calling the police. So I got a visit from one of the detectives, who wanted to go over all my notes. Ten years later, I'd ended up with more details on the case than they got at the time of the murders."

She stretched her legs out, then stole a pepperoni off of the last remaining slice of pizza. "Long story short…they solved the case. One of the three was already in prison for armed robbery. The other two were in Chicago. One was a bouncer at a strip club. The other was married with a family, had a decent job." She opened the water bottle beside her and took a sip. "Crazy how things turn out, isn't it? Anyway, that's what ignited my passion for cold cases. And I was totally amazed at how many unsolved murders there are. Unsolved crime, period."

"And the book?"

She laughed. "I'm not a writer, I'm a journalist. Big difference. I was writing the book as if I was filing a report for the newspaper. I think it took me longer to edit the damn thing than it did to write it in the first place."

"Success?" Kristen asked.

"It wasn't hugely successful, if that's what you mean. I would say mildly successful. But I learned I didn't sensationalize nearly enough. People want the blood and guts of it all." She fiddled with her napkin before continuing. "These cases—these victims—became very personal to me, so I found I wanted to protect them and leave out the most horrific parts of the crimes. It ended up being a little too tame."

"Well, this case would satisfy the blood and guts," Kristen said. "Literally."

"Yeah. But it'll be a while before I go through the rigors of another book. For one thing, it doesn't pay enough."

"So, are you still a news anchor?"

"No. Once I got a taste of being out in the field, I knew that's what I wanted to do. Once my contract was up, I went to work for the newspaper. I got to do some feature articles on other cold cases I'd found. Actually, most of my income now comes from magazines. A lot of the true crime magazines pay really well, and I've developed a reputation with cold cases so I don't really have to push my articles. And I still write for the newspaper on occasion."

"And you just travel around, picking cold cases that interest you?"

Marty laughed. "Not quite. Some of the ones that interest me the most are ones that will never be solved. This case, for instance, wouldn't have been one I'd pick because after reading the file there's just no evidence to go on, there aren't a ton of witnesses to pick from. But because Kesara was so *passionate* about it, I wanted to at least give it a look." She paused. "To be honest, the prospect of a police cover-up—or even misconduct—makes it all the more interesting. And no offense meant. I know these are your colleagues."

"No offense taken, I assure you." Kristen pointed at the pizza. "I'm done. You want that last one?"

"I shouldn't," she said, patting her full belly. But it looked good. "Hate to see it go to waste, though."

Kristen held up the cardboard pizza tray. "Take it. Then I'm going to have to run you away from my bed," she said, indicating the sofa. "I'm beat."

"Are you sure you don't want the bed?"

"No, this'll be fine. Especially since you found some sheets."

Marty took a bite of the pizza, which was now cold, then got to her feet. She took the cardboard from Kristen and folded it in half. "I'll clean up."

"Thanks. I'll hit the shower first."

Marty methodically made up her bed with a set of the sheets she'd found in the closet, listening to the water run as Kristen finished her shower. It had been a strange day all around, made more so by her admission of her foster care upbringing. While she had left out most of the horrors she'd faced as a child—feeling so lost, alone and rejected—it was still a subject she rarely broached. For some reason, she felt completely at ease with Kristen, almost as if they were old friends. And she appreciated Kris confiding in her about her mother's condition. Although, apparently the subject of her father and brother was off limits. She assumed they were estranged and had been for some time.

"It's all yours," Kristen called, interrupting her thoughts.

Marty grabbed her toiletry bag and the flannel pajama bottoms she usually wore, both summer and winter. Kristen was already on the sofa, the sheet covering her.

"How was it?"

"Passable. The towels are obviously meant for little people," she murmured as she rolled over.

Marty smiled, not caring. As long as the water was hot.

And it was.

CHAPTER FOURTEEN

"Okay, I'm officially bored out of my mind," Marty said after hours of alternating between sunbathing on the deck, surfing the 'Net on her laptop, attempting to work on her notes for the case, napping and finally flipping through the handful of magazines she'd found, most of them five years old or older.

"I thought your little phone card thing got you online," Kristen said. "You know, earlier you did the victory yell when you got a signal."

"That was five hours ago. I'm an Internet junkie, but even *I* have a limit." She stood and looked longingly at the water. "Are you sure we can't go swimming?"

"You don't really swim in the bay, Marty. You wade out there if you're going to fish. You take Jet Skis and play around. Kayaks. But you don't really swim."

"Okay, how about wading then?"

"It's April. The water's still a little cold. And even then, you'd want waders on. Jellyfish and man-of-war are pretty common in the spring," she said. "Wouldn't be pretty."

Marty sighed heavily, then put her hands on her hips. "I don't suppose you've heard from your lieutenant on when we might be sprung from this place, huh?"

Kristen laughed. "No, but I'll make sure you're the first to know." She pulled her sunglasses off her nose. "Is it too early for a beer?"

"No. Sounds good." She turned to go back inside to fetch them. "But if I drink beer, you're going to have to feed me an early dinner," she said over her shoulder.

"After that delicious brunch you whipped up, how can you possibly be hungry?"

Marty smiled at that, pleased that Kristen had enjoyed it. The'd lingered over coffee, it had been nearly ten. Instead of bacon and eggs and canned biscuits, she'd used the potatoes and cheese and whipped up a casserole with the bacon and eggs instead.

She smiled as she handed Kristen a beer. "That was hours and hours ago. Besides, I'm looking forward to your steaks tonight." She sat down in the lounge opposite Kristen and tried to relax. For some reason, she felt like they were wasting precious time being here. She had this nagging feeling that there was something she should be doing.

"You know, I never thought to ask," Kristen said. "You're not wearing a wedding ring, but do you have a boyfriend back in Atlanta?"

"No," she said, surprised by the question. "Why?"

"Well, the lieutenant whisked us out here so fast, we really didn't have time to call anyone, and I haven't noticed you on your phone."

"I guess I should pose the same question to you. I just assumed you were single, I don't know why."

Kristen nodded. "Single, yes."

"Why?"

"Why? Why is anyone single? Why are *you* single?"

"I'm sure my issues are completely different than yours," she said. "But you're very attractive, you're nice, you seem normal." She frowned. "Are you a player?"

Kristen laughed, a loud laugh that seemed to bounce across the deck. "A 'player'? Hardly." The smile left her lips, and she shoved her sunglasses on top of her head. "I was in a relationship back in Houston. But when I came out here, that ended."

"Long distance must be tough," she said.

"We never tried. Liz said if I loved her, I wouldn't leave. I said if she loved me, she'd come with me." She shrugged. "I can't blame her. All her family was there, her friends. She had a very good job, one I'm sure she couldn't duplicate down here."

"How serious were you?"

"We lived together. A little over three years."

"Why didn't you try doing the long distance thing then? There's so many means of communication now—webcams and whatnot—you could be in touch constantly."

"Call me old-fashioned, but those things can't replace a warm body. Besides, she wasn't receptive to long distance either. No, we amicably ended it and wished each other well."

"Do you keep in touch?"

"Not anymore. We did at first, but, well, she's moved on. She's seeing someone."

"Are you still in love with her?" Marty watched as Kris seemed to consider the question thoroughly before answering.

"No, I'm not. It was tough at first, but I realized that our relationship wasn't really all that I thought it was if I could just pack up and leave...and she could let me go without a fight."

"You haven't met anyone down here?"

"I haven't been looking. I haven't gone out anywhere to meet someone. At first, with my mother, there just wasn't a spare minute. Now...well, I know I won't be staying here, so there's no point. I'll probably go back to Houston."

Marty didn't say anything, reading between the lines, knowing

Kristen was only staying until her mother passed on.

"So what's your story, Miss News Anchor? Being on TV, you must have had guys falling at your feet."

"True." God, this was a subject she *never* talked about. Her normal response was that her career came first and she just didn't have time to devote to dating. And truth was, she did date. Sort of.

"But?"

She shielded her eyes against the sun, looking at Kristen, wondering again why she felt so comfortable with her. This was a subject she'd talked about at length with her therapist. Whether she wanted to share that fact with Kristen or not, she wasn't sure. Some people viewed seeing a therapist as a weakness. She didn't know what look she had on her face, but Kristen smiled gently, her eyes softening.

"Hey, if it's not something you want to talk about, don't. I was just curious, that's all."

"It's not something I normally discuss, no," she admitted. "I mean, I do date, if you want to call it that."

"Well, I'm sure you travel a lot. That must be hard to maintain a relationship."

So, Kristen had given her an out. She was surprised that she didn't want to take it. "That's not it exactly. I date men, go out to dinner, that sort of thing. I just don't sleep with them." She laughed as Kristen's eyebrows shot up.

"Don't like sex?"

"No, actually, I don't."

"Wow. What do I say to that?"

"Nothing. I have trust issues, or so my therapist said."

"From your childhood," Kristen guessed.

"Yes. When I was in high school, college even, I couldn't understand what was wrong with me. I had no interest whatsoever in dating. I had no interest in being a couple," she admitted. "I was used to being by myself, used to taking care of myself."

"And your hormones weren't raging?"

"No."

"Maybe you just never met the right guy. Or woman," she teased with a wink.

"Funny. Actually, I did sleep with a woman once. I met her at my first job in Atlanta. She made it known she was interested in me. I finally accepted a date from her." Marty looked away, recalling the night in question. "And we ended up in bed. It wasn't memorable."

"Why'd you do it? Did you think you were gay?"

"I'm not sure. I wasn't interested in guys, so I thought maybe—" she shrugged. "But no. She didn't do it for me either. I accepted the fact that I was asexual." She laughed at the look on Kristen's face. "I know what you're thinking. But I just had—*have*—no interest in a sexual relationship. Every time I tried, I felt violated afterward."

"Were you...were you abused as a child?" she asked gently.

Marty shook her head. "No. At first, I thought maybe I was and I'd just blocked it out. You know, you hear of people doing that. But I started seeing a therapist and talked it all out. There weren't any gaps or anything in my childhood that I didn't remember, there were no major, traumatic events. I mean, the accident with my parents, I certainly don't remember. I was two. But I got handed off so many times, so many people didn't want me—my aunt and uncle, my grandmother—I just never learned to trust anyone. Really trust, that is. That's carried over to all aspects of my life. I don't trust anyone with my body. I don't trust anyone with my heart." She held up her empty beer bottle and Kristen nodded. "I don't know if medically my condition is considered asexual in the traditional sense or not or if it's just the label my therapist and I came up with." She paused. "In my case, I'm certain it's more of a mental issue than physical."

"So you've stopped trying?"

"Yes." She went inside, wondering what was going through Kristen's mind. Did Kristen think she was some sort of freak? Marty knew from experience that it wasn't something normal people understood.

When she went back out with another beer for them, Kristen had put her sunglasses back on and was staring out at the bay. "I won't be offended if you want to ask questions," Marty said. Her comment was met with a grin.

"That's usually my line when someone without a clue discovers I'm gay."

Marty sat down again, watching Kristen, seeing questions form. She waited.

"So, like in college, there wasn't some cute guy that all the girls were swooning over, you included? I mean, swooning over in that 'oh, he's so cute' way. Not necessarily 'oh, I want to have sex with him.'"

"Well, sure, I've found people to be physically attractive. But none that I'm physically attracted to. Does that make sense?"

"I guess it's much like a straight woman might see a lesbian and think she's attractive, but that doesn't mean she wants to sleep with her."

"Exactly."

"But you've had sex?"

Marty laughed. "Yes, I told you I tried it. Several times. Well, not several, but enough to know it's not something I want, something I need and certainly not something I miss."

Kristen sat up and leaned closer. "So, you've never had an orgasm?"

Marty laughed again. "I'm fairly certain we don't know each other well enough to be having this conversation."

"You're right. I'm sorry. I just—"

"But yes, I had an orgasm once."

"*Once*? And?"

"And what? I was alone at the time."

"But…*oh*," Kristen said, and Marty was surprised by the blush that covered Kristen's face. "I see. You mean…"

"Yes."

Kris nodded. "You're right. We probably don't know each

other well enough for this conversation," she said with an embarrassed smile.

"I'm sorry. I didn't mean to be so blunt."

"No. I shouldn't have been so nosy," Kristen said.

Marty should just let it go, but, for whatever reason, it was important that Kristen understand it. Understand *her*. "You can't comprehend it at all, can you?"

"Not entirely, no. And I can relate to a degree. There have been times in my life where others I'm with will meet someone and just think they have this animal magnetism or something, and I'll look at them and…nothing," she said. "Not even a tiny spark. But to think that there was no one—*ever*—who turned me on," she shook her head. "Wow. I can't imagine going through life without that human contact."

"Yes. But that's because you've experienced it and you know what it is. And you know you'd miss it." She pointed at herself. "Me? No one's ever moved me that way. Ever. Kissing was as intimate to me as a handshake. Someone touching my breasts…well, they could have been rubbing my forearm and gotten the same reaction. There was no stimulation," she said quietly, thinking the conversation had gone on long enough. She certainly didn't want to get into the issue of the sex act itself, how she'd never been aroused and how terribly painful and dry it was.

"So you've accepted the fact that you're going to go through life without having a sexual relationship with someone?"

"Yes. But Kris, remember, you can't miss something you've never had. You can't long for something that you can't even relate to. It doesn't bother me anymore." *And it didn't, did it?*

"But it did?"

"Yes. I didn't feel normal. That's why I sought out a therapist. And before you ask, yes, I saw a medical doctor. I was convinced it was just a hormonal issue, in that I was lacking *all* of them," she said with a grin. "But I was perfectly normal." She put her beer down, no longer in the mood for it. "I know it's hard for others to comprehend, but it's not something I dwell on. It just *is*, you know."

"Well, I don't know if I should say 'I'm sorry,' or 'Aren't you lucky.' You won't have to deal with all the bullshit that goes with having a sexual relationship." Her smile faded. "I don't mean to make light of it. Really, I don't."

"No offense taken. Like I said, I don't normally discuss this with anyone. You're right. I do travel a lot. It's hard to maintain any kind of relationship that way—friends or lovers." She shrugged. "I don't think my personality fits my inner soul. I've learned to be outgoing, to talk to people, to even be gregarious on occasion. And all of that comes from having moved around so much as a kid. I wasn't the type to go into a shell. Yet at the same time, everything was always superficial. Because deep down, I didn't really believe anything people said. I never trusted anyone. Yet the friendships I made, I wouldn't say they were fake or phony. It just didn't get much deeper than the surface. I never really let anyone *inside*," she said, tapping her heart.

"Yet you don't appear to be lonely," Kris stated.

"No, not at all. My life is very fulfilling. My career is rewarding. I've met wonderful people along the way." She pointed at Kris. "You, for instance. I feel like I have a connection with you." She smiled. "And I don't mean to make you uncomfortable with that statement, but I feel very at ease around you." She laughed lightly. "I must. I've shared my most embarrassing secret with you."

Kristen sat up. "Oh, no. Please don't feel embarrassed by it. I...well, I appreciate you trusting me enough to share that. And like you, I feel very comfortable around you as well."

"Thank you."

Kristen stood up. "You ready to start on that early dinner?"

CHAPTER FIFTEEN

Bailey stood in the middle of the deck, absently listening as Marty piddled around in the kitchen, cleaning up after their dinner. The meal had been delicious, but simple. Steaks and baked potatoes only. But the conversation had been easy, light.

Now she stood outside, enjoying the beautiful, pleasant evening, the sun having set an hour before. April and May were two of her favorite months on the coast. The days not so blistering hot that you can't stand to be outside and the nights lacking that chill of winter when the breeze off the bay brings a coolness to the air. No, this time of year was nearly perfect. Low humidity, no mosquitoes, fresh air and clear skies. She looked overhead, seeing only a smattering of stars, the moon and the lights of Brownsville too bright for a full display. Despite the reason they were here, she could honestly say she was enjoying herself. Being on the bay brought back memories of her youth and happier times. Times when they'd come out here as a family, spending a nearly endless summer on the water. The old beach house was all she had left, and it had nearly killed her to have to sell it. But once her mother was gone, she doubted she'd want to come down here anyway. There were too many memories.

"Hey."

Bailey turned, finding Marty watching her. She walked closer, holding out a glass of wine.

"Thought you might like this."

"Thanks. I was just thinking how pleasant it is," Bailey said as she took a sip.

"Yes, it's a nice evening." Marty walked to the edge of the deck and leaned her arms on the railing, holding her own glass loosely in her fingers. "I've found I love the water," she said. "It's so calming. So peaceful." She glanced at Bailey. "I haven't really spent any time at all near water. I've been to L.A. a few times but never took the time for the beach. And the East Coast, well, I did make a trip to South Carolina. But it was raining the day I visited Myrtle Beach."

"The Gulf Coast is all I've ever known," Bailey said. "But I love the water. I could sit and stare at it, listen to it, *smell* it for hours on end." She moved to stand beside Marty near the railing. "I'm sorry you didn't get a chance to get out in it," she said. "Maybe you might want to take some time to hit Padre Island."

Marty turned away from the water. "Oh, I don't know. We'll see how this case goes. I have a feeling it's all but over."

"Like we're at a dead end?"

"Yeah. I was looking over my notes earlier. There's not really anyone left to interview. Quin Mendoza was going to be a good one, but that blew up." She sipped from her wine before continuing. "I'm not certain how much light he would have shed on it anyway, other than to say Carlos wasn't a part of that gang, which we already know."

"We could always try to talk to Juan Vargas and see what he remembers."

"Like your lieutenant is going to let me interview one of his

86

detectives. I don't think so."

"You could ask," Bailey suggested, although she figured Lieutenant Marsh wouldn't let Marty anywhere near Vargas.

"No. And I'm not sure if we've even accomplished anything, you know. I suspect that Carlos was clean. I'm fairly certain that he was an innocent boy at the wrong place, wrong time. But evidence to that effect?" She shook her head. "No. Because we haven't talked to anyone. We've been shot at, that's it. It's all so confusing. And I know there's something up with your department. There has to be a reason someone took the scorpion idol from the evidence box."

Bailey nodded. That had been bothering her too. She doubted just anyone would do that. Had to be Marsh or even Captain Diaz. Or at least they gave the order. But why? Why tamper with ten-year-old evidence? It did nothing but call attention to the fact that they didn't want Marty Edwards nosing around the case, as if they had something to hide. Which it looked more and more like they did.

"Of course, if this were a normal case," Marty continued, "I would just go to Lieutenant Marsh and report that something was missing from the evidence box."

"Yeah. And the way things are going, he'd probably accuse you of taking it. Or me," she added.

"Yes. Or maybe—" The ringing of a cell phone interrupted Marty. "Yours or mine?"

"Mine. Maybe it's Lieutenant Marsh giving us the all clear," she said hopefully as she headed inside. Her phone was on the bar next to her gun and holster, which she'd discarded earlier. But when she answered, there was no one there. Just silence.

"Bailey here," she said again with a frown.

At the sound of breaking glass, she whipped her head around, hearing a muffled scream from out on the deck. She grabbed her weapon and ran to the door, her eyes wide as she saw Marty in the grasp of a masked man, the knife at her neck shining brightly in the moonlight. One hand covered Marty's mouth, pulling her face up, exposing her neck to the blade.

Marty saw her and their eyes locked, Bailey seeing the fright there in the split second it took her to raise her arm. She fired twice. Time stood still as Marty's eyes closed from the impact, the assailant's weight taking them both down to the deck. It was deathly silent, and the bile rose in Bailey's gut as she feared she'd shot Marty in her haste. But finally there was a whimper, a moan and then a scream that echoed around them in the darkness. Bailey ran to her, pulling the man to one side, his lifeless body heavy to move, the gaping hole in his throat showing Bailey she'd hit her target. Marty was covered in blood, her mouth open but her screams now silent as her eyes found Bailey's.

"Help me. Get him off, get him off, get him *off*," she chanted.

"Are you hurt? There's so much blood," Bailey said, lifting Marty's neck, seeing the tiny slice across her throat.

"I don't know. Just get me up."

Bailey pulled Marty to her feet, then Marty held her hands up, the blood on them dark and sticky looking.

"Oh, my God," she whispered. She looked at her T-shirt, a once-white garment now stained a bright red. She turned away from Bailey, making it to the edge of the deck before she lost her dinner. The retching sounds of her stomach emptying made Bailey want to follow suit. Marty finally stood, tears streaming down her face, her hands trembling as reality set in. "Please," she whispered to Bailey. "The blood, get it off. Get it off."

Bailey grabbed her hand and pulled her inside, not pausing until she slid the shower curtain aside. She put the water on, then turned to Marty, her entire body now trembling, her teeth chattering, her eyes dull and unfocused, her clothing stained in blood.

"Sit down," she said softly, guiding Marty to the toilet seat. She took off her shoes, the sneakers splattered in blood. "Now stand," she said, Marty obeying silently. She pulled the bloody T-shirt over her head, smearing Marty's face with cold, damp blood, but Marty didn't seem to notice—her eyes remained unfocused. Bailey removed the rest of her clothing, finally guiding her into the now-warm shower. Marty stood still, her naked body dripping with streaked blood as it washed away.

They were making a mess of the bathroom, but Bailey hardly cared. She got nearly as wet as Marty as she washed her, taking the cloth and soap and scrubbing Marty's skin. "Turn around," she said, holding Marty's head to the water, wetting her hair. She squeezed shampoo into her hand, then lathered Marty's hair, doing the best she could to clean it. The water ran nearly clear now as she washed the last of the blood away.

She took two towels from the shelf, wrapping them around Marty as she led her from the shower. "Look up," she said. "I want to see your neck."

Marty stared at her for a moment, then slowly lifted her head. The cut was no more than an inch long, barely breaking the skin. Bailey nodded. "Good."

"I...I'm sorry," Marty whispered. "I—"

"Shhh, no." Bailey pulled her into a wet hug, her clothes and Marty's towel equally damp. "Come on. Let's get you dressed."

Marty sat silently on the bed, watching as Bailey rummaged in her bag, pulling out a bra and a pair of panties. She held up jeans and looked at Marty questioningly. Marty nodded. She walked over to her and laid the garments beside Marty.

"Would you rather dress alone?"

"No. Please don't leave me."

Bailey nodded. "I won't." She picked up the panties and handed them to Marty. "Here. Maybe you should do this part." She saw the flicker of a smile touch Marty's face, and she turned away, giving Marty privacy.

"You've just bathed me," Marty said, her voice quiet. "I don't think there's any room left for modesty."

"True." She turned back around as she heard Marty stand. Marty was slipping on her bra, and Bailey's gaze strayed to her small breasts before she pulled her eyes away again. "I need to call it in, Marty. I need to call Marsh."

Marty jerked her head around. "No," she said quickly. "I don't want to be in here alone." She glanced to the window, the blinds drawn tight. "What if—"

"Okay. It's okay. Get dressed. I'll wait for you."

Bailey didn't think there were two assailants. If there were, they'd already know about it. But she understood Marty's fear. So she waited while Marty finished dressing, then led her into the living room. "Sit here," she said, motioning toward the sofa. Marty's hand squeezed painfully around her own, not letting her go. "I'll be right here," she said. "Let me put some coffee on. Then I'll call it in, okay?"

Marty sat down, her hands clasped together, her eyes never leaving Bailey's as she nodded.

* * *

Marty sat on the sofa, clutching the coffee cup tightly in her hands, her eyes darting around the room full of men, looking for Kristen. She saw her through the kitchen window, standing on the deck talking to Marcos Fernandez, the man who had been introduced as her partner. The body had already been taken, thankfully. By whom, she didn't know. Kristen had told her that Cameron County had jurisdiction, but that Captain Diaz had cleared it so that his department could be involved. She'd given her statement to both a sheriff's deputy and to Detective Fernandez. Kristen had done the same.

The nightmare of the evening was slowly subsiding, but she still couldn't believe it had happened. It was one thing to be in the car and get shot at. Quite another to have a knife blade held to your throat. She touched the small bandage Kris had put there more for comfort than anything else.

"Miss Edwards?"

She turned, surprised to see Lieutenant Marsh standing behind her. "Yes?"

"Are you okay?"

She nodded.

"I must apologize. I was certain this place would be safe for you."

"Who was he?"

"Detective Fernandez says his tattoo indicates he's with *Los Demonios Rojos*."

"And that's who you said had targeted me?"

"Yes, Miss Edwards. I'm sorry we weren't able to protect you better."

"Better?" She set her coffee cup down and looked toward Kristen. "I think Detective Bailey did an admirable job. After all, I am still alive."

"Yes. You were lucky this time." He stood in front of her, blocking her view. "I'm afraid I must insist you give up this so-called investigation of yours and leave town. I can't possibly guarantee your safety after this."

Marty nodded. For once, she had to agree with him.

"I've taken the liberty of booking you a flight out. I thought it was the least we could do." He pulled an envelope from his coat pocket and handed it to her. "I've also booked you a room at a hotel near the airport. I have an officer standing by to drive you there. I've also instructed him to guard your room tonight and escort you to the airport in the morning."

"That's all very kind of you."

"Unfortunately, it's a six a.m. flight," he said. He motioned to the bedroom. "Why don't you get your things together, Miss Edwards? I'm sure you're anxious to get out of here. It'll be a while yet before they're through here."

She looked through the windows to the deck where no less than seven or eight people, including Kristen, were talking animatedly. She nodded and made her way to the tiny bedroom. There wasn't much to pack as she'd never really unpacked. The towels Kristen had used to dry her were tossed haphazardly on the bed, reminding her of the mess the bathroom must be in. She closed her eyes, remembering all the blood, the heaviness of the

man as he fell on her, the way her heart had stopped, thinking...
well, thinking she was going to die.

"You okay?"

She turned, finding Kristen watching her. "Yeah. Just a little
shaky still," she admitted.

Kristen closed the door and came closer, her eyes taking in
the luggage Marty had beside her.

"Lieutenant Marsh says you're leaving."

"Yes. He's arranged it."

"It's probably best, Marty."

"I know. Obviously, there's something going on with this
case." She turned away. "Carlos Romero won't get justice, but
it's not worth losing my life over," she said. "Or yours." She felt
Kristen come up behind her and she so wished she had the right
to ask for comfort from her. It had been so long since she'd
had that kind of human contact. She finally felt hands on her
shoulders, and she turned around, moving into the circle of
Kristen's arms, feeling them close around her. She wasn't going
to cry. She never cried. But her heart felt heavy, her emotions
raw. So she accepted the comfort that Kristen offered, if just for
a moment, pushing the horrors of the last few hours away. She
closed her eyes, feeling safe as she wrapped her arms around
Kristen's waist and held tight. "Thank you for saving my life,"
she whispered. She felt Kristen nod, but she said nothing. Marty
took a deep breath, then pulled away. "It was like it was all in slow
motion," she said.

"I know."

"You were there so fast. He grabbed me. I didn't have time
to think, to do anything. And there you were." She squeezed
Kristen's hand, then dropped it. "And it took an eternity. When
I saw you raise your arm, when I saw the gun, I thought there
was no way for you to shoot him without hitting me. I had time
to think all that," she said. "I was so scared. But I looked in your
eyes, you looked so calm, so sure. And then I heard the shot, saw
your arm jerk, felt his weight as he fell on me." She tried to smile.

92

"I still didn't know if I was shot or not. It took an eternity, yet it was only a split second."

"I'm sorry. I didn't—"

"Oh, God, don't say you're sorry. You were wonderful, Kris. You allowed me to have my little anxiety fit afterward, you took care of me." She met her gaze. "There aren't words to convey what I feel. A simple 'thank you' won't do it." When Kristen would have protested, she stopped her. "No. I owe you my life. I won't ever forget that…or forget you."

Kristen nodded, a slight blush covering her face. "Yeah, well, I'm glad I was here for you. I wish you well, Marty." She took a step back and smiled. "If you're ever again in Brownsville—"

Marty laughed. "I'll owe you dinner," she finished for her.

Her smile faded as Kristen closed the door behind her. She wrapped her arms around herself, wondering at the closeness she felt for Kris after such a short time. *Maybe a near-death experience does that to you.* She turned back to her bag and zipped it up, taking one last look around the room. The only thing left behind were the clothes she'd been wearing during the…well, the attack. She didn't know if they needed them for evidence or not, but she certainly didn't want them.

"Miss Edwards?"

"Yes, I'm ready," she called, opening the door to a young man, his uniform pressed and starched, looking brand new. She followed him to the front door, then paused, turning back around. The lieutenant was nowhere to be found. Neither was Kristen. She sighed, then walked out into the night and slipped into the patrol car.

CHAPTER SIXTEEN

"Who knew we were there?" Bailey demanded as she paced in front of Lieutenant Marsh's desk. She ignored the flash of anger in his eyes. "There's a mole in the department, Lieutenant. How else would—"

"You've watched too much TV, Bailey. A *mole*? Get serious."

"I am serious. Getting shot at could almost be explained as a coincidence. Tonight? No way. They knew where we were and that woman almost lost her life," she said, her voice loud.

"But she didn't." His smile was condescending and Bailey felt her fists clench. "Thanks to you." He scooted his chair closer to his desk in a manner that indicated she was about to be dismissed. "You know nothing of the gangs around here, Bailey. They're more high-tech than we are and much more sophisticated than you imagine. For all we know, they did GPS tracking of your cell phones. Obviously they knew your number. They called it."

"We don't know that it was them. It didn't register a call-back number."

"And the lab explained to me how easy it is to hide the number when making a call. Why are you trying to make it out to be something it's not, Bailey? Just like this case. Why was the reporter so convinced it wasn't a gang?" He opened a file, effectively dismissing her. "Now I'm tired and it's late. I just want to sign off on this and go home. You should do the same. It's been a long night."

Yeah, it had been a long night and she was exhausted. But she wanted answers and she wasn't getting them. And she knew she wasn't *going* to get them. She turned and left his office, finding Marcos at his desk.

"Anything?" she asked.

"No. But this guy's been around. I'm sure we'll get a hit on prints."

"When?"

"In the morning, Bailey. The lab's got everything, but it's not like it's a rush. He's dead. Our vic is alive."

"Yeah. I forgot we don't work 24/7 here," she said sarcastically. She didn't wait for a reply as she walked past him.

* * *

Marty paced across her room, her mind racing. Somewhere out in the hallway of the massive hotel was a uniformed police officer…she hoped. But as tired as she was, she couldn't sleep, armed guard or not. She just had a bad feeling about it all. Lieutenant Marsh, while trying to be accommodating, was perhaps a little too anxious to get her out of town. And like Kristen, she didn't trust him. At all.

So she crawled on the bed and shoved pillows behind her, pulling her laptop onto her lap. She had a plane ticket, yes. That didn't mean she had to use it. In fact, it was almost too easy to book another flight. She'd fly from Brownsville to Houston, then on to New Orleans. She didn't know where she would go after that, but Atlanta wasn't it.

With a new ticket purchased she went about rearranging her luggage. She dumped out the contents of all her bags—the laptop bag, the small backpack and the two pieces of luggage. Her tentative plan was to carry on only what she absolutely needed and have the hotel ship the rest of her luggage to Atlanta. She'd have someone pick it up for her there. She thought that was better than ditching it in New Orleans. She had an image of her bags spinning—unclaimed—on the luggage carousel, thus setting off a mad search for her whereabouts! No, she didn't want to call any attention to herself. Hopefully, her police escort wouldn't notice her lack of luggage.

She stood beside the bed, tossing her dress slacks and skirts to the side. Unfortunately, that didn't leave a whole lot. When she'd packed for this trip, she hadn't planned on needing casual clothes. At least not more than the two pairs of jeans she'd brought with her. She eyed the khaki pants but didn't want to have to take extra shoes, so she dismissed that idea. The backpack easily held a pair of jeans, her lone remaining pair of shorts, two shirts and her underclothes. She kept out the other pair of jeans for her flight tomorrow. The rest she folded neatly and repacked in her luggage. She then rearranged her laptop bag, putting her notes and papers in the zippered compartments so that she could easily get to the laptop when she went through security in the morning.

She eyed the clock, knowing it was far too late to call Mrs. Paulson, the older woman she rented an apartment from. While Mrs. Paulson was used to her coming and going, she wanted to let her know that she'd be gone longer this time. How long, Marty didn't know. She'd call her tomorrow, she decided.

She then e-mailed David, an old friend from the TV station. They didn't see each other much anymore and talked even less, but they kept up through e-mail. David would think it odd that she'd ship her luggage to him there at the station, but she had no doubt he would do as she asked. She made a mental note to let Mrs. Paulson know that he would be bringing it by. Lastly, she called room service, making arrangements to have the hotel concierge pick up her luggage in the morning.

With that, she shut down her laptop and secured it in the bag, setting it on the desk. It was nearly midnight and her new flight was at seven, not six. She'd leave at the previously arranged time, of course, since the police officer assigned to her would no doubt report back to Lieutenant Marsh after he dumped her at the airport. She settled under the covers, hoping to get a few hours sleep.

Unfortunately, when she closed her eyes, she felt a knife blade at her throat, and she kept hearing the loud, resounding pop as Kristen fired her weapon. She opened her eyes again, reality sinking in. If Kristen had been only a second or two slower, she'd be dead. A few seconds, the difference between life and death.

She let her eyes close again, this time focusing on the strength she saw in Kristen's eyes as she calmly raised her weapon, aiming at her assailant. The image eased her fears just a bit, though sleep still failed to claim her.

CHAPTER SEVENTEEN

Bailey stood in the doorway, feeling her heart break all over again as she watched her mother. She was in the same position as the last time she'd visited, sitting in the straight back chair, staring out the window, her face just a blank mask.

"Hi, Mom," she said quietly, moving to stand beside her. She touched her shoulder, getting no acknowledgment that her mother knew she was there...that she knew anyone was there. She pulled up another chair, sitting beside her. "Had a little excitement last week," she said. "Got shot at twice. Almost felt like I was back in Houston." She took her mother's hand, rubbing her fingers lightly across her knuckles. "I killed a man." She looked away. "He was...he was trying to kill Marty." She cleared her throat. "She's a reporter, I guess you'd call her. We spent a little time together." She smiled. "And I know what you're thinking, but it wasn't like that. I mean, I liked her, but, you know. Anyway, this guy grabbed her and he had a knife. It's a miracle I didn't shoot her in the process, but there was no time to think, only react." She shrugged. "I had to sit through an evaluation with a shrink," she said. "That wasn't a whole lot of fun. Remember back in Houston when I got shot? Remember how many psych visits I had? Well, I don't enjoy them any better now."

She reached out and turned her mother's face, trying to meet her eyes. She did, but there was no recognition there, no emotion, no expression. "Can you see me, Mom?" she whispered. "I know you're in there. Somewhere."

After a few moments, she lowered her hand and her mother's face turned back to the window, away from her. She squeezed her fingers, then stood. "I guess I should go." She moved the chair back and stood behind her mother again. "I'll see you next time," she said. She paused, her gaze lingering on her mother for a second longer. "I love you."

Outside her mother's room, a young nurse walked by, one who Bailey knew only in passing.

"Still no words for you?"

Bailey shook her head. "No. Nothing."

"I'm sorry. I wish I could offer hope but—"

"I know. I've accepted it. At least she appears to be comfortable. Thank you for that."

"For some reason, she wants to sit at the window and look out. I'm not sure she sees anything. But each morning when we come to check on her, she's already sitting at the window, just staring out."

"I guess her appetite is not any better. She looks so thin," Bailey noted.

"No. It's no better. Mashed potatoes seem to be her favorite. And she doesn't mind broth. I think she enjoys sipping through the straw."

"Okay, thank you, Alyssa. I'll be back in a few days or so."

"Of course."

She walked on. Bailey took one last look at her mother, then closed the door quietly behind her.

CHAPTER EIGHTEEN

The sun was warm on her face, even though it was barely ten in the morning. She crossed the busy street, holding her coffee gingerly in one hand so as not to spill it. In the other, she clutched the bag that contained two sinfully delicious cinnamon rolls. Marty had found the small bakery the first week she'd been here and had made going there a morning ritual. But usually only for coffee and something less fattening than the sweet, doughy cinnamon rolls that she'd chosen today.

As she climbed the stairs to her rented house, she tilted her head, looking past the row of houses in front of hers to view the beach. She would have loved to have an unobstructed view of the water, but her bank account would not allow it. So she'd settled for one block from the beach, where she was still able to hear the waves and smell the water and, if she positioned herself just right, see the water as she peeked around the stilted houses in front. Most were brand-new, having been built to replace those destroyed or badly damaged by Katrina. It was amazing how quickly the area had recovered.

After four weeks, she still didn't know why she'd chosen to go to Gulfport, Mississippi. When the plane had landed in New Orleans, she'd disembarked and headed for the rental car counters. No, she didn't know her destination, but she smiled as she told the attendant she was heading to Dallas. Of course, if anyone were truly tracking her, it would be easy enough to find out she returned the car in Biloxi, not Dallas. And she supposed they could also find out she'd taken a cab from Biloxi to Gulfport.

She knew her paranoia had caught up with her when she left her phone pocketed and used the public phone instead to call her landlord. Mrs. Paulson hadn't been concerned to learn she'd be away for a little longer than usual or that Marty had no idea how long she'd be away. A return e-mail from David assured her that he would leave her luggage with Mrs. Paulson. His tone was curious as to why her luggage had made it back to Atlanta and she had not, but she politely ignored his unasked questions and thanked him profusely, saying she owed him dinner when she returned.

Now, as she sat on the front porch of her house—its tall stilted feature adding to her limited views—she contemplated her future over coffee and cinnamon rolls. While she hadn't given up entirely on the Romero case, she hadn't been exactly working it either. Using a public phone again, she'd called Kesara, the sister, to let her know what had happened back in Brownsville. Which, of course, had only added to the sister's suspicions—and her own—that the police were somehow involved.

After four weeks without an incident, however, she had almost quit looking over her shoulder. Which meant it was time to move on and get back home to Atlanta. She decided to look at this as a working vacation. How else could she explain spending this kind of money on a beach house? It wasn't hard to sensationalize the events in Brownsville, but without firm answers to any of the questions they raised it still wasn't worthy of a magazine article.

So she'd spent most of her time in Mississippi putting the finishing touches on a two-part piece, this from a case she'd worked last year. The police in Toledo, Ohio had finally solved a six-year-old murder—after she'd started snooping around—and the trial was starting next month. It was a case she hadn't written about before, one without a lot of blood and guts. But the apprehension of a prominent businessman, after it had been discovered that the victim was his mistress, was proving to be the media event of the year—if not decade—in Toledo. She had had three offers for her account of the investigation. She'd taken the highest bidder, of course. Part two of the article would be about the trial. Which meant she would be sitting in a courtroom in Toledo for several weeks as the trial played out.

She would miss the gulf, the beach and the breeze though. Having never been around water, she was surprised at how quickly she'd grown to love it. It had a calming affect on her, something she'd discovered while holed up with Kristen outside of Port Isabel. Subconsciously—or perhaps consciously—she'd sought that out again when she'd chosen Gulfport as her temporary home.

And now it was time to leave, time to get back to her real life. The paranoid feeling she'd had earlier had all but disappeared. She no longer suspected someone was following her. She no longer worried that her phone was bugged. And she'd made do without a car. She'd ditched the rental as soon as she'd hit town, dropping it off at the airport. If someone were tracking her movements, she hoped they'd assume she was getting a flight out. She'd taken the shuttle back into town and had discovered a very usable—and friendly—public transportation system. Not that she had much cause to leave the beach house. Everything she needed was within walking distance.

She got out of her comfortable chair, knowing she'd wasted enough time out on the porch. She needed to make plans for her return to Atlanta. She had rented the house until the end of the week. Four more days. She thought she might actually take time out to place a call to Brownsville, to see if she could find Kristen, just to see if anything had ever come up with the case. Actually,

102

she was surprised no one had contacted her, surprised she hadn't heard from Kristen. Not that she'd ever given Kristen her cell number, but she assumed the detective could find it if she wanted to. Still, it seemed odd that the police hadn't needed anything more from her. After all, a man had been shot and killed. Surely the investigation didn't end with them hauling him away to the morgue? Then again, seeing how Carlos Romero's murder had been handled, yeah, she could believe the case was closed and buried.

Well, it wasn't her concern. The nightmares she'd lived with the first week had subsided, and she'd put it behind her. Perhaps it was a good thing she hadn't been contacted. It was a bad memory, one she'd just as soon leave tucked away out of sight... and out of mind.

CHAPTER NINETEEN

"Good morning, Reyes."

"What are you doing down here, Bailey?"

"Need an evidence box," she said, walking past him.

"On whose authority?"

"I'm a detective, Reyes. I don't think I need authorization to look at evidence."

He laughed. "Since when?"

She ignored him, walking along the shelves, looking for the Romero box. She'd had enough evasive answers from everyone. Yes, Armando Lopez had been identified as Marty Edward's attacker. Yes, he was a known member of *Los Demonios Rojos*. But no, they weren't going to pursue the gang's possible involvement in Carlos Romero's death ten years earlier. And no, there wasn't going to be an investigation into who ordered Armando Lopez to attack Marty Edwards. In fact, she doubted James Garza, the city attorney, had even been briefed on the attack. Despite the normal chain of command, it appeared that Lieutenant Marsh called most, if not all, the shots at the police department. Her pleas to find out who was behind the attack had fallen on deaf ears.

She stopped short when she found the empty spot on the shelf. She looked at the case number on the piece of paper in her hand, then glanced at Reyes. "Who's got this checked out?"

"Well, let's see." He flipped through the pages on his clipboard, a smug smile appearing on his lips. "Sorry. Can't say."

"What do you mean you can't say?"

"Confidential."

"Confidential? It's a ten-year-old case."

He shrugged and flipped the pages back down. "Sorry. Just following orders, Bailey."

Which meant Lieutenant Marsh had it checked out. She turned without another word, walking quickly back up to the squad room. She wasn't sure what she had planned to do with the file anyway. Marty had already told her everything that was in there. And what was missing—the scorpion idol.

"What's up, Bailey?"

She picked up her coffee cup, then stopped at Marcos's desk, leaning a hip against the side. "How long you been here? Twenty years?"

"Twenty-one."

"What do you know about the Scorpion?"

Marcos looked startled by her question. "What do you mean?"

"Oh, come on, man. There was a scorpion idol left at the scene of the Carlos Romero murder. The one the reporter was looking into."

"And? So?"

"Who is he?"

"I don't know who he is, Bailey. I don't even know if he exists."

"She said her research indicated that the scorpion was a signature of some kind. That it's been used for years. Surely you've come across it before."

He glanced over his shoulder, making sure no one was listening. "Look, Bailey. Let it go." He nodded. "Yeah, I've come across it before. It's bad news. Who he is or what he is, I don't know. But since I've been on the force, three cops have been killed. A scorpion was left at all three scenes." He stood up and pushed his chair away. "I don't want no part of it," he said quietly. "So you let it go."

Bailey watched him walk away, having more questions now than before. She put her coffee cup down and headed to the stairs, descending to the second floor. It'd been ten years, so she didn't know if Juan Vargas would remember the case or not. But her curiosity had gotten the best of her. Despite Marcos's warning, she didn't want to let it go.

Unfortunately, Juan Vargas didn't share her curiosity. In fact, as soon as she mentioned the case, he clammed up, claiming he had no recollection of it. When she mentioned the scorpion idol, he got defensive.

"I know nothing about that, Bailey. Nothing. And if you want to question me about an old case, you best have Lieutenant Marsh present. I don't have to talk to you." He left her standing at his desk as he walked purposefully into the men's room.

Great. Just great.

She walked back up the stairs, surprised to find Captain Diaz at her desk, chatting with Marcos. They stopped talking when she approached.

"There you are, Bailey. Lieutenant Marsh and I need a word with you," he said, heading to the lieutenant's office.

"Sure." She glanced at Marcos, but he had turned his gaze back to his computer, ignoring her. She followed Captain Diaz, thinking she was about to get her ass handed to her. One thing she'd learned, they didn't like people asking a lot of questions. And lately, that's all she'd been doing.

"Sit down, Bailey," Lieutenant Marsh said, waiting for Captain Diaz to shut the door. He folded his hands together on his desk, and Bailey looked from him to Diaz who still stood near the door.

"What's up, Lieutenant?"

"Well, we thought it was time we let you in the loop, Bailey. Apparently, this reporter was getting close."

"What do you mean?"

"We've been working the case."

"Carlos Romero? Since when?"

"For a while now, Bailey. It's not really your concern. We didn't ask you in here for that. But the reporter has uncovered something. She's agreed to come back here."

Bailey kept quiet, keeping her face blank as she'd learned to do.

"Needless to say, she's a little gun-shy." He cleared his throat. "She'll only come back if you escort her. Apparently, your little heroics with Armando Lopez impressed her."

Bailey nodded. "Okay. Where is she? Atlanta?"

"No. She's in Gulfport. In Mississippi."

Bailey frowned. "What the hell is she doing down there?"

"I didn't ask and she didn't offer. But we want you to pick her up and bring her back safely. We've got a flight booked. You leave first thing in the morning. She's expecting you." He handed over a folded piece of paper. "The information there is where she's staying and your flight info. There'll be a rental car waiting."

Bailey opened the paper, the address meaningless to her. She looked up. "There's no phone number here. Am I to call her when I hit town?"

"No need. She's expecting you."

"And the return flight?"

Lieutenant Marsh flicked his eyes to Diaz. "You'll have tickets waiting for them?"

"Yes. You can pick them up at the airport. You won't return until the next day."

Bailey folded the paper, her mind racing. Something didn't feel right. For one thing, if they had been working the case,

107

if Marty was in contact with them, surely Marty would have contacted her as well. It didn't make sense that she would deal directly with Marsh. Especially if Marty was requesting that Bailey be the one to pick her up.

"You can take the rest of the day, Bailey. I'll have an officer pick you up in the morning."

"That's not necessary."

"I insist."

Bailey met his cool gaze and nodded. "Very well."

"Good. Have a safe flight. We'll see you in a couple of days," he said, sliding his chair closer to his desk and picking up a folder, dismissing her.

She walked out without another word, slipping the paper into her pocket. Marcos was nowhere to be found when she stopped at her desk. She scribbled a note to him, not that she thought he'd miss her or anything. Just professional courtesy. But then again, he was tight with Marsh. He might already know.

She grabbed her keys from her desk, allowing herself a small smile. Regardless of the circumstances, she felt like she was at least contributing to the case in some way. And, it would be good to see Marty again. She'd never gotten her cell number and hadn't tried to find it, since it was obvious that Marty hadn't wanted to be in touch. After all they'd been through, that stung just a bit. But maybe that was Marty's way of coping with the attack. Out of sight, out of mind.

CHAPTER TWENTY

Bailey checked her directions again, turning off of East Beach Road to Allan Drive, row after row of beach houses bringing back memories of their own summer house back in Port Isabel. Even two years ago, when she'd first moved in with her mother, they'd still had happy times there. For a few months. But the happy times had faded. Now when she thought of the beach house, she remembered her mother wading into the bay without cause, she remembered her mother getting lost at the end of their road, and she remembered the first time her mother looked at her with that blank expression, the first time Bailey knew her mother didn't recognize her. The decline came so quickly that she didn't have time to contemplate keeping the house or not. They needed the money, and it had proved to be a good investment.

But the short time spent at Captain Diaz's house and now, driving just past the beach among the colorful stilt houses, made her miss the happy times, made her miss the carefree life on the water.

She spotted the beach house Marty was renting, pulled along the curb and stopped. Some of the windows were open, letting in the breeze, but there was no sign of Marty. Bailey got out and stood beside the car, taking in a deep breath of the gulf air. It calmed her somewhat, but she wasn't entirely certain as to why she was feeling nervous. She headed up the stairs, taking two at a time, pausing at the top to look around. The view of the water wasn't great, and she wondered why Marty had chosen this particular one to rent. If you wanted a beach house, you most likely also wanted the beach.

She took another deep breath before knocking, listening as she heard Marty moving about inside.

"Coming." Then, a pause. "Who's there?"

Bailey smiled. "Escort service back to Brownsville."

The door whipped open, and Marty stood there, her eyes wide with surprise. "Oh, my God! Kristen, what are you doing here? How'd you find me?"

Bailey frowned, then quickly pushed inside, kicking the door shut behind her. "You're not expecting me?"

"What? No."

"Son of a *bitch*," she said, grabbing Marty and shoving her forcefully to the ground. "Get down," she said loudly as she pulled her weapon.

"What the hell's going—"

Gunfire sounded, cutting off her words, shattering the windows and hitting the walls. Bailey dropped to her belly behind the sofa, crawling to Marty.

"Keep down," she yelled again, turning her face as the door exploded behind them. She tipped the sofa over, hoping it would provide more protection. She winced as a shard of glass landed on her arm, cutting her. Then the spray of bullets ended as quickly as it had begun. "Come on," she said, jerking Marty to her feet.

"Where?"

"Out the back. They're coming up to check on their work,"

she said. She held her weapon ready, looking over the back deck, but saw no movement. "Let's go."

"My stuff. My laptop."

"Leave it."

"Are you out of your mind?" she said as she ran back to her desk, her shoes crunching on broken glass.

"Goddamn it, Marty. Come *on*."

Marty shoved her laptop into the backpack hanging on the chair, then grabbed the wad of cables and power cord and pushed those on top.

They both looked up as they heard running footsteps on the stairs out front. Bailey grabbed Marty's arm, pulling her outside and to the edge of the deck. She swung her leg over and straddled the railing, then dropped to the ground, rolling once before coming to a stop.

"Come on. Come on," she said, waiting for Marty.

Marty stared at her. "I can't do that."

"We don't have time for this, Marty. Drop your backpack."

Marty turned back to the house and they heard voices inside. She looked back down at Bailey and nodded. She dropped her backpack into Bailey's arms, then quickly jumped the railing, landing roughly on the grass below. Bailey didn't give her time to recover, jerking her up and pulling her along, hiding behind the storage building of the house next door. She spotted her rental car on the street, now blocked in by two other cars, both with doors open and engines running.

Bailey turned in the other direction. "We need a place to hide," she said, walking fast.

"Down the street, there's a shopping area. Coffee shops, cafes, boutiques, things like that."

"Perfect. Let's go."

They hurried along, then Marty bumped Bailey's shoulder. "What's with me getting shot at whenever you're around?"

"I was about to ask you the same question." She looked back over her shoulder, but no one was following them. They heard the cars speed away, tires squealing on the pavement. "They're looking for us."

"Who the hell are they?"

"I don't know."

At the next block, pedestrian traffic increased. Bailey led them down the sidewalk, blending in, then ducked into a coffee shop.

"My favorite place," Marty said as they found an empty table away from the windows. "You're bleeding," she said, pointing at Bailey's arm.

"From the glass." She grabbed a napkin from the table and wiped at the blood, most of it dry now. "Where's your phone?"

"In my bag. Why?"

"We need to lose it."

"Lose it? Are you kidding me? Do you know how much stuff I have on this phone? I'd be lost without it. I've got as much on my phone as I do my laptop."

Bailey sat down across from her. "Listen to me. Someone's trying to kill us. Again. They can track you—with GPS—using your phone."

Marty frowned. "They *who*? And Kristen, what are you even doing here?"

"Look, you weren't expecting me, right? You've not been in contact with Lieutenant Marsh? You don't have new evidence?"

Marty slowly shook her head. "What are you talking about?"

Bailey met her stare. "I think my department is trying to kill us."

"The *police*?"

"I'll explain later. But we've got to get out of here." She pointed at the phone. "Get what you need off of there. But we've got to lose it."

Marty nodded, the fear showing in her eyes now. "I can...I can download what I need to my laptop."

"Good." Bailey pulled out her own phone and handed it to her. "Mine too." She stood. "I'll be right back."

She went down the hallway, finding the restrooms. Inside,

she quickly wetted her arm and washed the blood away. The cut wasn't long, just deep, and it bled again as she cleaned it. She grabbed some paper towels and held them to it, trying to stop the bleeding. She wanted to call as little attention to them as possible. Walking around with blood running down her arm was hardly inconspicuous.

Back out front, she stopped at the counter. "Do you have an ATM?"

The young man barely gave her a glance as he filled a cup with coffee. "The T-shirt shop next door has one out front," he said with a toss of his head.

She hated going back outside, but they needed cash. She stopped at the table where Marty had her laptop opened and running. "I'm going next door. I'll be right back."

But Marty's fingers wrapped around her wrist as she turned to leave. "What for?"

"Going to get some cash." As Marty's eyes widened, Bailey laughed. "ATM. That's all. I'm not going to rob anyone."

"Oh. Well, be careful."

Bailey pointed to the phone. "How's that going?"

"About done."

"Good."

* * *

Marty was surprised that her hands weren't shaking as she finished wiping her phone. It had all happened so fast, it didn't seem real. One minute she was packing her things, getting ready to head back to Atlanta, the next…Kristen was at her door. And they were getting shot at. Again. She hated to think she was getting used to it, but she'd simply acted on instinct, following Kristen's instructions without question.

And why was Kristen even here? She'd all but given up on the Romero case, having pushed it to the back of her mind weeks ago. Why would the Brownsville Police Department come looking for her now?

"All done?"

Marty nodded as she neatly folded the USB cable and slipped it inside her bag. "I want to know what's going on."

"Not now, Marty. We've got to get someplace safer than this."

"Yes, now," she said. She met Kristen's eyes across the table, waiting. "Please. I have a right to know why someone's trying to kill me."

"Look, I don't know what's going on. Lieutenant Marsh and Captain Diaz called me aside, said they'd been working the case. They said you'd uncovered something and you were willing to come back, but you wanted an escort. Me." She shrugged. "So they sent me to get you."

"But that's not true. I've not had any contact—"

"I know that now." She stood. "We can talk about this tonight. Right now, we've got to get out of here." Kristen reached for the phones, pocketing both. "Come on."

"Where are we going?"

"Shuttle. Do you know the routes?"

"Not really. I usually walk. There's a beach shuttle. And there's one that goes downtown. One to the airport, of course."

"Let's go downtown. More people."

Marty followed and didn't protest when Kristen grasped her hand. She ignored the curious stares of others and tried to pretend it was perfectly normal for her to walk down the street in Gulfport holding hands with another woman. Kristen was trying to appear nonchalant, but Marty could feel her nervousness as she constantly glanced over her shoulder. She wondered if the cell phones were acting like a beacon, enabling the killers to zero in on them. Her mind flashed to spy movies and tracking devices, and she squeezed Kristen's hand just a little harder.

"Almost there," Kris said as she hurried them along. The shuttle had just pulled to a stop and they waited while others departed before getting on. Kris led them to the back, near the side exit door. She pulled the phones out and held them, waiting until the shuttle was in motion before bending over and wedging the phones between the wall and the legs of the seat.

"So they'll track the phones, thinking we still have them."

"Yes."

"What makes you think they're tracking us with the phones?"

"Because it's an easy means of tracking. Of course, if you've been using credit cards down here, that's easy to track too. They had to have found you some way."

Marty stared at her. "I hate this spy stuff."

Kristen leaned back in her seat and appeared to relax. "So, how have you been?"

She smiled. "Oh, so now we take time for pleasantries?" She bumped Kristen's shoulder. "Well, I haven't been shot at since the last time I saw you."

"Why Gulfport?"

Marty shrugged. "I don't know, really. I was feeling paranoid and was afraid to go home. I switched flights from the one your lieutenant made for me. Stopped over in New Orleans, rented a car, got a map and here I am."

"A beach house that's not on the beach?"

"I enjoyed our short time down on the bay, enjoyed being near the water. But I found a house right on the beach was out of my price range, so I got the next best thing."

"It's probably best you were paranoid. Whatever's going on, Marsh is definitely in the mix."

"What happened? I mean, when I left, I thought everything was settled. Well, not the Romero case, certainly, but the attacks on us. On me."

"That's just it. Everything was settled too quickly, too neat. There wasn't any investigation as to *why* you were being targeted. There wasn't a consideration to try to link Carlos Romero's murder. Nothing." The shuttle came to a stop, and Kristen nudged her arm. "Let's get off here."

Back on the street, they walked in silence until Kristen ducked into a pharmacy. Marty followed, then laughed as Kris held up a cheap box of hair color.

"Are you insane?"

Kris ignored her. "You want brown or red?"

"Seriously, you want me to color my hair?" She ran her fingers through it, knowing it was past time for a trim, but her color would last another few weeks. "I pay a fortune for this lovely blond look. I don't care to go back to my natural brown."

"Yeah? And how do you think I'll look bleach blond?"

Marty was surprised at the seriousness of her tone. She took her hand, lowering the box of hair color. "Is this really necessary? I mean, what are we doing, going on the run or something?"

"Your rented beach house just got shot up as if we were part of a mafia hit. I suspect my own lieutenant of being involved." She looked around quickly, then back to Marty. "I don't know what we're going to do. Not yet. I only know I trust you and I trust me. That's it. That doesn't leave a lot of options."

"Okay. Then we need to sit down and go over everything and see if we can come up with an explanation. See if we can figure out what triggered this." She pulled a box of light brown color off the shelf. "I don't like this hair coloring thing one bit. But if I must, I'll go no darker than this."

"Deal. Let's find a room—a cheap motel—and talk this out."

"Does it have to be cheap?" Marty asked as she followed after Kristen, rolling her eyes as she picked up two toothbrushes and a small tube of paste.

"Cheap means no surveillance cameras."

"Oh, God, we really are in a spy movie, aren't we? Do I at least get clean underwear?"

CHAPTER TWENTY-ONE

Bailey closed the door and locked it, then went to the window and looked out, making sure they hadn't been followed. She had chosen this time, at near dusk, before the outside lights were turned on, in the hope of being less conspicuous. It wasn't like they had luggage.

She turned to survey the room, finding Marty standing near the lone bed, looking at it suspiciously. The cover was stained and rumpled, the pillows looked slept on. Their eyes met, then both slid a glance to the oversized chair against the wall.

"I'll take the chair," they said in unison.

Marty laughed. "Seriously, I got the bed the last time we bunked together." She pointed to the bed in question. "You take it this time. I insist."

"That's very kind of you. But I'm the one with the gun. I should probably take the chair so I can keep watch." She went to the bed and pulled the covers back. "See? Looks clean."

"No way. This motel probably rents by the hour." She opened the tiny door to the bathroom. "Okay. And no way am I taking a

117

shower in here." She turned back around. "Seriously. I wouldn't be surprised to see a rat or three dart across the room."

"I'm sorry. But we needed an out-of-the-way place without surveillance, not the Hilton." She peered over Marty's shoulder into the tiny bathroom and grimaced. The sink was rusted around the fixtures and a steady drip fell from the faucet. The linoleum was chipped and curling at the edges, the tiles in the shower stained with mildew. "Yikes."

"So, we won't sleep and we won't shower." Marty put her hands on her hips. "I'm starving, by the way."

"Okay, so this wasn't a great idea," Bailey conceded. She held up the paper bag. "We have clean toothbrushes."

"All right. Let's talk. Let's come up with a plan. Then let's get the hell out of here. I'd rather get shot at than stay here any longer than necessary."

Bailey nodded. "Okay. Take the chair. Let's talk." She pulled the covers all the way off the bed, revealing a semi-clean sheet before sitting down.

"First of all, are you sure we shouldn't call the police down here? The FBI? *Someone?* Surely they've been to the beach house. It's probably on the news. For all I know, I'm listed as a missing person."

Bailey stared at her, finally raising an eyebrow.

"You think I've seen too many TV shows?"

"You think?"

"No FBI?"

"What are we going to tell them? That my police department is trying to kill us? You think they might call them to check on that? So what do you think my department is going to say?"

"That you're smokin' crack and out of your mind?"

"Something like that, yes." Bailey leaned forward. "Marty, we're pretty much on our own on this one."

"Who was the man who attacked me at the beach house?" Marty asked suddenly.

"Armando Lopez. *Los Demonios Rojos*. Here's where they—

my department—dropped the ball. Lopez had a record an arm long, starting when he was an early teen. Armed robbery, assault, drugs, weapons charges, breaking and entering, possession to sell, you name it. But in the last five years, clean."

"Clean?"

"No arrests. Which I'm told means he was high enough up in the gang that he didn't have to do the dirty work any longer. At least, not the petty dirty work. Which leads to the question, why was he sent to kill you? Why not an underling? How high up was he and who called the hit?" Bailey got up and paced. "And why? Too many questions, yet they weren't interested in answering them." She paused. "Something else. The knife he was using, it had a scorpion engraved in the handle."

"So this gang, *Los Demonios Rojos*, is the Scorpion? Is that what you're saying?"

"I don't know. No one else thought it was significant. At least, not when I brought it up. And I couldn't get any answers from anyone. I asked my partner, Marcos, about the Scorpion. He wouldn't talk about it. So I went to Juan Vargas."

"One of the original detectives on Carlos's case, right?" Marty asked.

"Right. He wouldn't give me the time of day. You could see the fear in his eyes. Said he wouldn't talk about anything unless Marsh was present. And the evidence box was checked out. I wanted to pull it, to see if you missed something. Reyes told me it was 'classified,' meaning I didn't need to know who had it checked out."

"Marsh?"

"Most likely. That's when they came to me with this bullshit story about you wanting to come back."

"And they said I'd been in contact with them?"

Bailey nodded.

"But Kris, surely you knew I'd get in touch with you first. Right?"

Bailey shrugged and sat down again. "After the attack, I

thought maybe you wanted to remove yourself from that. And me, because I was too close to it."

"You saved my life."

"I did what I was supposed to do. My job. That's all, Marty."

"No. I have no doubt that if I had been with anyone else, I would have died that night. I think you know that too."

Yes, as Marty had said before, it had come down to a split second. And in that split second, there was not anyone else she would have trusted to take the shot, to *make* the shot. Actually, as she thought back on it now, was that the plan? To have Marty killed under her watch?

She met Marty's eyes. "They didn't think I could do the job," she said quietly. "They haven't let me be a cop, so they have no idea what my skills are." She stood again, pacing. "That's it. To them, I'm just a woman with a gun. They don't know I'm a sharpshooter. They don't know I scored highest in my class. They don't know I used to work undercover in narcotics. Hell, they probably never read my damn file. I transferred in, I pissed them off. End of story." She stood in front of Marty. "That's why they sent me this time. They wanted us both out of the way. I've been asking too many questions. Carlos Romero was a case that wasn't going to go away. Or so they thought. So send me after you, get us both together. Eliminate us. Have it look like a hit. After all, a gang has targeted us. They've tried to kill us before. It's just all so neat. Case closed. No questions asked."

"But why, Kris? Why is that case worth our lives? What is that case hiding?"

"I don't know. But we're going to find out."

* * *

"Do you really think this is a good idea?" Marty asked. Sure, it was nearly midnight, but Wal-Mart was still busy. It wasn't like they wouldn't be seen.

"We should be fine." Kris pulled her into the shadows of the building and pressed something cold into her hand. Her weapon. "Take this."

Marty shook her head. "No. I can't—"

"Marty, I can't very well walk into the store with it, now can I?"

"Oh. I thought—"

Kris gave a lopsided smile as she walked away. "Don't shoot anybody."

Marty wasn't exactly wearing clothing conducive to hiding a gun. She pulled her T-shirt out of her shorts and tucked the gun into her waistband, praying she wouldn't accidentally shoot herself. She knew little to nothing about guns. Of course, hiding in the shadows probably wasn't a great way to avoid suspicion. She nonchalantly walked to the outdoor garden center, her backpack slung over one shoulder, and pretended interest in the display of flowers. There was no one about. She wished she could transfer the gun into her already stuffed backpack, but she didn't want to risk being seen. She continued walking, her nerves on edge, expecting a security guard to come up and question her at any moment.

After what seemed like hours, she spotted Kris pushing a cart out of the store. She raised her hand, getting her attention, then went to meet her.

"Have fun?"

"A blast." Kris pushed the cart out to the parking lot, then grabbed three bags and handed them to Marty before getting the rest. "Let's just walk away. How much longer until the next shuttle?"

Marty glanced at her watch. "Twenty minutes."

"Okay. That'll give us time to eat. I got a couple of deli sandwiches. Can't guarantee how fresh they are."

"I'll eat anything. I'm starving."

They sat on the shuttle bench, and while Kris sorted through the bags looking for something, she ripped into the plastic-wrapped sandwich and took a bite. She nodded. "Fresh enough."

She pointed to a box Kris held. "What?"

"I got a phone. One of those disposable ones."

"It won't be traced?"

"No. Besides, we won't have it long enough. But I need to make a call."

"Now?"

"Yeah." Kris stood. "I won't go far."

Marty nodded, wondering why Kristen suddenly needed privacy for a phone call.

* * *

Bailey waited, letting it ring five, then six times. She knew he didn't use voice mail. He either took your call or he didn't. And being this late, chances were he wouldn't. If not, she'd try again in the morning. Finally, after eleven rings, a sleepy voice answered.

"This better be good."

She smiled. "Hey, Rico. It's me. Bailey."

There was only a slight pause, then she heard covers rustling, imagining him getting up quietly so as not to disturb his wife. "What the hell?" he whispered. "I haven't heard from you in two years."

"I know. I'm in trouble. I need help."

"Of course, Bailey. Anything for you. Where are you? Still in Brownsville?"

"Well, at the moment, I'm in Gulfport."

"Alabama?"

"Mississippi."

"Same difference. I have contacts, Bailey, but not in Mississippi. Tell me what you need."

"First, I need a car. Then…then I need to go under."

"What kind of trouble are you in, Bailey?"

"I'm not sure. Apparently there's a price on my head."

"And the police can't protect you?"

"I suspect they're involved."

A laugh. "I told you never trust the police. Can you make it to New Orleans?"

"Not unless I steal a car. I don't want to rent one. I don't want a trace."

"Bus?"

"Too dangerous."

He laughed again. "Guess you'll have to steal one, then. You probably haven't done that in a while. Don't forget to switch plates."

"Yeah. And this phone won't be good after tonight." She looked over at Marty, who was watching her with interest. "One more thing. There're two of us. We'll both need to go under."

"Credit cards, driver's license, passport? The works?"

"Three for each."

"Male or female?"

"Female. And I need money. I've got an account. It's joint with my mother. Can you find it?"

"Of course, Bailey."

"Transfer ten grand to a safe account."

"No problem. Now here's what you do. In New Orleans, there's a bar on the far west end, past the French Quarter. Mostly locals. No tourists. It's a Creole bar. Decoudreau's."

"I'll find it."

"I'll have someone meet you there. Noon. He'll have a clean car and take yours. Drive straight through to Corpus. I'll have everything ready for you."

"Thanks, Rico. I owe you."

"No, Bailey. You'll never owe me. Be safe, my friend."

The call ended, and Bailey stared at the phone for a second as old, old memories crowded in. She and Rico Ramos went all the way back to high school, two kids from different sides of the tracks. Two kids who had formed an unlikely bond. A bond that followed them from school, to the streets, to the police force and back to the streets. She took a bullet for him once. She did it out of love, but it was an act he felt indebted to her for. She'd never called in a favor before. That's why now, when she needed to trust someone, Rico was who she turned to.

"Everything okay?"

She nodded. "Yeah. Better." She took the water bottle Marty handed to her but shook her head at the sandwich. "Maybe later."

"I peeked through the bags."

"Yeah?"

"Hair clippers. Baseball cap. Water bottles. A few T-shirts." Marty grinned.

"And…underwear?"

"I promised you clean ones. And there're some jeans for you."

"Great guess on the size, by the way."

Bailey felt a blush light on her face, and she turned away. In the store, she had been contemplating the size, and her mind had flashed to the night in Brownsville when she'd undressed Marty and bathed her. While there was nothing sexual about the moment at all, she had observed enough to guess her size…and the fact that she wasn't a natural blonde.

"And Kris? Hair clippers?"

"For me. We'll do it tonight. Then we have to hit the road."

"Where to?"

"New Orleans."

"Are we going to rent a car? At this hour?"

Bailey bit her lip. "We're not actually going to rent one."

Marty stared at her. "And I don't suppose that means we're going to buy one."

"No."

Marty glanced over her shoulder nervously. "We're going to steal one?" she whispered.

"Yes."

Marty's gaze never left hers. "Who did you call?"

"An old friend. Rico Ramos. He has…well, connections. Once we get to New Orleans, we'll meet someone who will have another car for us. Then we'll head to Corpus Christi."

"I take it we're going back to Brownsville, then?"

"Yes. I don't know about you, but I don't like being hunted," she said. "I'd rather be the hunter."

"I don't understand. If we're not safe here, how will we be in Brownsville?"

"Because Marty Edwards and Kristen Bailey won't be in Brownsville." At Marty's blank look, Bailey smiled and took her arm, leading her back to the bench. "You'll have to trust me." She began gathering their bags. "Shuttle's coming."

"Oh, goody. Back to the wonderful motel room."

"Just long enough to open up the beauty shop, then we'll split."

Marty fingered her hair again. "I can't believe you're making me do this."

"You can take it out on me with the clippers and the blond dye."

CHAPTER TWENTY-TWO

"What's wrong?"

Marty stared at her, shaking her head as she took in Kristen's new short, very blond locks. "First of all, I hardly recognize you."

"I think that was the point. The brown color looks very nice on you, by the way."

Marty stuck her tongue out at her, then followed that with a quick hit on the arm. She hated her new hair color. "I've also never stolen a car before. It's kinda creepy."

"It's going to be fine."

"What if we get stopped?"

"I switched the plates. We won't get stopped."

"Our prints are in the car." She'd seen enough TV crime shows to know they'd catch them.

"Don't worry. This car will be taken from us, most likely sent to a chop shop. This car won't exist."

"That doesn't make me feel any better. This was someone's

car."

"That we took from a bar at two in the morning. He didn't need to be driving anyway. And he probably forgot where he parked it. Plus, if he's drunk, he's not going to call the police until the next day." She smiled. "See? We'll already be in New Orleans and have switched cars by then."

"Okay, good plan then." She sighed and leaned back against the seat. "I just can't believe my life of crime has been started by a cop."

Kris laughed. "Honey, by the time we're done, you can write a book on a life of crime."

"What does that mean?"

"It means we're going to get dirty." Kris glanced at her then back at the road. "We're going under. Meaning new identities, new looks. And we're going to know the streets, the drug dealers, the snitches and the suppliers. And we're going to find the Scorpion. He's got to have ties to the police. Whatever those ties are, whatever Carlos Romero's case means to it, we're going to find it. Because if we don't, if we run, then there's no hope. They'll find us eventually."

"What do you mean new identities? *Forever?*"

"Look, we're not safe like this. They tried to gun us down in a beach house in Gulfport. You think they won't find you in Atlanta? You think I can just waltz back to Brownsville and my job?" She shook her head. "No, Marty. Not until we take care of this, expose who is involved and find out why they're trying to kill us. Then—and only then—can you go back to being Marty Edwards, investigative reporter."

"And the guy you called? Rico Ramos? He's going to help us?"

"Yes. It's his specialty."

"I'm not sure I'm crazy about this plan."

"Are you crazy about being dead?"

Marty laughed. "God, you still have a sense of humor, sitting over there with your short, punked blond hair." She reached over and ruffled the top. "It's kinda cute."

Kris swatted her hand away playfully. "You'll mess it up."

Marty was surprised that the smile stayed on her face. She was scared. She was out of her element. She was on the run with a woman she barely knew. A woman she was trusting with her life. She rolled her head to the side, watching Kris as she drove. Yes, she looked different. The short hair, now unnaturally blond, made her look much younger. But the strong, firm jaw was still there, the straight nose, the mouth that naturally curved upward, giving her a pleasant, likable expression. And the eyes. Those warm, dark brown eyes, the ones that had convinced her all those weeks ago that Detective Bailey could be trusted—those eyes were the same.

"I feel like we're in a movie," she finally said, accepting the fact that they were racing to New Orleans to rendezvous with someone who would take their stolen car and most likely give them another stolen car. *Jesus, what have I gotten into?*

"With no script and no director."

"And no idea of the ending."

CHAPTER TWENTY-THREE

Bailey slowed the car as they neared New Orleans. They'd only been on the road an hour and a half, but Marty had fallen asleep before dawn. She straightened her shoulders, feeling them pop. She needed to grab a couple of hours sleep before they headed on to Corpus. They had six hours to kill before meeting their contact, but she wanted to hide the car as much as possible. Maybe they could find a busy lot with tourists mingling about, somewhere where the car would simply be one of hundreds.

"Hey, Marty," she said, gently shaking her arm. Marty sat up with a start. "It's okay. Sorry. But we're here."

"Already?" She rubbed her eyes. "I don't even remember falling asleep," she said around a yawn. "Are you okay? When's the last time you slept?"

"I don't remember."

"I'm sorry. I should have stayed awake with you."

"No. We shouldn't both be exhausted." She glanced over. "I

need to find someplace to crash for a couple of hours. A busy parking lot with a shade tree would do the trick."

"How far are we from the bar?" She asked as she yawned again.

"I'm not sure. But it's early. We have time."

"And how long a drive to Corpus Christi?"

"A good ten hours, at least."

"Okay. Well, we can take turns driving, right?"

"We'll see."

"I'm capable of driving, Kris. I don't want you to think I'm this damsel in distress. I mean, I'm not totally helpless."

"I never thought you were." Bailey sighed, too tired to argue. "And you're certainly welcome to drive."

"Thank you." She sat up straighter in the seat. "Then we'll find a spot for you to nap." She yawned again. "Sorry," she murmured.

Bailey hid her smile, knowing as soon as they stopped for her nap, Marty would be joining her. They'd been running on pure adrenaline for the last twelve hours. Marty had hit the wall. And she wasn't far behind.

They drove deeper into New Orleans, seeing the quiet streets coming alive as the workday beckoned for most. Bailey followed signs to the French Quarter, knowing the area would be busy with tourists no matter the time of day. She would find a place to park and rest for a few hours. Then find this Creole bar so they could ditch the stolen car and get a new one before heading to Corpus.

She glanced at Marty, who was still struggling to keep her eyes open. It would be a miracle, if between the two of them, they managed the ten-hour drive to Corpus without having to stop for sleep. She didn't want to do that. She wouldn't feel safe until she met with Rico, until they could go under with new names, new identities. Only then would she feel she could stop looking over her shoulder, thinking someone was hunting them.

Because she knew, right now, that someone was out looking

for Kristen Bailey and Marty Edwards. And that the hunt would escalate. Their one shot at an ambush had failed. They now knew that Bailey was on to them...and that Bailey was running. Would they think she would head back to Brownsville? Sure. Her mother was there. Her home was there. They would figure she'd return. What they didn't know was that her house, while she'd tried to make it a home, was just that—a house. There was nothing there she couldn't live without. No keepsakes she had to have, no important papers, no pictures. The most important papers were in a safe deposit box in Houston. And the keepsakes from her family, a few things from the beach house, old photo albums, things she couldn't part with, they were in a storage unit in Port Isabel with her mother's furniture. But her mother, that was another matter. It was something she'd have to work out once they got back. She wouldn't abandon her mother.

She drove slowly down Decatur, passing the French Market Place. She turned right on St. Ann, finding what she was looking for—a church parking lot that was about half full. She pulled into a spot near a huge magnolia tree, the shade welcome as the morning sun was already warming the day.

"Is this safe?" Marty asked.

"Should be." Bailey cut the engine and leaned the seat back, closing her eyes. "Sit back, Marty. Rest. I'm a light sleeper," she said.

"No. You sleep. I'll keep watch."

"Suit yourself," Bailey murmured, her eyes heavy as she drifted off.

CHAPTER TWENTY-FOUR

"That didn't take long," Marty said as they slipped into their new car.

"No. The guy's clearly done this before," Bailey said as she pulled out of the parking lot. "Look in the glove box."

Marty opened it. "A phone?"

"Yeah. He said it was clean." Bailey glanced at her. "Just in case."

"Okay. So now what? We head straight to Corpus Christi?"

"Yes. I-10 to Houston, then Highway 59 to Victoria."

"Ten hours?"

"At least."

"You didn't get much rest," Marty reminded her.

"I'm fine right now. We'll stop and get something to eat, and I'll get coffee."

"I can drive, you know."

"Yeah. Maybe when we get past Houston, you can drive to

Victoria." Bailey drove through the city, trying to remember the guy's directions for getting to the Interstate. "If you want to get some sleep now, you can."

"No. I'm okay." Marty leaned back in the seat, staring out the window. Then she turned and looked at Bailey. "I feel like a criminal," she said. "Do you?"

Bailey smiled. "Because we stole a car?"

"Well, that. And we're meeting questionable characters at bars, we're sneaking out of town, the police are looking for us. All those things."

"That doesn't make us criminals. Well, besides the car. But the rest, that's not of our doing. I'm just trying to keep us alive, Marty. We've got to stay on the move. My department is involved. Or at least, someone *in* my department. They obviously have connections here. Or else they sent someone from Brownsville after us. If that's the case, they're probably still looking for us, and they may be using police resources."

"What do you mean?"

"Checking hotel registrations. Looking for hits on our credit cards, things like that."

"The sleazy motel didn't have security cameras, didn't require ID and was happy to accept cash. So there are no hits on our names or credit cards."

"I withdrew cash at the ATM by the coffee shop, that's it. And I don't care if they know we were there. That's only a few blocks from your beach house. That won't help them, other than they'll know we have some cash."

"That won't get us far, Kris. I have a savings account. I can—"

"No. We have enough to get us to Corpus. Once we're there, Rico will have credit cards for us. And cash." Marty drew her eyebrows together in a frown. "That's what he does, Marty. He moves money around. People pay him to hide money in offshore accounts. People pay him to supply them with fake papers, driver's licenses, passports, things like that."

Marty stared blankly at her, then slowly shook her head.

"What are we getting mixed up in, Kris? I was a law-abiding citizen until yesterday. Now I've stolen a car and I'm on the run. And now you tell me we're about to meet up with this…this Rico person who's going to give us fake papers. And money."

"I would trust Rico with my life," Bailey said simply. "He's a friend."

"A 'friend'? He's a *criminal*. Good God, Kristen, you're a cop. How can we—"

"Marty, stop. He's not a criminal. Well, okay, maybe he is. But he's a good guy. And right now, he's the only one I trust."

Marty ran her hands through her hair nervously, finally taking a deep breath. "Okay, so I'm freaking out a little."

"You've got to trust me. This is the only way."

"I do trust you. I realize I don't know you all that well, but I do trust you."

"Good. And it's okay to freak out. I've taken you from your safe little world as a reporter and, well, you're right—we're on the run like common criminals. We're having to look over our shoulders. But we're going to be fine, Marty. We'll get to the bottom of it." Bailey gazed at her own reflection in the rearview mirror, wondering who she was trying to convince. Marty or herself?

* * *

It was eleven p.m., and Bailey's eyes felt like sandpaper. They had taken turns driving, but she hadn't really slept. And now, as the lights of Corpus came into view, she was afraid she couldn't make it the last few miles. She slapped her face several times, trying to wake up. She finally reached over and shook Marty's arm, waking her.

"What? What is it?" Marty said as she sat up.

"We're almost there."

"Already? But you were going to wake me in Victoria to drive again."

"I know. But you were all curled up and sleeping so soundly, I didn't want to wake you."

"Well, you look like hell," she said. She reached out and ruffled Bailey's hair. "But I still love your hair."

Bailey was too tired to respond. And she hardly recognized herself when she looked in the mirror. She'd never worn her hair short, and it had certainly never been bleached blond before. "Punked" blond, as Marty called it.

She turned off the Interstate onto Highway 358, then turned right on Old Brownsville Road and crossed the railroad tracks. She took Saratoga Boulevard to the south and slowed, looking for their turn.

"We take Greenwood," she said.

"I think that's it coming up."

She turned right on Greenwood, taking them away from the city. The small farm road was quiet and dark, and she looked for the tiny dirt road that would lead her to Rico's farmhouse. She allowed a small smile as she remembered all the high-tech gadgets he had inside, belying the nondescript farmhouse exterior.

"Here it is," she murmured, turning left and slowing on the bumpy dirt road.

"He lives out here?"

"No. He's got a house out near the bay. Wife, two kids. This is his office."

"Office?"

Bailey laughed quietly. "You'll see."

She relaxed as the house came into view, lights on inside as well as the porch light. She pulled to a stop beside Rico's truck, then finally let her breath out. They were safe for now. The front door opened and he stood there, a smile on his face. Bailey didn't realize she'd be this happy to see him, but she nearly ran up the steps.

"*Dios mio*, Bailey. What the hell did you do to your hair?"

Bailey ran her fingers through it. "Disguise."

"It's a good one. I hardly recognized you." He pulled her into a hug. "Good to see you, my friend."

"You too, man."

He held her at arm's length, his eyes raking over her. "When's the last time you slept?"

She shrugged. "Been a while." She stepped back. "This is Marty Edwards."

Rico shook her hand softly. "Welcome, Marty Edwards." He pulled her inside. "Tell me what kind of trouble this one has gotten you into, huh?"

Marty smiled. "I think I'm more to blame."

"Really?" He glanced at Bailey and winked. "She's cute."

"It's not what you think." Bailey closed the door behind her, looking around the large room. It was much as she remembered, littered with computers and monitors and camera equipment.

"Pity," he said, still smiling at Marty. "Well, I would offer you coffee, but I think you need sleep instead. Get some rest, Bailey. We'll talk in the morning."

"Yeah. I need a few hours at least." Bailey looked at Marty with raised eyebrows, but Marty shook her head.

"I'm fine. You go ahead."

"I'll watch out for her, Bailey."

Bailey pointed her finger at him. "Don't tell her any lies."

"No, no. We'll visit for a bit. Go."

Bailey met Marty's eyes for a second, making sure she was okay to be left alone with this "criminal," but Marty smiled and nodded, so Bailey headed off to the bedroom down the hall. She kicked her shoes off and stepped out of her jeans, then crawled under the covers. She was asleep before her head hit the pillow.

CHAPTER TWENTY-FIVE

"Come. You want coffee?"

Marty nodded. "That would be nice."

"Of course, if you're as tired as Bailey, then—"

"No, I'm fine. She's stubborn as a mule and would hardly let me drive. I slept a lot."

He laughed. "Stubborn, yes. That is my Bailey," he said as he handed her a cup of coffee. "Sugar?"

"And cream, if you have it?"

"Yes. Sit. I'll bring it."

Marty sat at the round table in the kitchen, watching Rico rummage in the fridge for the cream. The kitchen, as well as the fridge, appeared well-stocked. "Kristen said this was your office," she said.

He nodded. "You could say that. I spend a lot of time here."

"You're married?"

"Oh, yes. Emilia, she's lovely. And I have two daughters." He pulled out his wallet and plucked a picture out, showing it to Marty. "See? Beautiful."

Marty looked at the family portrait, smiling at the two beautiful little girls. She nodded. "Very lovely."

"They're my life," he said quietly, staring at the photo before putting it back.

"Do they know about your office here?"

He shook his head and grinned. "Oh, no. Emilia thinks I am a very successful real estate agent. And I admit, I do dabble in it some. After all, I have a license. I should at least use it, right?"

Marty sipped from her coffee, watching him. "Is it a license you produced?"

He laughed heartily and slapped the table. "I see Bailey has told you of my profession." But he shook his head. "It's a real license. When Bailey took me off the streets, I had to get clean, had to get a job. Bailey always said I could sell ice to Eskimos, so why not sell houses?"

"And did you?"

"For a while, yes." He tilted his head. "You have questions? You don't trust me, do you?"

Marty put her cup down. "Kristen said she trusted you with her life."

He nodded. "Yes. The feeling is mutual. Of course, she took a bullet for me so she's already met her part of the bargain."

Marty's eyes widened. "She was shot?"

"Oh, yes. See, I was her informant."

"On the streets?"

"Yes."

"That's where you met?"

"Oh, no." He smiled fondly. "High school. We had no business being friends. She came from a nice family. Her mother was a teacher. Her father a fireman. So was her brother. Mine?" He shook his head. "No. My father was a drug dealer and my brother was in prison. And I was a typical teenager with a bad attitude. But Bailey? Oh, she had a way about her, even then. She

always feels responsible for people, wants to take care of them."
He motioned to her. "Probably how you ended up here, no?"

Marty nodded. "Yes. But I'll let Bailey tell you that story."
She picked up her coffee again. "Tell me about her."

"The only reason I let her hang with us in high school was
because I had a huge crush on her." He laughed. "The one time
I tried to kiss her she bloodied my nose and said she'd 'break my
fucking neck if I tried that shit again.'" He got up and brought
the coffeepot back to the table, topping off Marty's cup. "I got
the message, but by then we were friends so it was too late for
me. Bailey stole my heart and she didn't even know it."

Marty smiled, picturing a young Kristen punching Rico in
the nose for trying to kiss her.

"Anyway, after graduation, we lost touch. Imagine my surprise
when she busted me one night for selling drugs on the street."
He shrugged. "You follow in your father's footsteps, I guess. It
was all I knew. But Bailey, she didn't haul my ass in. She said she
would give me one chance to make it right. She was working the
streets, undercover. Instead of selling, she wanted me to help her
clean up the streets. I could have told her it was a losing battle,
but she's stubborn, like you said."

"So you became her informant?"

"Yeah. I figured it beat jail. For the first time, I actually felt
good about myself. I got clean. I quit using. And I helped her bust
a lot of my so-called friends. Then one night, they were doing a
sting on a big-time dealer. I was supposed to set it up, then get
out of there. Well, I'm leaving, heading down the alley, and this
cop, he thinks I'm the dealer. He's got his gun on me, he's about
to shoot. Bailey comes out of nowhere, yelling at him to stop,
but he wouldn't listen. He told Bailey to get the hell out of his
way. He fired. I jumped, thinking 'where am I hit,' you know?
But it's not me. Bailey stepped into the line of fire, taking the hit.
She had her vest on, but he got her in the neck, right above her
collarbone."

"Oh, my God," Marty whispered.

"Yeah. It was bad. Real bad. But I couldn't stay. I took off running, afraid the dude was still going to shoot me. And afraid Bailey was dead."

Marty stared into her coffee cup, wondering what would make someone do that? Would she step into the line of fire for someone?

"I knew her mother," Rico said. "So at the hospital, I found her. I told her what had happened. And Bailey came out of it okay, just kept her out of commission for a while. The other dude, he lost his job, the bastard."

"That was the end of her undercover?"

"Oh, yeah. Mine too. I couldn't go back to the streets. My cover was blown too." He shrugged. "She helped me. I got a part-time job and went to school. Then got into real estate."

"And all this?"

"I don't deal with criminals, Marty." He smiled sheepishly. "Well, not real criminals. Most of my clients are immigrants. I dabble in new identities, but mostly, I move money around. It's very lucrative."

"How does one get into this line of work?"

"It's funny. You meet all kinds of people in your life. By chance, I met the man who ran this business," he said. "In Houston. We were still in Houston then. He told me you could be dirty and clean at the same time. Meaning never deal with criminals. You can't trust them. But lots of people for lots of different reasons are looking to move money, are looking for a new, or different, identity. He taught me everything, took me under his wing. And when I knew enough, when I had enough contacts, he rode off into the sunset with his millions, leaving me the business. But I wanted out of Houston. I wanted a fresh start. So here we are."

Marty nodded. "Kristen said she went to Brownsville to take care of her mother. She spoke briefly about her father and brother, but wouldn't tell me much. I assume they're estranged. Is that why she's looking after her mother alone?"

"She didn't tell you?"

"What?"

"Her father and brother are dead. They were killed in a big warehouse fire in Houston about ten years ago or so. Six firemen were killed."

"I had no idea. I knew they weren't a part of her life. I asked if they'd divorced. She just said no."

"They were such a close family. She and her mother had a hard time after that. Her mother couldn't stay in Houston. She moved to their beach house, but Bailey stayed. It took her a long time to get past it. I won't say she's over it. It was devastating. But she's moved on."

"And now her mother is so sick."

"What do you mean?"

"She has Alzheimer's. You didn't know?"

"Yes, that's why Bailey moved to Brownsville. But it was early stages, she said."

Marty shook her head. "No. She's in a...well, a care facility, I guess. Kristen said her mother hasn't recognized her in ten months, I think. In fact, I don't think she's even spoken a single word in months."

Rico leaned forward, resting his elbows on the table. "They were so close. She's all Bailey has left." He shook his head. "No family. No partner."

"That's why she told me she could relate," she murmured as she stared into her coffee, remembering their conversation back at the beach house.

"What?"

Marty looked up. "I have no family either. I was in foster care as a child. She told me she knew how I felt, not having a family." Marty pushed her coffee cup away. "I didn't really believe her at the time. I mean, people say things just to try to make you feel comfortable, you know?"

"Yes."

"Now I understand her devotion to her mother. But why do you think she wouldn't tell me about her father and brother?"

"Bad memories she'd rather not think about or talk about."

Marty sighed, then offered a small smile. "Thank you for telling me a little about her. We haven't known each other long, yet I feel very close to her."

"But…you're not involved?"

Marty frowned. "Involved? You mean romantically?"

"Yes."

"No. It's not like that. It's a professional relationship. I met her in Brownsville when I went down there to look at a cold case. I'm a reporter," she explained. "That's where this whole mess started."

"Well, I'll let Bailey fill me in later. Why don't you get some sleep too? It'll be a busy day tomorrow." He stood. "There is another bedroom. I'll show you."

She hesitated. "Actually, if you don't mind, I'd feel safer if I was with Kristen." She felt embarrassed, but nonetheless, she didn't want to be alone.

"I understand."

"Thank you for your hospitality, Rico. And for helping us."

"That's not necessary. I would do anything for Bailey. I owe her my life."

Marty nodded. "So do I." Several times over, Marty realized.

After using the bathroom, Marty quietly opened the door to the bedroom. She paused, watching Kris in the shadows, her breathing heavy and deep, her hand twitching involuntarily as she slept. Marty closed the door, then crept closer, quickly shedding her clothes before crawling under the covers beside her. The bed was warm, and she let out a deep breath, closing her eyes, feeling safe. It had been too many years to recall the last time she'd slept in the same bed with someone, but she doubted she had this same feeling of contentment then as she did right now. She shifted slightly, allowing her arm to make contact with Kristen's back. She lay still, letting sleep claim her finally.

CHAPTER TWENTY-SIX

Bailey rolled on to her back, her eyes still closed. She knew it was daylight, knew the sun was up. She also knew there was a warm body in bed with her. She relaxed, almost wishing there was more between them. How nice would it be to be able to take Marty in her arms and hold her? Her eyes popped open in shock. Yes, she found Marty attractive, but that was all. Even if the circumstances were different, there would be nothing to pursue. Regardless of her own sexual preference, Marty had made it clear that she had none.

She turned her head, surprised to find Marty so close. Her eyes lingered over her face, taking in the smooth skin, the flawless complexion, the small scar on her chin. She had a sudden urge to put her lips there, to touch the scar. She let her eyes drift to Marty's mouth, slightly parted in sleep. She was beautiful. Bailey made herself turn away, not liking the direction of her thoughts.

She eased out of the bed, careful not to wake Marty. She

gathered her jeans and shoes, then quietly opened the door, slipping into the bathroom without a sound.

Later, after a long, hot shower, she put her dirty jeans back on and went in search of coffee. She found it, and Rico, in the kitchen.

"You look better," he said as he typed on a laptop.

"Thanks. I slept like a log." She filled a cup, then added cream and sugar before joining him at the table.

"Kerry Thompson or Erica Jones?"

"Kerry."

"Melanie Nelson or Amanda Raines?"

"Amanda."

"Patty Stone or Emily Manning?"

She made a face. "That's the best you can come up with?"

"Just pick one."

"Emily."

"Thank you. I'm setting up credit cards."

"How does that work?"

"I've hacked into their system and set up new accounts. Three for you and three for Marty." He grinned. "You have a ten thousand dollar limit on all the cards."

"Wonderful. How long?"

"Three months. I have it set up to post a payment to the accounts each month, so the system will think the account is paid up to date. When they reconcile at the end of the quarter, they'll most likely find the bogus accounts and disable the cards."

"And if they find them sooner?"

"No way. They have millions of accounts. This is a legitimate account with a line of credit. When you use it, the store's computer will talk to their computer. It'll see that you have available credit and approve the transaction. Simple."

Bailey leaned closer. "How do you know how to do all this, Rico?"

"I know enough. But writing the program to get in? No. I hired a hacker to write it."

144

"Is that safe?"

"Of course. He lives in Hong Kong. College kid. He doesn't know who I am or where I am. Anyone can hide in cyberspace if you know what you're doing."

"Okay. And the rest?"

He nodded. "Driver's licenses, passports."

"Car?"

"SUV. Nice black one. Superloaded. You'll love it."

"Do I want to know where it came from?"

He laughed. "Don't ask. But it's clean. Tags are registered to Kerry Thompson."

"And my mother's money?"

"Yes. I found the account. I moved ten out like you asked. It's in an offshore account. I'll set up a local account under Amanda Raines, how's that?"

"Fine."

"The offshore account will feed it, if you need to withdraw cash. But use your credit cards. They're safe."

"I also need a couple of guns that can't be traced."

He stared at her. "You gonna tell me what's going on?"

She leaned back in her chair, thinking back over the last several months. "Marty came down to Brownsville to look into a cold case that was ten years old. A kid, a high school senior, was killed. The police labeled it as a gang kill, didn't even investigate it really. The family insisted the boy was not involved in a gang. He was an honor student, an athlete, he was going to college." She sipped from her coffee before continuing. "Anyway, my lieutenant was very nervous about Marty snooping around in the case and had me assigned to keep an eye on her. We got shot at twice. Then they put us up at a safe house, only to have someone try to kill Marty."

"You're kidding."

"He was a gang banger, had a knife to her throat. I shot him. Marty left town. Again, no investigation. They just shut the case. So I started snooping around. And everyone got nervous again.

145

They sent me to Gulfport to pick up Marty. They said she was coming back, that they were going to look into the original case." She shrugged. "Long story short, it was a hit, an ambush. I was able to get us out of there but I couldn't go to the police. I mean, obviously my department was behind it."

"Why do they want you out of the picture? What kind of case is it?"

"That's just it, it's a nothing case. My guess is, this kid saw something he shouldn't have and it got him killed. And whatever he saw implicates the police. That's the only reason I can come up with for all the cover-ups."

"And they got nervous when Marty started snooping around."

"Yes."

"So you're going back? To do what, Bailey?"

"To solve the goddamn case. And to expose the cover-up."

"How high up does it go?"

"My lieutenant for sure. And my captain. Higher than that, I don't know."

"And you're going to do this alone? With no help on the inside?"

"I don't know who I can trust, Rico."

"What about your partner?"

"I'm not sure. It's not like we were close, you know. Not like in Houston."

He watched her for a moment, meeting her eyes. Bailey saw the worried expression in them, but there was no other way.

"And where does Marty fit in with all this?"

"I'm trying to keep her alive, Rico. That's all." She stood up suddenly. "What would you have me do? Send her back home to Atlanta and wish her well?"

"No. She doesn't have anyone to turn to. I know that. But be sure of your motives, Bailey. To solve a case and expose corruption, that's great. But if you have a personal vendetta against your department—"

"Of course it's personal," Bailey said loudly. "I'm a fucking pawn in a game they're playing." She pointed down the hall.

"And Marty just happened to choose the wrong damn cold case. Here she's trying to bring closure to a family that is still hurting after ten years and she ends up being a target herself. Yeah, so it's personal." Her eyes narrowed. "I don't like getting shot at."

He finally nodded. "Okay, Bailey. You know best. Why don't you get Marty up and we'll get started. I'll need photos."

Bailey took her coffee cup to the sink and rinsed it out. "And we need to do some shopping. We left in a hurry, and we don't have any clothes."

"There's an older mall south of here, off Saratoga. You can try out your new credit cards."

"Yeah, we'll do that." She motioned with her head toward the hallway. "I'll wake her."

She found Marty in much the same position as she'd left her, other than Bailey's pillow was now pulled tight against her. She smiled, watching her for a moment before sitting down on the edge of the bed.

"Hey, time to get up," she said quietly, nudging Marty with her elbow. The only response was a deep sigh and a tiny moan. "We need to go shopping."

"I hate shopping," Marty mumbled, her eyes still closed.

"Well, I think we need some clothes, huh? And Rico needs to take some pictures for our driver's license and stuff."

Marty rolled over and opened her eyes, then shut them again as she stretched. Bailey couldn't take her eyes off the sleek form under the covers.

"So we get to come up with new names?"

Bailey laughed. "Too late. He had six identities. I picked the three best." She stood, looking down at Marty. "I believe one of yours is Patty Stone."

"Patty? I don't look like a *Patty*. Maybe Patricia."

Bailey turned away when Marty tossed the covers off, revealing long bare legs. "Feel free to shower if you want," she said at the door. "And there's coffee."

"Be right out."

Marty held up a pair of slacks, and Kristen shook her head. "Dark jeans, dark tops."

Marty frowned. "Not really my style."

"We'll be out at night. We want to blend in, not stand out."

"When you say out at night, what does that mean?"

"It means any investigating we do, any surveillance, will be done at night. Usually."

"Trust me, Kris, no one's going to recognize you with your cute little punked hairdo," she said with a laugh.

Kris leaned closer, her voice low. "My cute little punked hairdo will have to serve me well during a drug deal."

Marty's eyes widened. "A drug deal?" she whispered.

"Yes."

"Why a drug deal?"

"Because that's what it's about. That's where the money is. My guess is that Carlos Romero saw something—like a drug deal going down—and it cost him his life."

"And you want to jump into the fray?"

"It's the only way."

Marty didn't know enough about it all to voice her concerns, but playing with drug dealers didn't sound all that safe, even though she knew Kristen had experience. Instead, she pulled a dark blue shirt off the rack and held it up to Kris. "This would look nice on you."

"I'm not going for nice, Marty."

"I meant to say it would look cute on you."

Kris laughed. "And I'm definitely not going for cute." But she took the shirt anyway.

Marty moved on, seeing the wall of jeans. "You know, your friend Rico seems really nice. I'm sorry I freaked out and called him a criminal."

"Yeah, he's a good guy. I try not to think about his profession. And about what would happen if he gets caught," she added.

"He told me a little bit about how he got into it."

"Did he?"

Marty smiled slightly, meeting Kristen's eyes. "Yes. He told me about what happened. About you getting shot." She was surprised at the quick blush that covered Kristen's face.

"That was a long time ago." She shrugged. "I was young and stupid. Can't say I'd do it again today."

Marty moved closer, next to her, lightly grasping her forearm. "Now I know you're lying. I have no doubt you'd do it again. Don't make light of what you did, Kris. It's something most people can't even fathom." Again, she was surprised by Kris's reaction, surprised to see a hint of tears in her eyes.

"When I realized I'd been shot, when I felt my blood running between my fingers, I thought I was going to die," she nearly whispered. "And then I saw Rico running, not *to* me to help, but away from me. Running away. I hated him at that moment. I thought how little he must care about me to just leave me there to die, after I'd taken a shot for him."

"But—"

"I know. I know he found my mother. She told me what happened. But I was out of it for a bit, and she didn't tell me until nearly a week later. That's a long time to think about it." She looked away. "I never told Rico. We talked about the shooting, but I never told him how *hurt* I was. How betrayed I felt."

"I'm sorry," Marty whispered, squeezing her arm hard. "You never told anyone that, have you?"

"No. Although my mother knew, I'm sure." Kristen squared her shoulders and took a deep breath. "I'm sorry. I didn't mean to get all emotional on you."

"I wouldn't exactly call that 'all emotional,' Kris." She realized she was still gripping her arm and she let her fingers fall away. "Let's hope you don't get to witness me that way. Of course, you've already seen me hysterical." She winked. "I got a shower out of the deal." She didn't mean to make that night seem like it was no big deal, but she'd found she handled it better if she didn't dwell on the guy who had the knife. It was much easier to deal with thinking of the aftermath, of Kris stripping her naked to clean her, Kris as soaking wet as she was when it was all said and done.

CHAPTER TWENTY-SEVEN

Bailey pulled out of Rico's driveway bright and early the next day. She wanted to get an early start, find them a safe motel to begin with. Now that they had identities, had credit cards that couldn't be traced, she felt safer upgrading from the sleazy motel they'd chosen that night in Gulfport. That didn't mean Marty would be getting a suite with room service, a fact she'd already conveyed to her.

"I feel like we're going to war," Marty said as she went over the checklist Bailey had given Rico, a list he'd filled without question. "Although bullet proof vests sound good." She looked up. "You're not expecting me to know how to use these weapons, right?"

"You're going to have to keep a handgun, yes. I want you to feel comfortable carrying one. The rifles, no. I don't know that we'll need them, but I wanted to be covered."

"Night vision glasses?"

"A must."

Marty put the list down. "Do we have a plan yet?"

Bailey shook her head. "Not really, no. Number one priority is finding someplace safe to stay. I think we should start with looking up Rafael Ortiz."

"He was who again?"

"One of the original investigators."

"Right. He and Vargas. And you already spoke with Vargas."

"Vargas is still on the force and wouldn't talk. Ortiz is retired. He might be willing to shed some light on the case. If he remembers. He's probably early seventies by now. He retired right after this case."

"You think he might know who the Scorpion is?"

"I doubt it. There may be very few people who actually know who he is. But he might know who in the police force is corrupt. That would be a start."

"You mean besides Lieutenant Marsh?"

"Right. We can pretty much count him in. As soon as we're settled, I'm going to call in. I want them to think I'm afraid to come back."

"But you want them to know you think they're behind it?"

"Just sort of feel them out, that's all."

"And you're sure our phones can't be traced? Rico said something about the signal bouncing between towers."

"Yeah. They won't be able to get a lock on the signal, it'll just bounce around and they won't be able to get a fix on it. And if they trace the number, it'll come back to an account in California."

Marty shook her head and smiled. "I just don't understand all this spy stuff. And surprisingly, I'm not really afraid anymore."

"Afraid?"

"Yeah, afraid. This is your life, you're used to this kind of stuff. I'm a reporter. I'm used to sitting down and talking to people. And the fact that my beach house got shot up like we were in a gangster movie, well, I don't think that's even registered yet with me. I mean, we were running and hiding, I didn't even have time to consider what it really meant."

"That someone wanted you dead?"

"Yes. And the manner by which they were willing to go about it. It's crazy."

"Shooting up the place like that was more for show than anything. They wanted it to look like a gang hit."

"If you hadn't been so quick to realize it was a setup, well—"

"Yeah, we'd be dead," Bailey said. "It was just instinct. I saw the surprise on your face, the questions in your eyes. You weren't expecting me, which meant you'd had no contact with Marsh." Bailey glanced at her. "My instincts are usually very good, Marty. You just have to trust me."

"And you'll try not to get me killed?"

Bailey nodded. "I promise not to get you killed."

* * *

The three-hour drive was made quickly, the time passing with ease as Marty chatted about some of the cases she'd come across in the last few years—and the upcoming trial in Toledo she was supposed to be covering. As she told Kristen, maybe she could cover it through the news well enough to write the follow-up article.

"Do you have any idea where you want to stay?" she asked as they hit Brownsville, the highway littered with chain stores and restaurants, mile after mile.

"I'd like to go farther south, but still be near the highway. Before we can connect with the downtown dealers, we'll have to get to know those on the outside."

"I'm not crazy about all this drug dealer stuff, Kris. I know it's what you did in Houston for a while, and I guess you feel comfortable with it, but—"

"You never feel comfortable, Marty, because you can't trust dealers. But the two things going on down here that might cause the police to fidget—if they're involved—are drug trafficking

153

and human trafficking. There's money in both, but the big money obviously is drugs. Besides, I can't see someone in the police department actually being involved in human trafficking. Any hint of that and the Feds would be down here in an instant. Because if you're successful with it, you most likely have a Border Patrol agent in your pocket."

"Wouldn't that be the case with drugs as well?"

"Drugs are a lot easier to hide than humans."

Marty looked back to the sprawl of the city as Kris drove. She didn't like it, but she'd just have to deal with it. She would have to trust that Kris knew what she was doing. She also knew she'd have to get comfortable with a handgun. If this was to be their life until they broke this case, she didn't want to be the helpless female standing on the sideline.

"Will you teach me to use a gun?"

Their eyes met and Kris nodded. "Yes."

Okay. She turned back to the window, accepting that her normally passive, safe existence had changed. She was going undercover with a cop. She had to quit thinking like she was Marty Edwards and embrace this new life. Embracing it might be the only way to survive.

"There's a little outfit down the road here," Kris said as she exited off the highway. "Little cottages. Mostly fishermen stay there."

"You've been there before?"

"No. I've just driven past. They look clean, they're out of the way. And a cottage would mean we'd have more privacy." She slowed as they approached the entrance. "If I remember correctly, they're booked solid in the winter, but it's fairly quiet in the summers."

"You'd think it'd be just the opposite," Marty said.

"Winter Texans. They come to escape the cold and spend the winter, then head back north when it warms."

"Well, I only hope they're clean."

Kris parked at the first cottage, the vacancy sign flashing in the window. "I'll be right back."

Marty watched until Kris disappeared inside, then glanced around the place. It appeared clean and well-kept, with tiny freshly mowed lawns surrounding each cottage. Palm trees were planted along the road, reminding her that they were back near the coast. She turned as Kris came back out, holding up a key.

"Perfect," Kris said. "Only two of them are booked. We've got the one down at the end."

"The sign said 'kitchenette.'"

"Fridge, microwave, hotplate and toaster oven. A few pots and pans. Will that do?"

"Yes. Good."

"She said there's a grocery store just down the road. How about we unload our things and I'll let you unpack while I run to the store?"

"Okay. If you think that's safe."

"Yeah. We're out of the way here. It'll be fine."

"How long do you think we'll stay here?"

"I booked a week. Depending on what's going on, we could stay longer, but we might feel safer if we move on and not stay at one place too long."

Kris parked at the last cottage and they got out. Kris tossed the key to her, then opened up the back of the SUV and took out their two bags. Marty unlocked the door and smiled. The little cottage was quite homey looking...and clean.

"This is nice," Kris said as she tossed the bags on one of the beds. "Do you have a preference on which one?"

"It doesn't matter." Two beds. Marty nearly wished there was only one. She'd felt so safe sleeping at Rico's in the same bed as Kris. The first night there, she'd crawled into Kristen's bed without her knowing it. Last night, it was just assumed they'd share the bed as no mention was made of the spare room. She slept soundly, feeling the warmth of Kris beside her. She was being ridiculous, she knew. She would be perfectly safe with Kristen just in the next bed.

They went back out for the other bags, these containing most of the items Rico had packed for them.

"I'll leave the rifles concealed under the floor where Rico put them," Kris said quietly. "Unpack our clothes and things, but leave the rest of the stuff in the duffel bags. We'll need to take that with us each time we leave. We don't need a nosy maid snooping around and finding it."

"Okay. I'll get everything else put up."

"I'll be back in fifteen minutes." She tossed Marty a phone, then held up her own. "He stored all the numbers for each phone. Call me if you need me."

"I'll be fine." Although she slipped the phone in her pocket when Kris drove off. Just in case, she wanted it close by.

The wood of the dresser was chipped and stained, but the drawers were clean. She unpacked their things, putting the new clothes they'd purchased side by side, thinking how domesticated it was as she put her jeans beside Kristen's in the drawer. It was odd seeing all these new clothes, nothing familiar to her, nothing but the shoes she'd been wearing when Kris found her. They'd bought jeans and dark shirts, a few pairs of shorts, sturdy shoes for the streets, and a pair of flannel pajama bottoms for her. She smiled as she touched them. Not the soft, worn ones she'd had for years. Those had been left behind with the rest of her things at the beach house in Gulfport. She wondered if the police there had them stored as evidence or if they'd simply been given away to a needy family.

It seemed like so long ago, but it was only four days, four days since she'd opened her door to Kris, surprised—and delighted—to see the other woman again. Four days since her life had been turned upside down. Was she listed as a missing person? Had her colleagues in Atlanta been questioned? Had they been to see Mrs. Paulson? Marty fingered the phone in her pocket, wishing she could chance a call to her. But Kris had said no calls and no e-mails. They had to be totally "under," as Kris called it. Marty Edwards didn't exist right now. And that meant everyone in her old life didn't exist either.

Surprisingly, that wasn't quite as distressing to her as it should have been. Which, of course, basically meant that the relationships in her life were just as superficial as she'd always believed them to be. Sad as it was, it was still the truth.

And it was far too easy to cease being Marty Edwards, reporter…and morph into one of the women Rico had created for her. *Erica Jones, Melanie Nelson and Patty Stone.* Marty rolled her eyes. Names she would never have chosen for herself. But nonetheless, she carried their credit cards, their driver's licenses and their passports. They apparently were all very strong, very brave women, or so she hoped.

She sighed as she shut the drawers and carried their toiletries into the bathroom. This adventure she was on certainly would never have been one she'd have chosen. It's funny how things worked out. A cold case, ten years collecting dust, seemed like the safest investigation she would ever do, especially when she read the file and saw that there were only four witness statements, none of them with firsthand knowledge of the crime. She liked to think she was thorough, that she was a professional and good at her job, but even she had to admit that when she opened the evidence box and saw how little there was, she knew it was hopeless. She knew that very first morning that she would eventually call Kesara Romero and tell her that her brother's case would never be solved.

Yet things happen, don't they? Things like getting shot at, like being held at knifepoint, like going on the run with a beautiful cop. She looked up, meeting her eyes in the mirror, startled by her thoughts. *Beautiful?* Well, yes, Kris was very attractive. But since when did she go around describing women friends as "beautiful"? She tilted her head, her eyes questioning those in the mirror. Right now, at this very moment, Kristen was the most important person in the world to her. She was trusting her with her life. She was trusting her to get them out of this situation. She was the only person who mattered right now.

Another thought that made her realize how very small her world was. There was really no one in her life. She could disappear—she *had* disappeared—and no one would miss her. The newspaper would think she was off on one of her trips and would pop back in like she usually did. The few friends she kept in touch with at the TV station could go months without missing her, which was usually how infrequent their calls or e-mails were. Mrs. Paulson? Well, as Marty had told her, she'd be gone awhile and not to worry. And knowing Mrs. Paulson, she wouldn't. Magazine editors might try to contact her, wanting an article, nothing more.

And here she was, in a rented little cottage in Brownsville, Texas, waiting for the only person who was important to her. Kristen Bailey. A woman she barely knew. Yet a woman she trusted completely.

The sound of the front door opening brought her out of her thoughts, and she closed the bathroom door, rushing to help Kris with the bags.

"I got a little bit of everything," she said.

"I see that," Marty said, pulling items from the bags. Chips and salsa, bread, turkey slices, mustard and mayo. A bag of oranges. Coffee, cream and sugar. Six frozen dinners, two frozen mini pizzas and a container of potato salad. Bacon, eggs and a couple of cans of biscuits. A small tub of butter, a jug of orange juice and a package of frozen chicken breasts. Marty shook her head. "I think you should let me do the shopping from now on."

"You're probably right. Shopping was never my strong suit. I've just never been particular about what I eat."

Marty took the last bag, surprised to find three bottles of wine and a corkscrew. "Thank you," she said. "No beer for you?"

"No. Wasn't in the mood." She went to the small table where Marty had placed her backpack. "I need to use your laptop," Kris said. "I want to see if I can locate Ortiz. If so, I'd like to try to find him tomorrow morning."

"Sure, go ahead."

"I'm also going to call Marcos. See what's going on."

Marty put everything away, watching as Kris waited for the laptop to boot up. "Do you mind if I take a quick shower?" she asked. "It's warm. I think I'm ready for shorts."

"Oh, sure. That's fine. I didn't even think to put the AC on."

"It's okay. The windows were open."

"I'll shut them and put the air on. Go shower."

Marty was pleased that the bathroom was clean, the shower spotless. She washed her hair and put conditioner on it, hating the coarseness it had acquired since she'd put the cheap rinse on and covered up the blond she'd paid good money to have. She hadn't had brown hair since her first year in college, since she discovered hair color. She was quite used to seeing her reflection in the mirror and having a blond-haired woman look back at her. The brown she now sported, well, she hoped she never got used to that. Because as soon as it was safe, she was heading to a beauty shop to get rid of the mess.

She heard Kris on the phone, but she was speaking too quietly for her to make out the words. She was most likely talking to her partner, Marcos. And if they could find Ortiz, could talk to him tomorrow, then maybe things would start to make sense.

She slipped on a pair of the new shorts she'd bought and a T-shirt, then ran a brush through her damp hair. They'd tried to think of everything they'd need, but neither had remembered a hair dryer. Of course, with Kristen's now short hair, she wouldn't need one.

When Marty stepped out of the bathroom, she found Kris standing at the window, staring out, the phone held lightly in her hand. Kris didn't turn around as she approached.

"Did you find out anything from Marcos?" she asked.

"No, I didn't—" She cleared her throat but still did not turn. "I didn't call him yet."

Marty frowned, wondering at the thickness of Kristen's voice. She put a hand on her shoulder, gently turning her around. When their eyes met, the last thing Marty expected to see were tears. "What's wrong?" she whispered. Kris shook her head and tried to turn away, but Marty stopped her. "What is it?"

Kris closed her eyes. "My mother died."

Marty felt her heart ache for Kris. "Oh, no."

"I just called to check on her. We've had so much going on, I hadn't even thought of her. And she died. Three days ago."

"Oh, sweetie, I'm so sorry."

Marty pulled Kris close without thinking, cradling her head against her neck, feeling the wetness as Kristen's tears fell. She held her tight, her hands moving lightly across her back, trying to offer comfort.

"They cremated her," Kris mumbled against her neck. "They couldn't find me, they said they called my office and were told I was missing, that there'd been a shooting. They didn't know what to do, so they cremated her."

Marty's heart was breaking as she heard Kristen's anguish in her voice.

"All she wanted...all she asked of me was to make sure she was buried with Dad and Kevin. That was my promise to her. And now she's gone. It's too late."

She cried harder and Marty held her tight. "I'm so sorry, Kristen. So sorry," she murmured as she smoothed her hair, running her hand down the side of her face over and over again, wiping at the tears that fell as she held her. Her lips moved across her face, kissing her lightly, hoping to soothe her pain. She didn't know what to say to her. How did someone without a family relate to this sorrow?

Kris pulled out of her arms, wiping her eyes with the back of her hand. "I'm sorry. It's just, for so long, she's been there, not talking, not seeing, just sitting in her chair staring off into space. And I wanted her to die, I wanted her to find peace." Kris met Marty's eyes, her own still swimming in tears. "I just didn't expect it to happen so soon. I guess I wasn't as prepared as I thought I'd be."

"I don't think death is something you can ever prepare for."

Kris ran her hands through her hair, and Marty could see she was trying to think, trying to make a decision. "I need to make arrangements, I need to instruct them—"

"Do you want to go by there?"

"No. We can't take a chance. If there's any place they'd expect me to go, it'd be to see her." She shook her head. "No. I'll have them send her…her ashes, to Houston, to the same funeral home that handled my dad and Kevin's funeral. I'll ask them to keep the ashes until I can get there. Until I can do a proper funeral."

"I'm so sorry."

Kris tried to smile as she considered her words. "A 'proper funeral'? I don't know who would go. My mother lost touch with all her friends in Houston years ago. There are no brothers or sisters or aunts or uncles. No cousins. She moved down here and just existed. The only time she had a semblance of life was when I visited, which wasn't often enough. We'd go out to eat, or we'd go and buy fresh fish and shrimp and cook at the beach house. And we'd get out on the water. And we'd talk and reminisce, the only time we talked about Dad and Kevin."

"The beach house was her safe haven," Marty guessed.

"Yes. The beach house was our summer place, fun and sun. It was full of laughter and happy times. Houston, well, Houston was home, but Houston was full of death. The house there, she just couldn't stay at. So she retired from teaching and went to the one place she knew happiness." Kris turned back to the window. "Only the beach house was a reminder of her loneliness too. The laughter and happy times didn't exist any longer."

Marty didn't have any words that could ease Kristen's pain, so she said nothing, offering only comfort as her hand rubbed lightly against Kris's back.

"Thank you for allowing me this time," Kris said quietly. "I know we have to—"

"No, we don't. We take care of your mother first. The rest can wait."

But Kris shook her head. "No, I have to deal with this, then move on. We can't afford any breaks, Marty. I won't put our lives in danger because of this."

Again, Marty didn't know what to say. So she let her instinct take over. She slid her arms around Kristen's shoulders, pulling her close in a hug, relishing the closeness she felt, trying to offer her comfort…and yet taking it at the same time.

"I'll be okay," Kris murmured, her own arms snaking around Marty, squeezing her tight. "We'll be okay."

"I know."

Kris pulled away, walking into the bathroom. Marty heard the water running in the sink, and she imagined Kris splashing her face, washing away her tears. She didn't know what to do, didn't know what Kris expected, so she sat down on one of the beds and waited. When Kris came back out, her face was washed and dried, her eyes clearer. She offered a weak smile.

"I'll be okay, Marty. Don't worry."

"I know," she said again.

Kris pointed to the laptop. "Rafael Ortiz. Why don't you try to find him? I'm going to call Marcos."

"Are you sure you don't want to wait? I mean—"

"No. My mother's been gone for a long while now. It just took a little time for her body to go with her." She turned away and picked up the phone. "I can't dwell on that, Marty. It is what it is."

Marty wasn't an expert on grief. In fact, the losses in her life were of the living, not the dead. She certainly didn't remember the car accident that took her family's life when she was two. But she knew enough about grief to know that Kris was trying to get over the death of her mother in a matter of minutes, not days. So she stood up and went to Kris, taking the phone from her hands.

"No."

"No?"

"No. One more day is not going to set us back. You can't just get news like this and expect to go on about our business."

"Marty, let me handle this my way."

162

"No. Your way is not healthy." Marty ignored the flash of anger in Kristen's eyes. "You let me think your brother and your father were alive. Back in Port Isabel, when we talked, you never indicated they were dead. Rico had to tell me what happened."

"I didn't want to talk about it."

"No. You wanted to sweep it away, like your mother did. You said you didn't talk about your father and Kevin. That the only time you reminisced was when you went to the beach house. Other times of the year, it was like they never existed. And now you want to do the same thing with your mother."

"That's not fair."

"No, it's not. And I'm sorry. But you can't just not dwell on it. It's not going to go away, Kris." Marty gripped both her arms hard, squeezing until Kris looked at her. "You're going to call and make the arrangements that you need to make. And then we're going to open a bottle of wine and you're going to tell me all about your mother and about your father and Kevin. We'll have our memorial service tonight." She dropped her hands from Kristen's arms, hoping she hadn't overstepped her boundaries with her. "Tomorrow we can get back on track."

They stared at each other, Kristen's eyes defiant, but Marty refused to look away. Finally, after long seconds of quiet battle, Kris nodded.

CHAPTER TWENTY-EIGHT

Again, Bailey woke as sunshine streamed in through the mini-blinds, and again there was a warm body next to her. She squeezed her eyes shut against the headache that roared to life, brought on by tears and too much wine. And she remembered now how she'd asked Marty to sleep with her. She wanted—needed—to have that human contact. Not in the next bed, but right beside her. And again, there was nothing sexual about it. She just wanted the closeness. Marty had understood, crawling in beside her and holding her hand until they drifted off to sleep. Now Marty was curled on her side, her hands tucked to her chin, resting lightly on Bailey's shoulder. It felt nice.

And it had felt good to talk last night. Marty had prompted her by asking questions of her childhood, digging out long-buried memories. Bailey had cried...and she'd laughed. One bottle of wine turned into two as she said her farewells to her mother, easing some of the guilt she felt at not being there when she died.

But today was another day, and it was time they got back to business. She'd called yesterday and made the arrangements for her mother's ashes, asking that they bury them in the plot next to her father. Yes, she felt guilty for not being there for some sort of service, but not as guilty as she'd feel if she asked them to hold the ashes until she could get there, not knowing when that would be. She wanted her mother, what was left of her, to be at rest near her father, not sitting on a shelf somewhere waiting on her.

With all that done, it was time to get back to the task at hand. And that was finding Rafael Ortiz.

"Are you awake?"

Bailey turned, finding Marty staring at her, her eyes half-closed. Bailey nodded.

"How'd you sleep?"

"Good. You?"

Marty rolled to her back and stretched, her legs brushing Bailey's in the process. "Great." Marty propped herself upon her elbows, watching her. "I'm starving, though, and I need some aspirin. Chips and salsa and two bottles of wine make for a raging headache."

Bailey laughed quietly. "Good. I was hoping I wasn't the only one in pain." She paused. "Thank you. Thank you for last night. You were right. I wasn't dealing with it very well."

Marty reached across the bed and touched her arm, rubbing it affectionately. "You were hurting, and you were just trying to brush it away. It broke my heart."

Bailey closed her eyes and turned away, nearly mesmerized by the feel of Marty's fingers brushing her skin. "I'm better today," she said. It had been so long since someone touched her like that. More than two years since she and Liz had ended things, but if she were honest, Liz had never been all that affectionate. Their sex life was great. What was missing were the small, incidental touches that went beyond the sex, that went deeper. Maybe that's why it had been so easy for them to end things—their love went only as deep as the sex. She kept her eyes closed, imagining that Marty's touch went deeper than just that of comfort. Imagining there was some emotional attachment in her touch.

When the fingers stilled, she opened her eyes, meeting Marty's gaze. She was surprised at the confusion she saw there and at the slight blush that covered Marty's face. The other woman pulled her hand away quickly, moving to the side of the bed.

"If you let me shower first, I'll do breakfast," Marty said, tossing the covers off. She glanced at her, arching an eyebrow.

"Sure," Bailey said. "I'll start coffee."

* * *

Marty shut the door to the bathroom, nearly afraid to meet her eyes in the mirror, afraid of what she'd see there.

"Don't be stupid," she murmured, finally facing the mirror and looking at herself. Yes, she looked different. Her hair was light brown, not blond. But that wasn't enough to account for the fact that she seemed to have suddenly acquired a libido.

What was it about Kristen that drew her? Why did she feel the need to touch her? Why did she have this…this crazy urge to be close to her? And why did she find such contentment when sleeping next to her? Was it an attraction that was becoming physical? Maybe it was just a sense of bonding. After all, someone was trying to kill them. They had no one to turn to, no one to trust but each other. It couldn't be sexual. It just couldn't be. It was *never* sexual for her.

"What if it is?"

She met her eyes again in the mirror, staring into them, remembering the sudden flush that had heated her, had moved over her body, had made her fingers tingle where she touched Kris, remembering the distant ache she felt, not knowing what it meant, but knowing it was a longing to touch, to be touched.

This can't be happening. Not now. Not when someone is trying to kill us.

She stripped off her clothes and stepped into the shower, turning the water on full blast and sticking her face into the stream, chilled by the cold yet shocking her system back to reality. She and Kristen were professional allies, nothing more. She wouldn't mistake her natural instinct to offer comfort to the other woman as something it wasn't. Comfort was emotional as well as physical. And Kris had needed both last night.

She turned around in the shower, tipping her head back and wetting her hair, her eyes closed tight.

Then why does it feel like we're more than just professional allies?

Finally, her body was showing signs of coming alive, of responding to another person. Should she just ignore it? Should she just assume it was the circumstances and nothing else?

She reached for the soap, not having any answers to her questions. She moved soapy hands over her breasts, over her nipples, shocked by their hardness, shocked by the lingering tremors of desire. It felt good.

It felt *really* good.

* * *

Bailey paced, waiting as the phone rang for the third time. Finally, Marcos answered.

"It's me. Bailey," she said.

"My God. Where are you?" he asked, his voice low. "They think you've been abducted or something."

"Yeah. Or something."

"Are you okay?"

"If you call getting shot at okay, I guess."

"What happened? The gang carried out their hit?"

"I don't know, Marcos. How would the gang even know I was there?"

"They know more than you think, Bailey. You need to get back here. Marsh has you in the database as a missing person."

Bailey flicked her glance to Marty, who was leaning a hip

against the small kitchen counter, listening.

"I'm not coming back, Marcos. It's not safe."

"Of course it's safe. Where else can you go? Back to Houston?"

"Not Houston, no."

"What about the reporter? She's missing too."

"She's alive, yes," Bailey said, smiling at Marty.

"What should I tell Marsh?"

"Tell him we survived the attack. And tell him we're going to find out who did it."

"So you're still in Gulfport, then? The police there said they had no trace of you. What about—"

"I better go, Marcos. I just wanted to let you know that I'm okay. I'll be in touch."

"Wait, Bailey—"

She disconnected before he could say anything else.

"Well?"

Bailey shrugged. "Hard to tell. He asked a lot of questions. He thinks we're still in Gulfport."

"That's good then, right?"

"For now. But they're not stupid. If we don't show up on the radar in Gulfport, they'll assume we're not there any longer."

"And they'll know that we're hiding?"

Bailey shook her head. "They won't think we've gone under, no. Why would they? They'll think we're running. And they'll continue to monitor our credit cards, our names, thinking they'll get a hit eventually."

"But they won't think we've come back to Brownsville?"

"Not at first, no." Bailey grabbed a piece of bacon from the plate and took a bite. "I like bacon. I just don't ever buy it or cook it. This is good."

"Thank you." Marty turned back to the two-burner hotplate. "Scrambled or fried?"

"Whatever you're having. I'm not particular."

"We'll do fried." Marty pointed the spatula at her. "Next time we shop, get me some green onions, mushrooms and spinach."

"I thought you were doing the shopping from now on?"

"I'll make the list and you shop. I cook." Marty pointed to the laptop. "Find Rafael Ortiz."

CHAPTER TWENTY-NINE

"What makes you think they're watching him?" Marty asked.

"Because if it were me, I'd be watching him. He's the only link to the old case who's no longer under their control."

"So what's the plan?"

Bailey pulled to the curb, two blocks from Ortiz's house. "I'm going to do a little surveillance on foot," she said. She reached into the backseat and grabbed one of the backpacks. She pulled out a baseball cap and a pair of small binoculars. She slipped the cap on her head and pulled it down tight. "Come drive. Keep your phone ready. If they make me, or if we have to get out of there in a hurry, I'll call. Drive like hell and pick me up."

"How far are you going?" Marty asked as she got out and walked around the SUV to the driver's side.

"Close enough to see his house and see what he drives. And to see if they've got it staked out. I'm certain they've got his phone tapped."

"Okay. Please be careful."

"Always."

Bailey waited until Marty was behind the wheel, then closed the door before heading down the sidewalk. It was an older residential area with large trees and big front yards. There wasn't much foot traffic, and she felt conspicuous with nothing to blend into. But she didn't have to go far. As soon as she hit the corner of Ortiz's block, she made out a beige unmarked car parked four houses down. She stopped, moving next to the shrubs that lined a fence across the street. She bent lower, using the binoculars to scan Ortiz's house. An older model white Ford Taurus was parked in the driveway, but the blinds were drawn and she saw no movement.

She turned on her heels and made her way back to Marty, slipping quickly into the passenger's seat.

"Anything?"

"They're watching his house."

"So now what?"

"We watch them watch him."

Marty stared at her. "Can we do that?"

"Their car is facing east. We should be able to go around the block and park on the corner behind them, out of their line of sight. We'll be able to see if Ortiz leaves."

"But won't they follow him?"

"Yes. So will we."

Marty started the engine and pulled away. "Okay, so maybe I've seen too many movies. Won't they see us?"

"No. Because they're not expecting to be followed. Their focus is on Ortiz."

"But they think we might try to contact him?"

"My guess is that they think if we do try to contact him, we'll do it by phone. If they follow him when he leaves, they're probably following his car more than following him."

"What do you mean?"

"I mean, if Sunday morning comes and he goes to church,

they'll follow him to the church, but won't follow him inside." Bailey pointed to an overhanging tree at the corner. "Pull over there."

Marty eased the SUV closer to the curb, stopping when Bailey put her hand out.

"See the car? Beige sedan."

"Yes."

"Okay. Count four houses down from where they are. That's Ortiz. We're now behind the surveillance car. Their focus is up ahead, not behind. So we can watch them and watch Ortiz at the same time," she explained.

Marty shifted in her seat, turning sideways to face her. "So this is the exciting police work that you do?"

Bailey laughed. "Oh, yeah. Stakeouts are always boring. That is to our advantage. If those guys have been watching Ortiz for any number of days, they're probably bored out of their minds. Which will make them sloppy."

"So if Ortiz leaves, we follow, hoping he goes someplace public where we might have a chance to talk to him?"

"Right." Bailey leaned back, trying to ease her tension. Stakeouts were her least favorite part of the job. Sometimes you'd sit for hours, day after day, with no activity. She hoped that wasn't going to be the case here. But Ortiz was over seventy years old. He might leave his house only once or twice a week. She smiled as she heard Marty sigh. "Bored already?"

Marty laughed quietly. "It looks more exciting on TV." She glanced at Kris. "Although it beats getting shot at."

"Yeah. That hasn't happened in a few days."

"That's a record for us, isn't it?"

Bailey relaxed against the seat, holding the binoculars lightly in her hands. "I'd like to promise you that you wouldn't get shot at ever again," she said. "But I can't."

"I wouldn't expect you to. I know this is a dangerous game we're playing."

Bailey nodded. "When you work narcotics—undercover—

172

you realize how many truly *bad* people there are. It's one thing to read about it in the paper or see it on the news, quite another to be face to face with them, to look into their eyes and see the evil there, to know they'd put a bullet in you without a thought, without remorse." She looked at Marty, capturing her eyes. "It's a very dangerous game, yes. But it's a game I've played before."

"I trust you."

Bailey looked away. "You trust me because you have to. You don't really have a choice. But what if there were other options, Marty? Would you still trust me?"

"You saved my life. More than once, Kris. It's you who's stuck by me, not the other way around. You could have left me in Gulfport. You could have sent me home to Atlanta." Marty reached over and squeezed her hand. "You care about me. I know that. I care about you too. I want you to be safe, just like you want me to be. I trust you. And you trust me."

Bailey stared at their clasped hands, then squeezed back. "Simple as all that, huh?"

Marty smiled slightly. "I told you once that I never trusted anyone, that I never learned to. I was handed off from family to family, place to place. There was never any security in my life. I learned to recognize their lies when they said I was welcome in their homes or that they'd take care of me. I learned not to be surprised when I was told I was going to a new place." Marty's grip tightened on her hand, and Bailey kept quiet, waiting for her to finish her thoughts. "It's different with you," she nearly whispered. "Whether it's real or my imagination, I don't know. I feel safe with you. I feel secure. I *believe* what you tell me because I know you're sincere." She looked away, her voice quiet. "For the first time in my life, I trust someone completely. It feels...it feels good."

Bailey didn't know what to say as she watched Marty's fingers slip away from her own. She couldn't relate to Marty's childhood, couldn't imagine going through life alone and able to depend on no one. Couldn't begin to understand the feeling of never being able to trust anyone. It must have been exhausting for her to live her life that way.

Bailey didn't know what to say to Marty, so she said what she was feeling. "I want to hold you."

Marty turned back to her, surprised. "What?"

Bailey felt embarrassed but didn't look away. "I…I want to hold you," she said again.

Marty smiled. "Like a hug?"

"Yeah. Like that."

"Kinda hard to do with the console."

Bailey moved closer, reaching for her anyway. She wrapped her arms around Marty's shoulders and pulled her as close as the console would allow. She felt Marty's fingers digging into her back.

"You're not alone anymore, Marty. I'll be here for you. I promise."

Bailey was surprised to feel dampness against her neck where Marty's face was pressed. She continued to hold her, feeling her quiet tears. She suspected Marty rarely cried, having learned long ago to harden her heart. But Bailey was offering her something she'd never had before, and it apparently softened her enough to bring on tears.

"I'm sorry," Marty murmured against her skin. "I didn't mean to—"

"No. It's okay. You don't have to say you're sorry."

Marty pulled away, wiping at her eyes. "I feel so alone sometimes. Not really lonely. That, I've learned to live with," she clarified. "But there's never been anyone I could count on, no one I could lean on. It just hits me sometimes. I'm sorry."

"You can count on me."

"I know I can. That's why I cried."

Bailey nodded, understanding her tears weren't from grief, but from relief.

"Thanks for the hug," Marty said. "I needed it."

"Anytime."

Bailey turned her gaze back to Ortiz's house, absently raising the binoculars, looking for movement. She lowered them again, glancing at Marty who seemed lost in thought. Bailey wondered what was going through her mind. For that matter, she wondered at her own thoughts. She was becoming very fond of Marty. In fact, under other circumstances, she knew "fond" wouldn't be the word she'd use. She found Marty attractive, both physically and intellectually. She appreciated her spirit and her toughness. She had never once complained about the situation they were in. She accepted it, just as Bailey had done.

Marty was still scared, that much was evident from her crawling into Bailey's bed the two nights at Rico's. And both of the following mornings Bailey had relished the closeness of the other woman. Their sleeping together last night had nothing to do with Marty being scared, though, and everything to do with Bailey wanting her near, needing her comfort. She wondered if that was a pattern they would stick to. She would welcome it, she knew, but it could turn into a dangerous habit. While she knew their relationship could never be physical—Marty had made it plain she didn't have physical relationships—an emotional attachment could be just as detrimental. She needed to stay focused on the task at hand.

"There's movement."

Bailey looked up, realizing it was she who had drifted away in thought, not Marty. She used the binoculars to get a better look, seeing someone who she assumed was Ortiz getting into the white Ford.

"No offense, but I think I should drive," she said.

"Of course."

"Let them pull away before you get out. I don't want them to notice us."

Ortiz backed out of his driveway, then headed south, away from them. The unmarked car followed. Marty quickly got out and hurried around to the passenger's side while Bailey simply crawled over the console. She sped after them as soon as Marty closed the door.

"I see them," Marty said. "About two blocks ahead."

"Okay." Bailey slowed, not wanting to get too close. The residential area faded as Ortiz led them toward Southmost. As the traffic light turned from green to yellow, Ortiz put his brakes on as if to stop, then sped through the light at the last minute, leaving the unmarked police car stuck in traffic. "I'll be damned," she said. "Pretty slick for an old man."

"Now what?"

Bailey turned right at the next street, speeding through the intersection before turning left again. "He's got to head south. There's nothing to the north except the shortcut to Port Isabel."

"There," Marty pointed. "The white Ford."

Bailey smiled as she turned right, now only two cars behind him. She glanced in the rearview mirror, seeing the beige sedan trying to catch up. She slowed as Ortiz's blinker came on. He turned into a local grocery store's parking lot. She drove past, turning at the next block and pulling into the lot at the opposite end. Before she could ask, Marty had reached into the backseat for the backpack.

"Thanks." Bailey pulled out the wireless headset and handed it to Marty. "Put this on." She then pulled out a tiny earpiece and inserted it in her ear. Then she clipped the wireless microphone on her watchband. "Test it," she said.

"Can you hear me?" Marty asked softly.

"Loud and clear. Me?"

"Yes."

Bailey got out, walking away from the car. "Record the conversation like Rico showed you. We may need to go over it later. You look for the other car. Make sure they don't see you with the headset on. Warn me if they come inside."

"Ten-four."

Bailey smiled. "Cute." She paused at the entrance to the store, looking around, then grabbed a red basket from the stack by the door and went inside. The store was small, and she had no doubt she'd find him, but after going down a third aisle without spotting him, she was beginning to worry that her window was closing. If her guess was wrong and they followed him inside, she would have no chance to talk to him.

"The beige car just pulled in," Marty said in her ear.

"Copy that," she said quietly, then heard Marty's amused chuckle.

She finally spotted Ortiz as he perused the vegetables, turning each potato over in his hand before selecting it. He was a small, slight man, his hair totally gray, his face lined in wrinkles. She walked casually beside him, picking up an onion and tossing it into her basket.

"Rafael Ortiz?"

He turned. "*Si*. Do I know you?"

"No, sir, you don't." She glanced around them. "I need to speak with you in private."

"Does it have anything to do with those yahoos who have been staking out my house for the last week?" He moved past her, inspecting the peppers much as he'd done the potatoes.

"Do they know you made them?"

"I doubt it. I spotted them the first day. Hell, thirty years on the force, you'd think they'd know I could spot a tail."

"I need some information, Mr. Ortiz."

"Who are you?"

She hesitated. "Kerry Thompson," she said. "It's about an old case of yours. Right before you retired."

"Information for what?"

She ignored his question. "Carlos Romero. Do you remember the case?"

"I should. It was the last one I worked. Seeing that boy laying there on the street with his guts ripped out gave me nightmares for months after."

"It's a cold case. Labeled as a gang-related killing, nothing more."

"What are you? A reporter or something?" He walked on,

going to the fruit.

"Not a reporter, no. I'm trying to find the Scorpion."

He stopped and spun around. "Listen, little girl, you don't want to go there. I don't know who you are or what you're after, but you don't 'find' *el Scorpion*."

"Tell me about the scorpion idols that are left at crime scenes."

"How do you know about that?"

"There was one left with Carlos Romero. Does the Scorpion leave the idols to mark his kill?"

"'Mark his kill'?" he scoffed. "No." He glanced behind them, then moved on after placing two oranges in his basket. "They make fresh tortillas right here in the store. You should try some. They're as good as the ones my dear wife used to make."

Bailey followed him, trying not to lose her patience.

"He leaves the idol for the police," he said quietly.

"I don't understand."

"If a scorpion idol is left at the scene, the police are to ignore the crime and not investigate, not solve, not work it. Or worse, frame some innocent."

"He controls the police?"

"Yes."

"How high up?"

Ortiz shrugged. "High enough."

"And everyone goes along with it? That's incredible."

"Not everyone, no. But those poor souls are dead, ripped up much like your Carlos Romero was. And each with a scorpion left at their side. Doesn't take much more than that to learn to keep your mouth shut."

"But who gives the order?"

"There are no orders. You just know. My first time to see one, I was probably only on the force a few years, it was this plastic orange thing. But my partner knew what it was. I didn't want to go along with it, no. It was some woman with her throat cut. But he told me what the scorpion meant, told me about other cops getting killed who didn't heed the warning." He shrugged. "I was

178

on the force thirty years. And I probably saw thirty scorpion idols at crime scenes."

"Who is he?"

"Who knows? I sure don't."

Bailey walked beside him as he went to get tortillas. "Drug lord?"

"If that's the case, he's in his eighties by now. I've heard other cops say the scorpion has been a signal going back fifty years or more."

Bailey stood back as he placed an order for three dozen tortillas. If the scorpion idol had been around that long, then the Scorpion wasn't a man. Not in that sense. The scorpion simply represented power. And whoever had the power controlled the police just by leaving a scorpion idol at the scene.

"So you going to tell me who you really are?"

Bailey gave him a short smile. "You're safer if you don't know."

"Safe? Just telling you the little that I have could make me a marked man. But hell, thirty years on the force and I was terrified of *el Scorpion*. I ain't going to let that follow me forever." He handed her a package of the tortillas. "Try them."

She took them and nodded. "The police? They got your house bugged too?"

He nodded. "And my phone." He went toward the checkout, but she hung back. "You know why they're watching me?" he asked.

She nodded. "They're looking for me."

"Smart girl, contacting me this way."

"Thanks for the information, Mr. Ortiz. You take care now."

"Remember what I said. You don't find *el Scorpion*. He finds you."

"I'll remember that."

He paused. "*Buenas tardes.*" Then, "*Vaya con Dios.*"

She bowed slightly. "*Gracias.*" She turned away, but he called her back.

"Miss Thompson?"

"Yes?"

"I shop here every Thursday. Same time."

"I'll keep that in mind."

"If you should need something else," he added. "I'm old, yes. But I'm still a cop."

"*Buenas tardes*," she murmured, turning away and walking back to the produce section. "Marty? You copy?"

"I'm here."

"You get all that."

"Yes. Fascinating."

Bailey stopped, glancing at the mushrooms. "So, you need mushrooms, green onions and what else?"

Marty laughed. "Spinach."

"Okay. I'm seeing an omelet for breakfast tomorrow."

CHAPTER THIRTY

Marty sat on the bed and turned on the TV, flipping through channels without interest. What did interest her were the enticing smells coming from the Mexican food they'd picked up for their dinner. She walked over to the tiny kitchen, intending on sampling the chips and salsa. The paper bag the chips had been poured into was dark with oil, attesting to their freshness. As she passed the bathroom, however, her eyes were drawn to the door, which was slightly ajar. She felt her breathing catch as she spied Kris in the shower, the glass door hiding nothing. She watched—transfixed—as the water cascaded over Kristen's small breasts, her nipples hard and taut from the water. Her eyes followed the length of Kris's sleek, wet body, and she felt her pulse spring to life, felt unfamiliar arousal at the sight. Stunned by her reaction, she knew she should turn away before she was caught staring, but she couldn't pull her eyes from Kris's body. Finally, Kris turned, sticking her face into the water, and Marty made herself move. She leaned against the wall, trying to make sense of what she was feeling. And trying to get her breathing back to normal.

Long forgotten were the chips and salsa as she closed her eyes, the image of Kris's naked form etched in her mind. She was still leaning against the wall when Kris stepped out, her short blond hair in disarray. Without thinking, she reached out and tried to put some order to it, her fingers lingering in the damp hair.

"Yeah, there wasn't a comb or brush in there," Kris said, her voice low, vibrating through her as their eyes met.

Marty pulled her hand away, embarrassed. "Looks kinda cute," she said. "I'm finally getting used to it." She moved into the tiny kitchen, putting some space between them.

"Glad you are," Kris said, her fingers plucking at the short strands. "I don't know if I ever will." She motioned to the bathroom. "You want to shower before we eat?"

"No. I'm starving. I was just about to attack the chips and salsa," she said, her voice hinting at the nervousness she felt.

"You okay?"

Marty jerked her head up. "Of course. Why?"

"I don't know. You seem a little fidgety."

"No. I'm fine." She turned her back to Kris, finding a couple of plates in the cabinet. She poured salsa into a bowl while Kris heated their plate of enchiladas in the microwave. The Styrofoam containers with the rice and beans still felt hot so she carried them to the table and waited.

"Here we go," Kris said, placing the tray between them. "You want something to drink?"

"Oh, just water is fine."

Kris nodded, pulling two water bottles from the fridge. Marty took one from her. But the food, while excellent, didn't have quite the appeal it had had earlier, before her stomach had been tied in knots by the sight of Kris in the shower. She moved her food around on her plate, forcing down bites despite the turmoil inside her. She looked up, seeing Kristen's questioning gaze, but she looked away quickly. She was surprised by the light touch on her hand, even more surprised when she jerked her hand away from Kristen's fingers.

"I'm sorry," Kris murmured.

Marty quickly reached across the table and squeezed Kris's hand. "No. I'm sorry," she said.

"What is it? This case finally getting to you?"

Marty stared at her. *The case? No, my body is like a stranger to me now, and I can't seem to look at you and still breathe at the same time.* But no, she couldn't very well blurt those words out. So she nodded. "Well, if I think about it too much, yeah," she said and tried to smile. "So let's don't." She pushed her plate away and leaned her elbows on the table. "Tell me about your ex."

"Liz?"

"Yes."

Kris took a swallow of water, then cleared her throat. "What do you want to know?"

Marty shrugged her shoulders. "Just curious, that's all." Truth was, she wanted to know more about Kris, not her ex.

"Well, she's a good person. I certainly don't have any ill feelings about her. She was fun. She liked to party, liked to share dinner with other couples. We entertained all the time." She pointed at Marty's plate. "You going to eat that?"

"No, it's yours," she said, pushing the plate closer to Kris.

"We had a large circle of friends. Most of them hers." Kris grabbed a handful of chips. "Like I said, she was fun to be around."

"But you ended things so easily."

Kris paused. "She's a computer programmer, works for a large corporation in Houston. She would only make a fraction of her salary down here. That was the excuse for not moving."

"Meaning?"

"Meaning our relationship wasn't quite as deep as I imagined it was. Apparently for both of us. I mean, I walked away, not her. And I didn't exactly beg and plead for her to come with me."

"And she's moved on," Marty said, remembering Kris had said Liz was in another relationship now.

"Yeah. And I wish her well. Like I said, she's a good person. But now that I'm removed from it, I realize what we had wasn't that of lifelong lovers."

Lovers. For the first time in a long, long while, Marty wondered what it would be like to have a lover. After accepting the fact that she wasn't normal, not in that regard, she suddenly found her body alive...and wanting. She shoved away from the table quickly. "I think I'll shower now."

She gathered her flannel pajama bottoms and a T-shirt and escaped into the bathroom. She felt Kris's eyes on her, knew they would be filled with questions. Questions that she didn't dare give answers to.

The bathroom was no safer, she discovered. As she stripped down to her skin, she stared into the mirror, studying herself. She wasn't as tall as Kris, wasn't as sleek, yet she'd always taken pride in her body, something she found ironic. It wasn't like others saw her body, it wasn't like she had a lover. She slid her hands to her breasts, surprised again by the sensitivity of her nipples, surprised by the way they hardened. She dropped her hands, embarrassed, and quickly got into the shower, rushing through her routine, not wanting to think.

After she dried off, she hung her towel next to the one Kris had just used. She hadn't realized the intimacy involved with sharing a small living space, sharing a bathroom, sharing meals. She'd never had a roommate except for the one year in the college dorm. That had been enough to convince her she never wanted another one. Of course, back then, she still had held out hope that she'd meet someone who would stir her libido just a little, just enough to make her want a sexual relationship. It wasn't until she was twenty-six—after yet another disastrous attempt at sex—that she had sought out a therapist. After three years of discussing her childhood, her rootless existence, her lack of stability, she'd finally accepted the fact that her physical, mental and emotional states weren't in sync. "Trust issues," they'd labeled her condition.

184

She brushed her teeth, pausing to meet her eyes in the mirror. Did she still have trust issues or not? She rinsed her mouth, then leaned on the counter, staring into the mirror but seeing nothing. She trusted Kristen...completely. Was that why the wall she'd built around herself was beginning to crumble? Was that why she'd let Kris inside? Because she trusted her?

She sighed. That seemed far too simple an answer, but she was too tired to explore it further.

When she walked out of the bathroom, Kris was on the phone, pacing back and forth in front of the beds.

"You're a hacker, for God's sake, Rico. How hard can it be?" She shook her head. "I don't have time for you to get your Hong Kong friend to do it." Kris covered the speaker with her finger and smiled at her. "I'm getting Rico to hack into the police database."

"Whatever for?"

"Drug dealers." She turned back to the phone. "Yes. Arrested but not convicted. Get the file that's got their last known address." She paced again. "I know that, Rico, but some will be accurate."

Marty stood between the beds, watching Kris, free to observe her and she did. By the look on Kris's face, she was playing this almost like a game, a cat and mouse game that she was enjoying thoroughly. She was a cop and she was using her skills, something she'd not been allowed to do for the last couple of years. But now they had a cause—a mission—and you could see the excitement on her face. It was because of that, the confidence she saw there, that Marty wasn't really afraid of the situation any longer. Kris could handle herself. And Kris would protect them.

"E-mail Marty the file. Yeah, to Patty Stone," Kris said, flashing a smile at Marty. It was the least favorite of her new names and Kris knew it. "Thanks, buddy." Kris placed the phone on the table, then pointed at the bathroom. "Gonna brush my teeth."

Marty nodded, still standing between the beds. Well, there was no reason for her to get into the bed they'd shared last night, so she dutifully pulled her eyes to the other bed and sighed.

She couldn't for the life of her understand why she craved the closeness of a warm body—a female body—when she'd spent her whole adult life dodging that closeness that came with dating. She pulled the covers back and crawled in, fluffing the two pillows before lying down. She sighed again as she stared at the ceiling, wondering if she should tell Kris the directions her thoughts had taken lately, tell her about the confusion in her mind and body. But no, she didn't need any added embarrassment. It was hard enough looking herself in the eyes.

She rolled her head to the side when Kris walked back, looking at her briefly before turning away.

"You gonna be okay over there?" Kris asked nonchalantly as she went to her own bed.

"I'll be fine."

"Okay. Well, goodnight then."

Kris turned the lamp off, and the room was plunged into darkness. Marty stared at the window, her eyes adjusting as a faint glow shown through the blinds from the porch light outside. She wasn't afraid. But she was alone. She quietly turned her head, seeing Kristen's silhouette in the shadows. After last night and Kris's tearful farewell to her mother, Marty supposed the proper thing to do would have been to offer to sleep with her again and let Kris be the one to say "No, I'll be fine." She turned her head away and forced her eyes closed. No, she was being ridiculous. They were both grown women, not teenagers hiding from the dark.

So, she rolled to her side, trying to get comfortable, trying to fall asleep. It was an act she repeated many times into the wee hours of the morning, her mind refusing to shut down, her body refusing to drift off to sleep. Hours later, she was still awake, still tossing in her bed while Kris slept peacefully only a few feet away.

It took all of her willpower not to go over and crawl into the bed with her, knowing it would be warm there...and safe. And knowing she'd fall asleep instantly.

CHAPTER THIRTY-ONE

Bailey looked up from the computer, watching as Marty rolled over, her legs stretching out under the covers. Bailey's eyes lingered for a second before she pulled them away. It was after nine, but she wasn't going to wake her. She knew Marty had had a fitful sleep. Each time she'd awoken, she'd heard Marty fidgeting in her bed. She'd damn near asked Marty if she wanted to sleep with her but thought that might be a bit forward of her. There was no logical reason for them to share a bed. So she'd let Marty toss about as she fell back to sleep. When Bailey got up at six, Marty was finally sleeping soundly. So soundly, in fact, that Bailey was able to sneak away to the taco stand down by the grocery store for breakfast.

She sipped her coffee as she went back to the e-mail Rico had sent. The file wasn't large, containing only fifty names or so, but it was useful. Not only had Rico managed to get all the information she'd asked for, he'd also located a file with known associates that was cross-referenced with the arrests. Just from that file alone, she'd targeted who she believed to be the top three dealers in the Valley. Not that she would start with them, no. But it helped to know the pecking order. The man she wanted to start with was Fabio Perez, a mid-level dealer who just might be hungry enough to do business with her—a woman and a stranger to him.

The only problem with the plan, he liked to do business at *El Pirata del Parque*. The Pirates Park, the one where they'd gotten shot at, whether to warn them or to warn *Los Rebeldes* not to speak to them. Either way, she knew Marty wasn't going to be crazy about the idea.

She glanced over to the bed, seeing the other woman stir. Marty rolled onto her back, her legs stretching out under the covers. Then she sat up quickly, her disorientation obvious.

"Good morning," Bailey said quietly, trying to ease her fears.

Marty brushed the hair away from her face and rubbed her eyes. "What time is it?"

"Almost nine thirty."

Marty fell back to the pillow and groaned. "I can't believe I slept this late. Why didn't you wake me?"

"You didn't sleep well during the night. I didn't want to wake you when you were finally sleeping soundly."

Marty tossed the covers off and sat on the edge of the bed. "I'm sorry if I kept you awake."

"No, I slept fine." She stood. "I'll get you some coffee."

"Thanks."

Marty got up and stretched again, raising her hands over her head. Bailey smiled as she pulled her eyes away from the sight.

"What's that I smell?" Marty asked as she followed her into the kitchen.

"I went down to that taco stand we saw by the grocery store. Got a few breakfast tacos."

"They smell great." She headed to the bathroom, then paused at the door. "If you want to go ahead and eat, you can. I won't mind."

"I'll wait."

She poured them both a cup of coffee and carried them to the small table where she'd been reading. She moved the laptop out of the way, stacking her notes neatly to the side. Then she unwrapped four tacos and put them in the microwave to heat while getting plates and napkins out. By the time Marty came out of the bathroom—her hair brushed to some semblance of order, her eyes looking not quite as sleepy as before—Bailey had the table set and hot tacos waiting.

"Thanks," Marty said as she reached for her coffee.

Bailey sat down opposite her, grabbing one of the tacos off the plate. "You know, the beds are queen," she said before taking a bite.

Marty put her coffee cup down, taking a taco as well. "Yes, I know." She raised her eyebrows questioningly.

"I just mean, I wouldn't mind if you wanted to share," Bailey said quickly. At Marty's startled look, Bailey wished she'd kept her thoughts to herself. So Marty had a fitful night's sleep? There was no guarantee sharing her bed would put an end to that. Although the three nights they'd slept together, Marty had appeared to sleep soundly.

"So I did keep you awake?"

"No. It's just…if you'd feel more comfortable—safer—in my bed, I wouldn't mind it if we shared." Bailey noticed the slight blush on Marty's face and again wished she'd just kept her mouth shut.

"Thank you," Marty said as she took a bite of her taco. She moaned and closed her eyes. "This is wonderful."

"Yes, it is." Bailey wasn't sure if the "thank you" was for the offer of her bed or the taco.

"Did you get what you needed from Rico?"

"Yes, he sent some good information," she said.

"So, do we have a plan?"

"I don't know if you'd call it a plan or not, but I have someone targeted who I'd like to hook up with. But it may involve going down to *El Pirata del Parque*."

Marty's eyebrows shot up. "That's the park where we went that first night?"

Bailey nodded.

"Are you *crazy?*"

Bailey smiled. "I figured that'd be your reaction."

"Well, *yeah*."

"We'll talk about it. But we have to start somewhere, Marty. Based on Ortiz's description of the Scorpion, it's not really a person, but rather an entity, especially if it dates back fifty years or so."

"How can we find someone when nobody knows *who* he is or *what* he is?"

"He's the one with the power. And to have the power, you have to have the money. To have both, then you deal in drugs. My guess is that maybe, years and years ago, there was a man who perhaps called himself Scorpion. Maybe he died and passed the title on. Or maybe he was killed and someone took it from him. Maybe every time the scorpion idol changes, say from paper to plastic—now to a glass paperweight—maybe that's a different man being the Scorpion. Who knows?"

"And the police? Is it really possible to have this much corruption, for this long?"

"Why not? Brownsville is stuck down here on the border, all by itself. It's a small city, high unemployment, a struggling economy. So fifty years ago, you might own a few street cops and they let you sell drugs and turned the other way. Then maybe you go higher up the chain. You have the money and they're willing to take it. Maybe just by chance one of them decides to come after you. So you kill him. And you leave your mark. Maybe it did start out as a warning."

She drained the last of her coffee and leaned her elbows on the table. "So now you have a cop who went up against you and is brutally murdered. Fear grows. It's safer to let you do your thing than to try to take you down. Years and years pass, you now control the police completely." She shrugged. "The new guys on the force may not even know you, but they know the Scorpion. Ortiz was on the force thirty years and he's seen cops murdered. Marcos told me the same thing. He's been here twenty years. Neither of them knows who the Scorpion is, but they know what he does. If I was a local, born and raised here, if I came on the force at twenty-one and learned these things, I don't know what I would do. I might just turn the other cheek too."

Marty shook her head. "No. I don't believe you would. It's not your nature."

"I'd like to think I'd do the right thing, Marty, but who's to say? I'm an outsider and I can look upon this with disbelief. How could all these cops, for all these years, let themselves be controlled like this?" Bailey got up and took their dishes to the sink. "They didn't all want to be controlled. Obviously some stepped forward. And those who did are dead. Fear breeds fear."

"So the police, Lieutenant Marsh, they're trying to kill us, eliminate us, why? Fear?"

"Perhaps."

"Or is the Scorpion calling the shots and he gave the order? Again, why?"

"I don't know why. Carlos Romero saw something he shouldn't have. Whatever that was, they don't want us to know."

"But how would we know? Carlos is dead."

Bailey stared at her, her mind spinning. "Maybe that's not it at all," she said. "We keep saying this is a nothing case that appears to have no significance. Why this case?" She turned, pacing across the room, feeling Marty's eyes on her. "Maybe we're too preoccupied with this case to see the big picture." She stopped, feeling certain she was on to something. "Think about it. The Scorpion can control the local police. But when you came here and started snooping in the case, when you hinted to Marsh that there was a police cover-up and corruption, well, then you're raising the possibility of getting outsiders involved. And outsiders don't play by the same rules as the locals."

191

"You're not a local either. So what's to keep us, you and me, from going outside the local police? What's to keep us from bringing attention to this?"

"Exactly. We might go to the newspaper. Or maybe we might go to Austin and get politicians involved, get the attorney general to investigate. The Scorpion doesn't have control any longer."

"So eliminate the two outsiders," Marty said. "Then you eliminate the threat."

Bailey nodded. "It could have absolutely nothing to do with Carlos Romero."

Marty smiled. "Speculation and theory. But where does it get us?"

"Nowhere. We might be way off the mark. But I still think power, money and drugs—that's the bottom line." She took Marty's arm and pulled her to her feet. "Now, enough of that. Let's take a play day."

"What do you mean?"

"Let's go to the island. We can walk the beach, relax. We'll have a late lunch."

"But what about—"

"We have time. We won't go out until late tonight." She waited, seeing the bright smile that flashed across Marty's face. "Is that a yes?"

"I'd love to."

CHAPTER THRTY-TWO

Marty followed Kristen's lead, taking her shoes off and sinking her bare feet into the warm sand. It felt good—the softness of the sand, the splashing of the water against her ankles, the breeze filled with salt air brushing her skin. She turned her face into the wind, relishing the feel of the sunshine as it warmed her. A play day, Kris had said. Marty knew they shouldn't be out frolicking about like they didn't have a care in the world. But it felt good, it felt normal. They were just two people walking the beach, like so many others were doing. Two people enjoying each other's company, the silence between them comfortable now.

They'd driven the short stretch between their cottage and Port Isabel chatting away like old friends—or like the new ones they'd become. She felt completely at ease in Kristen's presence, and she wondered if that was the source of her affection. It had been so long since she'd felt this comfortable with another person—if ever—that she didn't want to mistake that for more.

Yes, her body felt more alive than it had ever been. Her senses were heightened, her mind clear, yet it was her libido that was jumping up and down screaming to get noticed. She glanced quickly at Kris, taking in her softened features, the contented look on her face, her lips turned up in a natural smile. No doubt Kris needed this break as much as she did.

"Tell me about your family," she urged.

"Funny, I was just thinking about them." Kris bent down and picked up a broken sand dollar. She studied it for a second, flipping it over with her fingers, then letting it fall back to the sand. "My mother had a huge collection of sand dollars and shells. She had them in jars and bowls all over the house. Once a week, she'd get us up before daylight and we'd drive to the island, trying to beat the crowds so we'd get the best shells. Then she'd treat us to breakfast. Pancakes. The only time we got pancakes."

"Your brother was older than you?"

"Yes. But we were close. Closer in the summers because we didn't have the distraction of school and outside friends. Once he got into high school, he didn't stay out here as much, but I did. I stopped spending my summers here the year I started college."

"Lazy summer days?"

"Oh, yeah. Sunbathing, Jet Skis and more sunbathing."

"What about your father? You don't mention him much," Marty noted.

Kris shrugged. "Just habit, I guess. After the fire, after the funeral and all, we just couldn't bear to talk about them." She looked at Marty quickly. "As you said, not healthy. But it was just me and my mother then, and we coped the best we could."

"You were close to your father?"

"Yeah. I didn't spend nearly as much time with him as I did with my mother, of course, but yeah, we were close. He took two weeks off every summer to stay out here with us. That's the only time we went fishing." She laughed. "I hate to fish, always have. But he insisted it would grow on me. So for two weeks each summer, we'd put on those hideous waders and walk out in the

194

bay to fish."

"And were you successful?"

"Most times. I'm sure there are pictures to prove it."

Marty stopped when Kris did, both of them staring out into the gulf as the waves crashed to shore. Pelicans and terns dove into the surf, looking for lunch, and hundreds of tiny shorebirds ran on the beach away from the wave, then chased the water back down as they rapidly dug into the sand for their own morsels of food.

"I can't imagine not having those memories, though," Kris said unexpectedly. "Your childhood memories are more painful than anything."

Marty nodded. "That's true. But our life experiences are what shape us, what makes us who we are. As idyllic as spending the summers on the beach sound, I didn't know any better. Living on an Iowa farm was what I knew. Being shipped from family to family, that was my life. It made me stronger, it made me learn to depend on myself and no one else, and it taught me resilience. Would I have liked to have had a normal childhood and a stable family? Sure." She started to walk again and Kris followed. "But then what? Would I have married the son of a farmer? Would I be working our farm with my husband and three or four kids?"

Kris laughed. "God, that's your alternative?"

Marty playfully bumped her arm. "Yes, that most likely would have been my fate."

"No TV news anchor job?"

"Hardly. And I certainly wouldn't be here, walking this lovely beach with you now." She smiled. "It's funny where life takes us, isn't it?"

"It certainly is."

They both jumped as a surprisingly strong wave brought the water up to their knees. They hurried out of its way, running up onto the dry sand. Marty felt as relaxed and carefree as she could ever recall being. Whether it was Kris's companionship or the serenity of the water, it mattered not. At that moment, she was simply a young woman enjoying the company of another. For a few hours, at least, they could put their "mission" behind them and enjoy the warm sunny day on the beach.

"I could get used to this," she said.

"What? The beach?"

"Yes. Now I know why some call it therapeutic. You can just lose yourself out here, can't you?"

"Yeah, you can. It's hard to hold on to problems out here. Your mind won't let you. You're watching the waves, watching the birds, enjoying the sound of the surf, the breeze…it's almost an overload to the senses."

"Which was why you thought this would be good for us today, huh?"

Kris shrugged. "I just thought we could use a break."

"And tonight we look up a drug dealer?"

"Yes. Back to the mission at hand." Kris stopped walking again. "You about ready for that late lunch I promised you?"

Marty wasn't nearly ready to leave the beach, but she knew they had to. Kris must have seen the wistful look on her face as she took in the scene around them.

"We can go back down to where the condos are," Kris suggested. "There's an outdoor patio café. We can still watch the water."

Marty grabbed her hand and squeezed. "Sounds great." She was surprised when Kris's fingers intertwined with her own. They walked several steps together, fingers clasped, before they separated. Was it an innocent gesture or a show of affection? She decided it didn't matter. She was growing closer to Kris with each passing day, each passing hour.

And tonight she would go with Kris out into the darkest part of the city, to try to connect with a drug dealer. That seemed so far removed from where they were now, out here on this sun-filled beach. And after that, they would retire to their little cottage and their two queen beds, and she would stand between them, wondering if she dared take Kris up on her offer to share,

196

knowing she would sink into a deep, peaceful sleep beside her. Or would she opt for another sleepless night in her own bed, too stubborn and too scared to crawl into bed with Kris?

Stubborn, no. Scared? Plenty.

CHAPTER THIRTY-THREE

"Are you okay?"

Marty nodded. "Nervous."

Bailey reached across the console, touching Marty's shoulder, then lower. "Wanted to make sure you remembered your vest."

"And you?"

Bailey tapped the hard material under her shirt. Marty was white as a sheet, and Bailey was having second thoughts about taking her along. Not that she could have left her behind. She knew Marty would never have gone for that. The best thing she could do now was keep her mind occupied.

"You have the headset?"

"Yes."

"Give me the earpiece and microphone. We'll test it." She held her hand out as Marty found the pieces in the backpack. She inserted the tiny earpiece into her right ear, then clipped the microphone to her watchband.

"Can you hear me?" Marty nearly whispered.

"Perfect. You?"

"Yes. You want me to record this too?"

Bailey nodded. "Yes. We need to have a record of everything." She slowed as they approached the park. "You have your weapon?"

"Yes. But—"

"Just a precaution, Marty. You may not think you can use it, but if it came down to life or death—yours or mine—I have no doubt you'd pull the trigger."

"Thank you for the vote of confidence," she said. "But I'm scared to death."

"Nothing's going to happen. We look for him on the street. If he's not out, then we go to his house. It's only two blocks from here."

"You don't know this man, Kris. How can you just walk up to him and—"

"I know what I'm doing. Money is all that matters. These guys live to make a sale. So if I show up wanting to buy, they're not going to turn me away."

"What if they suspect you're the police working undercover?"

"Not in this town. They don't have drug stings. Probably because our friend, Mr. Scorpion, controls the drug trade." She drove slowly through the park, surprised at the lack of activity. It was nearly eleven. She'd expected the dark corners to be alive with sales, not empty and quiet. Maybe the park had evolved into a playground for gang wars, moving the drug trades into the city.

"It looks awfully quiet."

"That's what I was thinking." She drove on through, seeing only a couple of shadows that ducked from her headlights. "Something's going down tonight," she murmured.

"What do you mean?"

"I can feel it. The park's nearly empty. Those that are here, they're hiding."

"What does that mean?" Marty whispered.

Bailey ignored her question as she left the park, turning

right. Fabio Perez lived down this street. And it too was empty, quiet. She killed the lights as she drove, then pulled to the curb, parking in the shadows. She reached overhead, disabling the interior lights.

"Is this his house?"

"Yes."

"There aren't any lights on," Marty noted.

"Stay in the car, leave it running," Bailey instructed. "You listen to me," she said. "If something goes wrong, you get the hell out of here."

"No. I'll—"

"You'll do as I say, Marty."

"I won't leave you here."

Bailey gripped her arm hard. "Nothing should happen. But if it does, you leave here. You go to the cottage and get our things, then you contact Rico. He'll get you back to his place safely. You can trust him."

"Kris—"

"I'll be fine." Bailey got out, then ducked her head back inside. "Get behind the wheel, Marty. Lock the doors." She closed the door, then heard Marty's whispered voice in her earpiece.

"Please be careful."

"Copy that."

To say she had a bad feeling was an understatement. The air was thick with tension, you could almost see it. What it meant, though, Bailey had no idea. She stayed in the shadows, hugging the side of the house. In the distance, she could hear a dog barking, the only sound disturbing the eerie silence. As she neared the back of the house, she heard angry voices, two men speaking Spanish. Instinctively, she pulled her weapon out, holding it close to her side.

She slipped behind the lone shrub, crouching low to the ground and out of sight. She brought her wrist up to her mouth. "I'm at the back. You copy?"

"Yes."

"There's someone inside with him. Sounds like they're arguing."

"Kristen, please don't do anything crazy. Maybe you should—"

Her voice was drowned out by two loud shots. Bailey slammed against the wall, her weapon ready.

"Kris? Are you—"

"Shhh."

She waited until the door opened, then rounded the corner. As soon as the man there saw her, he raised his gun. She fired once, knocking him back into the house.

"Jesus Christ, what the hell happened?" Marty's urgent voice sounded in her ear.

"Stay put. I'm fine," she said. "Give me twenty seconds."

She stepped over the body in the doorway. Her shot had hit him in the forehead, killing him instantly. Still clutched in one of his hands was a large duffel bag. She nudged it away with her foot, then bent to open it. She wasn't surprised to find it stuffed with money. Farther inside the house was another body, this one of Fabio Perez. He had taken one to the chest and one to the head. But her eyes were drawn to the scorpion idol resting on his bloody shirt. So that's why the park was empty. The Scorpion had had a hit on Perez, and everyone knew it was going down. She wondered why Perez didn't know.

"Marty, you copy? Any activity?"

"No. And will you hurry it up, please."

"I'm on my way."

She grabbed the duffel bag and took one last look around the room. On a shelf not far from where Perez lay was a stash of liquor bottles. She walked closer, smiling when she saw the unopened bottle of Hennessy Cognac.

"Thank you very much," she murmured. She shoved it into the duffel bag, then hurried back out into the night.

* * *

201

"So that's your version of 'nothing's going to happen'? Two men dead and a bag full of money?"

Kris held up the bottle. "Don't forget the cognac."

Marty put her hands on her hips. "Are you going to tell me what happened or not?"

Their eyes held for a second, then Kris nodded. "Very well." She went into the kitchen and took two glasses from the shelf and poured a generous amount of liquor into each. "Sit," she said and pointed to the floor. "We should at least count the money."

The women leaned against the bed, the duffel bag between them. Marty took the drink Kris offered, sipping slowly as her eyes widened. "Wow."

"Excellent stuff," Kris said. She pulled the bag closer, exposing the money. "Drug money," she said. She emptied the contents of the bag between them, and Marty stared. She'd never seen that much cash before. "How much?"

"A couple hundred thousand, I'd guess."

"Good Lord. What are we going to do with it?"

"Well, I would say we were going to use it to buy drugs, but that may not work now."

"Why?"

"Because the guy who killed Perez left a scorpion idol on his chest. And I killed him *and* took their money."

"And they're going to want it back."

"Yes."

Marty shook her head, finally understanding Kris's meaning. "No. You're not going to deal with these people. No. I won't let you."

"How else are we going to get close to the Scorpion?"

"They're not going to let you get close to him." Marty gripped her hand tightly. "How does this happen? You picked Perez's name out of a hat, yet on the very night we go to contact him, he's killed. How is that possible?"

"Luck?"

Marty released her hand. "Tell me what happened," she demanded again.

"There's not a lot to tell. They were arguing. I couldn't understand what they were saying. Then two shots. When the guy came out of the house, he saw me. I fired before he could get a shot off. He had the duffel bag and was on his way out. When I went inside, Perez was sprawled on the floor, a pool of blood around him, and there was a scorpion idol on his chest."

"The same kind? A glass paperweight?"

Kris nodded. "Yeah."

"So pure coincidence?"

"Normally I'd say I don't believe in coincidence. But in this case, since we're working independently and no one knew our target, then yeah, coincidence." Kris poured more cognac into her glass. "And maybe it's more than just luck. I picked Perez because he was a mid-level dealer and he had known associates all common to the big guys."

"Big guys?"

"The file Rico sent us had a lot of information. In fact, it read more like a scorecard than a police report." She sipped from her glass and smiled. "Smooth. Good stuff."

Marty wrinkled up her nose. "It makes me hot." As soon as she said the words she wanted to take them back. Especially when she saw the mischievous look in Kris's eyes.

"Makes you hot, huh? Please explain."

Marty blushed and hit Kris's knee with her own. "Stop it. You know what I mean."

"Yes, I do. I didn't mean to tease."

Marty leaned back, sipping from the very liquid she said made her hot, and watched as Kris flipped through the money—one hundred dollar bills bound together in groups, more money than she could comprehend. It dawned on her that she wasn't even fazed by the events of the night. Two men dead. One killed by Kris. And one giant bag full of money. Maybe she wasn't fazed by it for the same reason Kris wasn't—the dead men were drug dealers. Drug dealers with guns, one of which had been pointed at Kris.

And now, here they sat on the floor, surrounded by money and guns. It was an adventure she would have never believed possible. Maybe in the movies. But not for her. Yet here she was, sipping cognac and watching the woman who—for some reason—brought all her senses alive. The sight of whose breasts in the shower had made her question her entire existence. The woman who made her wonder what it'd be like to have a…a lover.

Kris turned as if sensing her thoughts, her eyes searching. Marty was afraid of what she was revealing to Kris, but she couldn't stop her wayward thoughts, not even when Kris leaned closer. She knew what was happening, knew she could turn away if she wanted. But her eyes were drawn to the lips that were so close, and she waited, mesmerized, as they drew nearer.

The touch was so light, so feather-soft that Marty almost thought she'd imagined it. But when she opened her eyes, Kris was there, closer still. Her lips came again, and this time Marty moved to meet them, shocked by the thrill of heat that coursed through her. She parted her lips at Kris's urging, feeling Kristen's lower lip fitting between her own. She moaned, surprised by the unfamiliar sounds coming from her and simply stunned by the hammering of her heart from such a gentle touch.

Before she could take another breath, she felt the barest of touches from Kristen's tongue, and she thought she might very well faint dead away. But no, she realized she was gripping Kris's neck, pulling her closer.

She came to her senses and jerked away, embarrassment washing over her as she touched her hot face. "I'm…I'm sorry," she murmured as she tried to turn away from Kris's knowing eyes. She wondered why she was sorry. It was the most incredible feeling she'd ever had.

"No. It's okay," Kris whispered, her hands moving softly across Marty's face. "It's okay." Kris leaned back against the bed, pulling Marty with her. "Come here."

At Kris's guidance, Marty sat between her legs, her back resting soundly against Kris. She trembled as Kris's arms wound around her, pulling her back even tighter.

"Relax," Kris whispered in her ear. "Just a kiss. It's okay."

Marty thought the way her body was responding was anything *but* okay. She was scared. She didn't know what to do. The safe little wall she'd built around herself was crumbling, and she wasn't even trying to repair it. She felt silent tears fall down her cheeks, and she squeezed her eyes tight, willing them to stop. She was literally petrified by what she was feeling. She felt like a stranger had invaded her body, and she didn't know what to do.

That was a lie, though, wasn't it? She knew what to do. She certainly knew what she wanted to do. She was just afraid to do it. For so many years she'd longed for her heart to race from someone's touch. She'd dreamt about a lover's hands on her body, bringing her alive. Hoped and wished and prayed, yet never believed it would ever happen. Not to her. She'd lived too long in this frigid state to ever think the day would come that she'd crave the touch of someone—a woman. She took a deep breath, moving her hand, tentatively touching the arm that was around her waist, pressing it closer to her, feeling safe. It was ironic—the one person who could turn her insides into a tumultuous bundle of nerves was also the only one who could calm her.

Kris didn't comment on her tears, she just held her. Marty sighed as she felt Kristen's kisses move lightly over her hair. They sat that way for a long time, Kris just holding her, nothing more. When Marty felt she'd recovered enough, she turned her head, meeting Kris's eyes.

"This is nice," she whispered. Kris nodded but said nothing. She let her eyes slip closed, totally relaxed now in Kris's arms, the gentle caressing at her waist soothing her. She turned her head again, this time not wanting to meet Kris's eyes, yet wanting to know. "Why did you kiss me?"

She thought Kris wasn't going to answer. There was no sound from her other than a quiet sigh. Then Kris shifted, moving her arm so that her fingers tangled with Marty's.

"Because this time I couldn't resist."

"This time?"

"Shhh," Kris murmured against her hair. "Let's don't talk about it now. I'm sorry. It won't happen again."

Marty's eyes closed and she didn't fight it. She felt safe and warm, and she pulled Kris's arm tighter around her. She was too tired to think about it anymore.

CHAPTER THIRTY-FOUR

Bailey paced across the room, her eyes shifting between Marty's sleeping form and the bag of money. Nearly three hundred thousand. Not the kind of money a drug dealer was going to forget about. Which was why they needed to be on the move. Even though they'd switched plates last night, the black SUV couldn't be used again, not if she wanted to do a buy. She'd already put in a call to Rico. A red Mustang would be here by noon. A red Mustang with a false floor in the trunk. After they'd moved everything to the Mustang and hit the road, someone would be by to pick up the SUV. And she was anxious to get going.

Again her eyes lighted on Marty, the even breathing telling her she was still sound asleep. Bailey had held her for hours last night, slumped against the bed, until the pain in her arm became too much. Marty had barely woken as she'd pulled the covers back and laid her down in the bed. Her own bed, not Bailey's.

She turned away, wondering at her sanity last night. *A kiss? What was I thinking?*

Apparently the same thing Marty was thinking. When she'd turned and found Marty staring at her, staring at her lips, kissing was surely on her mind as well. And as Bailey had said last night, she just couldn't resist. What was she supposed to do? Ignore it?

But after all was said and done, it was a kiss, sure, but it was a fairly chaste kiss. Even so, Bailey had kissed enough women in her time to know when one was responsive to her. And Marty was definitely responsive.

Which led to another question. Since when did Marty respond to sexual overtures? She'd said her body was dead in that regard. But the tiny moan she'd heard, the desperate grip Marty'd had on her shoulder—all provided evidence that her body wasn't dead at all.

Why are you thinking about this now? Focus on the mission.

Yes, the mission. They had no time for Marty to suddenly have her sexual being awakened.

But Bailey grinned as she turned away and headed to the kitchen for more coffee. *No time, no. But God, how much fun could that be?*

CHAPTER THIRTY-FIVE

Marty laughed as they sped away in the bright red sports car, the top down and warm sunshine beaming down upon them.

"This is fun," she said loudly as she tried to tame her hair.

Kris smiled back at her. "It's not supposed to be fun. We're running from drug dealers, remember?"

"So I should not look at this like a vacation?"

"I doubt this would be your chosen spot."

"No. Instead, I'd have you take me to a secluded beach in Mexico. Pacific coast, preferably." Marty laughed again. "Provided you were still at my disposal."

Kristen's grin was wicked. "Am I at your disposal?"

Marty knew she was blushing and she looked away quickly. When was she going to learn to *think* before she spoke?

Kris reached over and patted her thigh. "I'm just kidding, you know. But I take that to mean you're not ready to talk about it?"

Marty raised her eyebrows.

"The kiss," Kris clarified.

Marty blushed anew but managed to smile, albeit sheepishly. "No."

"Okay."

Time to shift gears, Marty thought. *I am not ready to have this conversation.* "Do you have a plan? I mean, as far as where we're going to stay?"

"No. I liked our last setup, with the privacy and all, but I think we should stay closer to the highway. In case we need a quick escape route."

"So a hotel?"

"No. We have to stay under the radar, Marty."

"Okay." She reached into the backseat for her laptop. "I'll find something." Anything to keep herself busy, her mind occupied. It was all she could do to make it through her shower this morning. Left alone, alone with her thoughts, the only thing filling her mind was the kiss she and Kris had shared. The kiss that made her heart race, her pulse pound. The kiss they hadn't yet talked about. Because what would she say? "Gee, I think I do like kissing after all?" Or how about "the thought of having sex with someone—with *you*—is making me crazy with desire"? She paused, her fingers on the keyboard of the laptop, her vision blurring as she pictured making love with Kris.

"Everything okay?"

She blinked several times, clearing the image from her mind. *Okay? No, everything definitely is not okay.*

"Marty?"

She turned finally, meeting Kris's questioning gaze. "Kissing. It was always as thrilling for me as watching paint dry."

"Oh, yeah?"

"So last night, I didn't know how to handle it when it really felt...*thrilling*."

"I thought you didn't want to talk about it."

"I don't." She went back to her laptop, wondering what thoughts were flying through Kris's mind about now. Could you

210

call an innocent kiss with no tongue "thrilling"?

* * *

"Will this do?"

They were a little farther from the highway than Bailey would have liked, but the cabins, while small, were certainly charming. They were in a wooded area north of town, more rustic cabin than tropical beach cottage. There was not a palm tree in sight, belying their close proximity to the gulf. But again, she suspected the place catered to fishermen and winter Texans, which meant few summer residents.

She pulled up to the office, noting the quiet. "Yeah, this'll work. Not much activity."

"I'll go in," Marty offered. "How many nights?"

"Book a week."

Marty smiled as she got out. "I think I'll be Erica Jones today," she said as she held up a credit card. "I'm tired of being Patty."

Bailey was still amazed at how unfazed Marty was with this game they were playing. They had traded their comfortable SUV for a fast red sports car, one that was hiding rifles, handguns, surveillance equipment and three hundred thousand dollars in drug money. And if she was reading Marty correctly, she was less concerned with all that than she was the tiny kiss they'd shared the night before.

She tapped her fingers on the steering wheel, glancing into the office as she waited. Tonight, she would go downtown. She would let it be known she had the money. She wasn't foolish enough to think the man behind the scorpion idols would show himself. For all she knew, he operated on the other side of the border. But if he wanted his money back, no doubt he would make the decision on how to get it, not some subordinate. The scenario she pictured was them offering a sale, then an ambush that left her dead with an idol on her chest, warning the police to leave it alone.

But what she *hoped* would happen was that she and Marty could tail their contact back to someone higher up the chain, perhaps use the surveillance microphone Rico had rigged for them and eavesdrop on a phone call. Or better yet, have the keypad number tones tell them the number. She rolled her eyes. She was actually buying into Rico and his spy toys. She only hoped Marty remembered more than she did from the crash course he had given them.

She raised her eyebrows expectantly when Marty opened the door and got in.

"Very nice lady," Marty said. "Talkative."

"And?"

"They only have one other cabin booked this week. Elderly gentleman. He just lost his wife to cancer. He's going to spend the summer with them and get in some fishing in the gulf."

"And we're booked at the opposite end from him?"

"Yes. He's right here by the office. We've got the last cabin around the end of the circle drive," she said, pointing in the direction Bailey should drive. "There's not a grocery store close by, but there's a little mom-and-pop café down the block that serves breakfast and lunch."

Bailey grinned. "You tired of cooking for me already?"

"No. I've hardly cooked for you at all." She glanced to the backseat where the contents of the fridge were piled in bags. "And we've got a lot of food."

"Well, you can cook today. We'll have an early dinner. Then we'll need to go out."

"You have a plan?"

"Sort of. Maybe we should spend the afternoon going over the surveillance equipment Rico gave us."

"Fine. But I want to know your plan." She motioned to the next cabin. "Number Fifteen." She turned back to Bailey. "I told you last night, I don't like the idea of you just offering yourself up to these guys. They're not going to let you get close to him."

"I know. That's why we need surveillance." She pulled to a

stop at Cabin Fifteen. "This is great. Private."

"And it has a full kitchen," Marty said as she opened the trunk and took out the bags of groceries.

Bailey followed, taking out the two large backpacks with their clothes and the duffel bag of money before locking the car. She stopped when she got inside, following Marty's gaze. There was only one bed. A large king, but still—one bed.

"I told her two adults. I guess she just assumed..." Marty said, her voice trailing off. She met Bailey's stare. "We can go see if she's got something with two beds."

Bailey shook her head. "This is fine. We've shared a bed before," she said reasonably. But that was before *The Kiss*. "Unless you'd rather—"

"No. This'll be...be fine. Just fine."

Bailey tossed their bags on the bed, then went to Marty, who still stood rooted to the floor, the grocery bags looking heavy in her arms. Bailey took the bags from her and set them on the counter in the small kitchen, finally rousing Marty from her thoughts. They silently put the food up, sidestepping each other in the tiny space.

"You want to talk about it yet?"

Marty shook her head. "No."

Bailey sighed. "What are you afraid of?"

Marty spun around, facing her. A hint of anger sparked in her eyes, then disappeared just as quickly. "I'm afraid...I'm afraid of myself. I'm afraid of you. I'm afraid of these...these *feelings* I'm having all of a sudden. I'm afraid that I don't know myself any longer. I'm afraid of a lot of things, Kristen." She looked away. "I'm afraid I'm getting too close to you. I don't ever get close to people. It just doesn't happen. And we're chasing drug dealers, for God's sake," she said, meeting her eyes again. "I'm terrified something is going to happen to you."

Bailey stepped closer. "Come here," she said, pulling Marty to her. Marty's arms snaked around her waist tightly. "All of that, huh?" Bailey whispered. "And here I thought you were just afraid

213

of my kiss."

Marty laughed quietly against her chest. "I am *petrified* of your kiss."

Bailey pulled back far enough to see Marty's face. "Because I'm a woman?"

"No. Because you made me *feel* something."

"That's a bad thing?"

Marty slipped out of her arms with a sigh. "I guess we're going to talk about it after all."

"I'd like to clear the air, yes," Bailey said.

Marty went back into the main area of the cabin, sitting down on the bed. Bailey followed, choosing the chair by the window instead. She sat quietly, crossing her legs, waiting for Marty, who appeared to be gathering her thoughts. She finally looked up, and Bailey was surprised to see the nearly panicked look in her eyes.

"I told you about, well, about my life. About my *issues*," she said.

"Yes." And now Bailey realized the panicked look in her eyes was swimming in embarrassment.

"I've never met anyone who…who *stirred* something in me. Ever. And so I was shocked to discover that now…well, now my body seems to have a life of its own." She glanced away quickly. "You…being with you, near you…" she paused, pulling her eyes away, a bright red flush crossing her face.

"Marty, please, you don't have to be embarrassed."

"Of course I do." She stood quickly, pacing. "I have zero experience in this. I don't even know what the hell is happening to my body. I feel like I'm in a stranger's body, not my own." She stopped, pointing at Bailey. "And you, I don't even know what you think about all this." She stared at her. "Why did you kiss me?"

"Because right then, at that moment, that's what your eyes said. 'Kiss me.'"

"Oh, *God*," Marty whispered, covering her face with her

hands.

"Marty, why is that such a bad thing? Why are you embarrassed by this?" Bailey got up and went to her, again seeing the panic in her eyes. "Do you think I'm disgusted by the fact that you wanted to kiss me?"

"I don't know," Marty whispered. "I don't know how this is done."

Bailey reached out a hand and cupped Marty's face, rubbing her cheek lightly with her thumb. "I said last night that I couldn't resist. That was the truth. I've wanted to kiss you before but didn't dare." She lowered her hand. "Because of your 'issues,' I didn't think you'd ever be in a position to welcome my kiss. So I ignored this attraction I have for you."

"*What?*"

"Why? Do you not think I could find you attractive?" Bailey frowned. "Or, because I'm a woman, you didn't think you could find *me* attractive?"

"No, that's not it." Marty moved closer, her fingers finding Bailey's. "I do find you attractive. Am I surprised? Yes. But not because you're a woman. It's just I'd given up on ever having sexual feelings for anyone. To have them now, with all that's going on, and for you, not knowing whether you think I'm crazy or not," she said with a smile.

"And so with all of that, then opening the door to the cabin and finding only the one bed—"

"I kinda panicked."

"Afraid you might attack me during the night?" Bailey teased. But Marty's face turned scarlet. "God, no, I just—"

"I'm just teasing," Bailey said.

Marty pulled away. "Do not tease me about this. I told you I don't know what the hell I'm doing. I don't know how I'm supposed to act, what I'm to say, what I should *do*. I just—"

"Marty, stop," Bailey said, trying desperately to keep a smile off her face. "Let's just play it by ear, okay? And I totally give you permission to kiss me anytime you're feeling the urge."

Marty finally laughed. "You're right. I'm making this out to be some horrible, *horrible* thing."

"Right."

"And so we'll just play it by ear," Marty said. "Of course, since I have no experience in this, I'm not really sure what that means. I guess I'll follow your lead."

Bailey stared at her, totally captivated by the child-like wonder on Marty's face, her eyes bright with excitement, her face still slightly flushed. "You are so adorable," Bailey murmured. Marty met her gaze, her eyes steady as she walked closer. Suddenly it was Bailey who was afraid.

"I think I want to kiss you now," Marty whispered.

Bailey nodded, watching Marty move close, feeling her breath on her face, smelling the scent she'd come to recognize. Yes, now it was she who was afraid. It had been so terribly long since she'd kissed someone, since she'd even been interested. More than two years had passed since she and Liz ended things, and she hadn't been with anyone since. And now here was Marty, a woman who was experiencing her first sexual awakening. A woman who Bailey suspected would be ravenous, having been starved for too long of human intimacy. A woman Bailey found herself extremely attracted to. A woman who now wanted to kiss her.

So she welcomed her, guiding her near, lowering her head to meet Marty's lips. They opened without urging, and Bailey moved across them, nibbling gently, feeling Marty's fingers as they dug into her arm. The quiet moan she heard sent her blood boiling, and she gave up all pretense of taking things slowly. She pulled Marty closer, feeling her breasts press against her own. She opened her mouth, her tongue at last making contact with Marty's, sliding slowly into her mouth.

Marty moved closer, her breathing ragged as her hips instinctively pressed hard against Bailey. This time it was Bailey who moaned. Her hands found their way past Marty's waist, gripping her hard as she pulled her tight against her, hearing Marty whimper as her pelvis arched into Bailey—once, twice,

216

three times as she tried to get closer.

It felt so good…But they were going too fast and going into uncharted waters as far as Marty was concerned. So she eased back, tempering their kisses from a "I'm about to rip your clothes off" tempo to one of a simmering passion that promised much more to come. Later.

"You okay?" she finally asked, her lips moving to Marty's ear.

"I'm not sure," Marty admitted. Her hands still clung to Bailey, her fingers still gripped her arms. "At least I can breathe again."

Bailey laughed quietly, squeezing Marty tight in a hug before pulling away. "We were…we were going too fast."

"I know. I lost total control." She stepped out of Bailey's arms, moving away as she plunged her fingers into her hair. "Is this what it's like? Is this what it feels like?" She met Bailey's eyes searching. "Is this what people feel when they…"

"When they what? Have an attraction? Want to sleep with someone?" Marty's face turned scarlet again and she turned away, but Bailey stopped her. "Marty, don't be embarrassed. This is perfectly natural."

"Not necessarily natural for me."

"I think it is. And for whatever reason—your body, your mind—you've just been repressing it all these years. It's a wonderful thing, Marty, to want to share yourself with someone."

Marty looked at her shyly. "And do you?"

"Want to share myself?" Bailey nodded. "Very much so," she whispered.

"With me?"

Bailey smiled. "Yes, with you."

Marty took a step back, her face breaking into a grin. "Okay, I think I'm really scared now."

"Then I'll give you a reprieve. How about we practice surveillance?"

Marty took a deep breath and looked relieved. "Oh, yeah. We are kinda on a mission, aren't we?"

CHAPTER THIRTY-SIX

"I'm not crazy about this idea," Marty said for the fifth time.

Kris nodded but said nothing as she drove down the dark streets of the old warehouse district.

"You don't even want to argue with me?"

"Will it do any good?"

"No."

"Well, then?"

"I want you to tell me everything's going to be fine."

Kris laughed. "The last time I said that you accused me of pacifying you."

"I'm just really worried. You may know what you're doing, but I do not. You're used to going out and doing this with real backup. And I'm just clueless about all this police stuff." In fact, knowing she had a handgun strapped to her back made her even more nervous.

"I don't need backup. I just need someone to run surveillance.

And that, you know well. We went over it countless times. You've got it down."

And she did, she knew that. Besides the normal wireless microphone and earpiece Kris wore, there was a tiny camera on the fake glasses she would wear, as well as another camera on the back of her jacket that gave Marty a view of the surrounding area. As an added precaution, they'd installed a GPS tracking device in Kris's shoe. Just in case.

Yeah, in case they abduct her and haul her off, I will be able to track them to find where they dump her body.

Marty took a deep breath, knowing thoughts like that would just make matters worse. As Kris had told her, focus on the mission at hand, nothing else. And that meant parking several blocks away, setting up the portable satellite dish and homing in on Kris's location with the "super-duper amplifier," as Rico had called it. She would be able to hear—and record—conversations within a six-block radius. And as scary as that sounded, they'd tested it at the cabin, listening to the owners discuss the plight of their recently widowed tenant and his success at fishing. The conversation was so clear, they could have been in the same room with them. Rico had walked her through it all, even how to adjust the frequency to weed out conversations you didn't want and to tap into those you did.

"I'm going to park here on Merchant Street," Kris said quietly. She pulled into an alley between two buildings and stopped, killing the lights. "I think this is too close to International Boulevard for there to be much activity on this block. You should be out of sight." Kris turned to her. "You remember the drill?"

"Yes. Secure the satellite, then back in the car and lock the doors."

"If someone spots you or comes over for a closer look, simply drive away." She pointed up ahead. "This alley comes out on Twenty-third. Go one block to the left and try to find another place to park. Got it?"

"How far are you going?"

"I'm going to walk down about four, five blocks."

"Kris, this thing only has a six-block radius."

"That's just for the audio with the satellite and the camera transmission. Our regular wireless setup will go for half a mile. As long as I can hear you and you can hear me, we'll be fine."

Marty waited while Kris secured the tiny microphone to her watch and fitted the earpiece in her ear. Marty already had her receiver on.

"Test one, two, three," Kris said quietly.

"Copy."

Kris grinned. "Excellent." She pulled her weapon out and dropped the clip, inspecting it before slamming it back into place. She sat up, fixing the weapon into the small holster strapped to her back. "Now remember, if anything happens, you get the hell out of here. Same drill. You get our stuff from the cabin and call Rico."

"I hate when you say that."

"I just want you to be prepared, Marty."

"But nothing's going to happen." She gripped Kris's arm. "Because I'm just now feeling alive. *Alive*. Because of you."

Kris smiled. "Then I'll try not to screw that up."

Marty leaned closer. "Please don't," she whispered, brushing her lips across Kris's.

Their eyes held, and Marty had to suppress the urge to gather Kris close and beg her not to go out. But she knew that wouldn't happen. The sooner they finished this, the sooner they could...what? Get on with their lives? Go their separate ways? Kris pulled her eyes away, fumbling with the fake glasses, and Marty sat back, her heart heavy.

"Remember, you're not just watching me," Kris said. "Keep an eye out here too. If you feel threatened in any way, just drive away."

Marty nodded, clutching the portable satellite dish in her hand. As soon as Kris walked away, she got out, securing it between the window and the roof like they'd practiced. She went around to the driver's seat, got in and dutifully locked the doors. Her laptop was already up and running, and she plugged the USB cable from the satellite into it, waiting for it to load.

"Are you up?"

"It's loading now," she said. She heard Kris's footsteps along the sidewalk and at least felt connected to her. Finally, an image on her screen came into focus, and she adjusted the setting. "I'm up," she said. "Picture is clear."

"Copy that."

The satellite picked up both cameras, and she toggled between the one on Kris's back and the one in her glasses, shrinking both screens so that she could watch them at the same time. "You've got company," she said. "Behind you. Two guys. They just stepped out. It looked like from a doorway or something."

"Copy," Kris whispered.

"They look like thugs," Marty said, her voice low. "I'm going to try out this amplified microphone of Rico's."

That too was dependent on the satellite, and she pulled the black box onto her lap, using the dual cord from her headset to tap into it. She turned the dial slowly, searching for sound. There was a chorus of muted voices, the words Spanish and meaningless to her. She found the frequency of Kris's microphone and amplified the power, amazed that she was able to hear their footsteps. She glanced to the screen, knowing that Kris had slowed her pace. The guys were nearly upon her.

* * *

Bailey turned quickly, startling the two guys following her. "What the hell do you want?"

The taller of the two stepped forward, his smile showing off dirty—and missing—teeth. "Late for a woman to be out on the streets, *chica*. Anything could happen."

"You're not my type. Beat it."

"Oh, she's a feisty one, Tony. And she has no manners. Here

221

we only wanted to ensure your safe passage. These streets aren't safe."

Bailey took a step closer, able to smell alcohol on their breath. "Unless you can make a deal, I don't want to talk to you."

"A deal?"

"I want to make a buy."

"A buy? I don't know what you're talking about," he said. "We don't mess in that shit."

"Right. Then beat it. I want to talk to someone who does."

He rubbed his face, pulling on his goatee. "I may know someone, chica. How much?"

"It's not for personal use." She smiled. "I aim to turn it for a profit. I have several hundred thousand dollars to deal with."

"I see." He turned to his friend, their Spanish quick and quiet. Bailey wasn't able to follow. "You go on. Ridgely. Ask for Cesar. You tell him I sent you."

"And you are?"

"Lucero. He'll know."

She nodded. "*Gracias.*"

She walked on, leaving them behind her. When she was a safe distance away, she brought her wrist to her mouth.

"You copy that?"

"Yes. They've turned back. He's on a cell phone now."

"Can you hear?"

"Spanish."

"He's probably calling this Cesar person." She slowed her pace. "One more block to Ridgely."

"Ridgely is where Carlos was killed," Marty reminded her.

"Yes."

"Be careful."

"Promise."

She stood at the corner of Ridgely and Twenty-second, looking around, seeing no one. She turned, intending on going down the easement between two buildings when a voice called to her.

"*Buenas noches.*"

She spun around, seeing movement in the shadows. "Cesar?"

"*Si*. And you are?"

"Raines. Amanda Raines." He stepped closer, and Bailey was surprised at his age, his hair silver, the stubble on his face shining in the streetlights.

"A word of warning, *senora*. This is a man's world, not fit for a woman. Especially if you want to do business."

Bailey smiled. "What? My money not good enough for you?"

His expression did not change as his eyes stared into hers. "You wish to turn a profit, yes? Where do you plan to do this?"

"Well, here in Brownsville, of course."

At this, his lined face broke into a grin. "Here?" He laughed. "You must be new."

"There's always a market, Cesar. Brownsville is big enough to accommodate several sellers, isn't it?" She stepped closer. "I recently came into some cash. Three hundred thousand, in fact. I wish to...*trade* it."

"Three hundred thousand?"

"Yes. And I think we both know where I got it."

"So, you are the one. And here you come down to the streets, you wish to make a sale?" He laughed. "I could kill you right now."

"So it's your money?" She held her hands out. "I don't have it on me."

"No, not mine. But the man that it belongs to, he is not happy with you." He rubbed the stubble on his face. "What do you really want, *senora?*"

"Like I said, I wish to trade. Perhaps you and I could do business and this other man need not know?"

"And like I said, you must be new in town. There is no business that happens without 'the man' knowing."

"Who is he?"

Cesar shook his head. "*Vete, nina.* You run along now. I don't wish to see you dead with *el scorpion* as your marker."

223

"*El scorpion?*" she asked.

"The death sentence. He is ruthless. And he doesn't play games. He wants his money back."

"And I'm just supposed to walk down here and hand it over?"

"No. They will kill you for sure." He shrugged. "Of course, he will kill you anyway."

Bailey watched as he turned and disappeared back into the shadows. She continued on, not wanting to go back. No doubt someone would try to follow her, and she didn't want to lead them back to Marty.

When she was a safe distance away, she said, "You copy that?"

"Yes. That was kinda creepy. But you're getting too far away. The picture is a little grainy. I'm going to lose you soon."

"Use the satellite microphone. See if you can pick up anything from our friend, Cesar."

"Hang on."

Bailey paused, then walked on slowly. "Anything?"

"Cell phone."

"Could you pick up the tones?"

"I don't know. It's very faint. He's speaking Spanish. But that was quick."

"What do you mean?"

"Call ended."

"Okay. Any problems for you?"

"No. Quiet."

"Good. Leave the satellite on the roof. Just drive slowly out of the alley. Turn left. Do you remember the day we got shot at down here?"

"Who could forget?"

"Find Harrison and Nineteenth. I'll meet you there. Just park. If I feel like someone is following me, I'll let you know to drive on. We don't need them to make our car. I doubt Rico could get us another one by tomorrow."

"Okay. I'll leave now. Where are you?"

"I'm still on Ridgely. I'm going to Nineteenth from here,

then head up to Harrison. Copy?"

"Yeah, copy."

Bailey heard the car start and breathed a sigh of relief. For as exposed as she was out here, it was really Marty she was worried about. If anyone had a mind to jack with her, jack with the car, she doubted Marty could have gotten out of the situation. Not without gunfire. And as much as they'd practiced with her weapon—loading and unloading—it wasn't the same as firing it, feeling the power in your hands. She knew Marty was still uncomfortable with it.

"Okay, I'm away. I don't see anyone."

"Good. Park under a light on Harrison. Keep your eyes open. Just pull away if you see anyone on the sidewalk."

"How much longer?"

"Give me five minutes."

"That's an eternity. Oh, wait, you're getting closer. The satellite has picked up the camera again."

"Copy that. Watch my back. I can feel eyes on me."

"You're right. Someone's following you. Three guys."

"Same ones?"

"No. They're to your right. Hugging the building."

"Copy," she said quietly. She could feel their presence now, but she sensed they were following only. She didn't have the money on her, and he wanted the money. Or she assumed he wanted the money. "How many paces behind?"

"I'd say thirty feet."

At the corner of Nineteenth, Bailey went right. Now it was she who was hugging the building, staying in the shadows. She pulled her weapon, waiting in the doorway of one of the old abandoned buildings.

"Kris?"

"Shh."

"You're pissing me off."

Bailey smiled. "Copy that."

"Please don't do anything stupid."

225

"Too late," she whispered. When she heard the footsteps round the corner, she stepped out, holding her gun against the first man's forehead, between his eyes.

"Whoa, lady."

"Don't move." She moved her eyes, seeing one of the others reach for what she assumed was his own weapon. "Don't try it, Blondie, or your friend here gets a bullet to the brain." He stopped, showing her both of his hands. "Now, you go tell 'the man' that he's not getting his money."

"I...I don't know what you're talking about."

"Then why the fuck are you following me?"

"Hey, we're just out for a stroll."

Bailey smiled. "Yeah. And I'm Goldilocks. What are you? The three bears?"

In a flash, the blond man reached again for his gun, pulling it out from behind his back. She turned and fired, knocking him to the ground, then she whipped around, holding her gun against the man's head again.

"Oh, that's right," she said. "I told him I'd shoot you if he tried that shit." She smiled when his eyes widened in fear. She glanced at the man on the ground, who was holding his shoulder. His gun was ten feet away. "Damn, I missed. I was aiming for your head." She flicked her eyes to the third man, who had remained silent. "You want to try something?"

"No. I'm cool."

"Good." She lowered her weapon. "Like I was saying, tell him he's not getting his money. Now get the hell out of here while I'm still in a good mood."

The blond man got to his knees and headed toward his gun.

"No, no, Sonny. Leave the gun."

Their eyes met.

"You're dead," he said.

Bailey laughed. "What? You going to do it?" She shook her head. "You better go see a doctor about that shoulder, son."

"Fuck you."

Then he turned, hurrying after his buddies who were already a block away. She took a deep breath, then turned, picking up his discarded gun before continuing up Harrison.

"Marty, you there?"

"Yeah. And I hear sirens."

"Copy that. Take the satellite off the car, then come back this way and meet me. We can't have cops."

"I understand."

"Hurry."

The sirens were louder now, but she hoped they'd go down Ridgely. Of course, if they'd been tipped, they'd know to come down Harrison. Then they'd be sitting ducks. She broke into a run, seeing Marty's headlights. She ripped the fake glasses off her face and shoved them into her pocket. Marty came to a stop and Bailey jumped in, barely getting the door closed as Marty took off again.

"Easy now," Bailey said. "Take it slow."

"Are you okay?"

"I'm fine."

"Good. Then I can continue to be pissed at you."

Bailey smiled as they turned on International Boulevard. She could see the flashing lights of the police cruisers as they crossed behind them, going straight down Harrison. Yeah, they had been tipped. She glanced at Marty. "Why are you pissed?"

"You pull your weapon on three thugs? Are you insane? And then you shoot one of them and then *tease* them? You could have gotten killed."

"I couldn't let them follow, Marty. This is the only car we have. And I love Rico to death, but a bright red sports car is hardly inconspicuous."

"You could have gotten killed," she said again.

"Marty, you've got to trust me. I can handle this."

Marty turned, meeting her eyes. "Well, maybe I can't."

CHAPTER THIRTY-SEVEN

"You want to talk about it?"

Marty moved through the small cabin, stopping to get a water bottle from the refrigerator. "No," she said, her back to Kris.

"Are we having our first fight?"

Marty shook her head. "I'm tired." She took a deep breath. "And I was scared." She felt hands on her shoulders, turning her around. She slipped into Kris's arms, pressing her face against Kris's chest, feeling safe again.

"I'm sorry," Kris murmured.

"I just feel so helpless. I can hear you. I can see what you see." She closed her eyes. "I'm watching the computer screen like it's a TV. But it's real. And you've got three thugs surrounding you and—"

"Marty, you've got to quit thinking I'm going to get shot every time I go out."

"I know." She pulled her head back, finding Kris's eyes. She tried to smile. "Maybe I *have* watched too much TV."

Kris touched her face lightly, her gaze drifting to her mouth. Marty held her breath, thinking Kris was going to kiss her. But her hand dropped and she moved away.

"Come on. It's very late," Kris said. "I need a shower."

Marty leaned her hip against the counter, listening as the water turned on. She stared across the room, seeing nothing as her mind's eye flashed back to when she'd spied Kris in the shower, the water cascading over her breasts, traveling down the endless length of leg, the skin smooth, tan...and wet.

She blinked several times, chasing the image away. But as her vision cleared, she saw the bed instead. A bed they would be sharing. She made herself move, collecting her things for her own shower. What did she think would happen? Was tonight the night?

Don't be silly.

As Kris had said, it was late. Nearly two. They were both tired. She sighed, then glanced at the closed door to the bathroom. Late, yes. But for her, it was really, *really* late. Late as in fifteen years late. And now that she felt something, now that she'd had a taste of what desire did to her body...well, now she wanted to feel that again. She wanted her body to come alive, to pulse with desire. She wanted to get naked and wild. She wanted to have an earth-shattering, toe-curling orgasm.

She realized she had two problems with that. One, she wasn't sure Kris was ready. She didn't seem like the type for casual sex. And two, she had no idea how to have an earth-shattering, toe-curling orgasm. She only knew she wanted one.

She visibly jumped when Kris opened the bathroom door, and she immediately felt her face flush with embarrassment, as if Kris could read her mind. Kris cocked an eyebrow at her but said nothing. She quickly hurried into the bathroom and closed the door, nearly laughing when she saw her expression in the mirror.

Okay, so maybe tonight wasn't the night for sex. Judging by the frightened look in her eyes, maybe it was she who wasn't ready.

She stared into her own eyes. No, she was ready. Her fear was what it always was. That her body wouldn't respond, that she'd freeze up, that she'd go through the act without...well, without that earth-shattering orgasm she craved. Which, of course, was silly. She knew her body would respond. She'd practically melted just from their little kissing session that morning.

Again, a flush covered her face as she remembered her body taking on a life of its own, her hips trying to...to what? Mold themselves to Kris? When Kris's hands had cupped her, had pulled their bodies together in the most intimate of ways, Marty had wanted to be inside her. She wanted to do things with Kris— to Kris. She had no idea where those thoughts came from, but she wanted to *do* them.

She quickly stepped into the shower, trying to curb her thoughts. After years of playing dead, her libido was now apparently on overdrive. She stood under the water, the spray hitting her sensitive skin like a caress. She closed her eyes as her hands covered her breasts, finding the nipples hard, responsive. She imagined Kris touching them, imagined Kris's mouth and tongue covering her nipples—sucking them. A jolt of arousal went straight to her core, and she put her hands out against the shower wall to steady herself as her knees nearly gave way.

She held her face up to the warm water, a slow smile forming. *Scared? No. Aroused? Definitely!*

But when she stepped out of the bathroom, the cabin was quiet and dark, the lone lamp left on at the far side of the bed. Kris lay on her side, her breathing even, her face relaxed.

Asleep? Please say no.

Marty tried to ignore the disappointment she felt. It was late. They were both tired. No sense rushing things. But still, her body was humming, demanding attention. She assumed for the first time in her life she was about to experience sexual frustration at its worst. She grinned in the darkness as she turned the lamp off. Sexual frustration? She'd been suffering from it all of her adult life. What she wanted to experience was sexual relief.

She pulled the sheet up to her waist, staring at the dark ceiling, feeling herself being pulled to Kris's warm body like a magnet. She lay still, hoping sleep would claim her. She was surprised when Kris rolled over onto her back, even more surprised when she felt Kris's hand touch her arm.

"Are you tired?"

The question was innocent enough, but Marty didn't pretend not to understand the underlying meaning of those words. She was nearly embarrassed at her quickened pulse and the rapid breaths she was taking.

"I'm...I'm not tired," she whispered. "Are you?"

Marty could tell Kris was smiling as she leaned up on her elbow. Marty turned toward her, a soft moan leaving her lips as Kris's hand snaked under her T-shirt, touching flesh for the first time.

"Not tired at all, no," Kris murmured.

Marty gasped as Kris's hand brushed her breast, and she waited, aching for her touch. But Kris hesitated.

"Tell me to stop and I will."

"No. Don't stop..." Marty managed to whisper before Kris's mouth covered her own. There was nothing tentative or shy about their kiss as mouths opened and tongues did battle. Marty was on fire and she had no desire to put the flame out. She wanted it to burn deep within her. She couldn't stop the moans, couldn't stop the primal sounds as Kris's hand cupped her breast, her fingers capturing her nipple, turning it rock hard. *God, yes.*

It was everything she'd imagined, yet so much more. She had no idea another's touch could make her tremble with want, make her body sing, set her soul free. No idea that a touch upon her breasts would ever arouse her to the point of pure ecstasy. Then she realized she didn't know what ecstasy was at all until Kris shoved her shirt higher, exposing her breasts. Their eyes met in the darkness, the only sound, that of their breathing...and the rapidly pounding heartbeat that vibrated through her. By the time Kris lowered her head, before her mouth and tongue even touched her nipple, Marty was gasping for air. And when that warm mouth closed over her, the low guttural sound that escaped was surely not from her.

Oh, but it was, and she arched closer, her hands finally moving, holding Kris hard against her, urging her to...to what? She closed her eyes, reveling in the fact that Kris was at her breast, her tongue teasing, then sucking her nipple into her hot mouth. At that moment, Marty wasn't sure she could take any more.

Then Kris lifted her head, her hands fumbling with Marty's shirt, pulling at it. Marty sat up, letting Kris remove it, exposing her upper body to the cool night air—and Kris's knowing eyes. Kris pulled her own shirt off, tossing it off the bed before turning back to Marty.

"You okay with this?" Kris whispered, her hand finding Marty's breast again.

Marty nodded. "Yes. And afraid," she admitted.

"What are you afraid of?"

Marty closed her eyes and moaned as Kris brushed her nipple with her fingers. *Yes, what am I afraid of?* She opened her eyes again. "I'm afraid I won't...I mean, what if my body...what if I'm not able to—"

"To climax?" Kris asked gently.

"Yes. And with you, I want to so badly."

Kris took her hand, guiding it to her breast. Marty's fingers closed around it, Kris's nipple hard against her palm. She heard Kris's quiet moan, and her mouth opened as Kris came to her again, her tongue delving inside. Kris pulled back slightly, her lips gently moving across her face.

"Do you trust me?"

"With my life."

"Then trust me with your body," Kris murmured into her ear as she pressed close, her bare breasts touching Marty's, flaming the fire again. "I'm going to make love to you." Kris's mouth moved along her jaw, then lower, suckling the hollow of her

232

throat. "Close your eyes, Marty. Just feel me. Feel my hands. Feel my mouth."

Marty did, feeling the warm mouth at her breasts again, first one, then the other, her nipples aching and hard. She was nearly writhing with need when she felt Kris's hand move lower, under the waistband of her flannel pajamas. Off. She wanted them off, she wanted to be naked, she wanted to feel Kris's equally naked skin against her own.

"Please take them off," she said. "Please hurry."

Her hands shoved at them, then Kris pulled them down her legs, freeing her. Kris must have sensed her need, as she removed her own panties, leaving them both naked. Marty pulled Kris back to her, her body arching, her legs opening as Kris urged her thighs apart. She could feel her own wetness, could feel Kris's wetness against her skin, and she couldn't get nearly close enough. Her hands moved, cupping Kris, pulling her hard into her parted thighs, desperate for relief, nearly delirious in her desire.

"Slow…slow," Kris whispered. "Let me."

"Not slow, no," Marty countered. Her body wasn't hers to control any longer. She didn't know how she knew, but she wanted Kris inside her. Now.

She didn't have to wait long as Kris's hand moved between them, her long fingers slow and sure as they moved through her wetness. Marty's hips jerked, her clit feeling swollen, hard, sensitive…and oh, so alive. Her moan turned into an outright groan as she felt Kris filling her.

"You're so wet," Kris murmured. "So ready," she said, her mouth again finding a nipple, her teeth teasing it.

Dear God, yes, she was *so* ready. The sound of the wet slickness of their skin, the sound of Kris's hand as it plunged inside her—out and back in again—the sound of their breathing, their moans…all was an overload to her system. She didn't think she could take one more minute of this sweet torture called lovemaking. She didn't have to. Kris's hand was like lightning now, moving deep into her, her thumb hitting her clit with each pass. She was panting, she knew, her body taking on a life of its own, her hips meeting each thrust of Kris's hand, deeper and harder.

Her orgasm hit with such blinding speed—no warning, no time to prepare—just an explosion of light behind her eyes, an explosion of her senses. She couldn't stop the scream, the thrill of it touching her to her core. She felt her body clenching and unclenching, tightening around Kris's fingers, not wanting to let her go.

She opened her eyes when she felt Kris's mouth move past her breasts, her tongue wetting her skin, moving lower. The realization of what Kris intended to do to her sent her senses reeling, her body trembling at the thought. She whimpered when Kris's fingers slipped from her, but the anticipation of what was about to replace them was nearly her undoing. Her fingers threaded through Kris's hair as she felt her warm mouth nibble above her thigh. Kris lifted her head, her eyes clouded with desire.

"Is this okay?"

"Yes," she whispered, the word echoing around them in the dark room. She stared in fascination as Kris moved lower, her hands spreading her thighs as she knelt between them. Marty's breath came in short gasps as Kris moved to her. Instinctively, Marty raised her hips, offering herself to Kris. She didn't know what she expected—this was an act she'd never experienced—but the first touch of Kris's hot mouth and tongue sent a bolt of adrenaline through her. Her hands curled into fists as she clutched the sheet, her hips jerking uncontrollably until Kris gathered them to her, holding her tight against her mouth. Incoherent sounds came from her at the pure pleasure of feeling Kris's tongue circle her clit, feeling her mouth close over it, sucking it, teasing back and forth. This time, Marty felt her orgasm building, felt the thundering roll as her body pulsed. She took a deep breath, holding it, her hips straining against Kris's grip...then from deep within her soul she climaxed, the sound of satisfaction—and fulfillment—wrenched from her as she collapsed with Kris's mouth still on her.

She opened her eyes, her lids heavy. The last thing she remembered was looking into Kris's eyes as she drifted off to sleep.

CHAPTER THIRTY-EIGHT

Bailey sat in the chair, still mesmerized by Marty's sleeping form. The sheet had slipped to her waist, and her breasts were visible, her nipples erect. She made herself turn away, needing to focus, needing to plan. It was too dangerous for them to go out again as they had last night. Most likely they—or she—would be killed on sight, whether she had the money on her or not. She assumed she had pissed them off sufficiently enough, at least, that they wouldn't be willing to make a deal with her. They needed a new plan. She couldn't seem to come up with one, though—her mind was still very much on Marty.

Like it had been doing all morning, her gaze drifted to her again. Marty had literally passed out, not waking even when Bailey had crawled beside her, pulling her close as they slept. At eight, Bailey made herself get up, reluctant to leave the warmth of Marty's naked body, but knowing if she stayed, she would wake her, wanting to make love again. She wanted to give Marty some space, some time. She was afraid of what Marty's reaction was going to be in the light of day. Would she be embarrassed? Or worse—ashamed?

Oh, but she had been just as passionate as Bailey imagined she'd be. And as much as she'd enjoyed making love to Marty, bringing her to orgasm, seeing—and hearing—the pleasure she was giving to her, she could only dream of what it would be like to have Marty love her for the first time. Would she be tentative? Afraid? Or would she be adventurous and ravenous, taking Bailey with a passion too long denied? Bailey closed her eyes, fantasizing the latter.

She opened them again when she heard Marty stir. She watched as Marty rolled onto her back and stretched. Then she sat up, leaning on an elbow, her eyes finding Bailey's. Bailey waited, seeing the recollection of their lovemaking cross Marty's face. Then Marty smiled, a shy smile, and Bailey returned it.

"I kinda fell asleep."

"Uh-huh."

A quick blush and Marty looked away. "It...it was incredible. And beautiful."

Bailey let out a relieved breath. "Yes, it was."

Marty brought her gaze back to Bailey. "Are you sorry?"

"God, no. I was afraid you would be."

"No. I'm only sorry I fell asleep. I think I missed out on some lovely things I was going to do to you."

Now it was Bailey who blushed. "I think maybe we can try it again, then." She was surprised at the relief that showed on Marty's face. "What?"

Again, Marty looked away. "I was afraid you wouldn't want to...I mean, I thought maybe just the one time would be...well, I'm not exactly experienced at this. And you probably didn't—"

"Marty, one-night stands don't really do anything for me. I'm attracted to you. Physically, intellectually. Emotionally. I care about you. And I know you care about me. A sexual relationship only heightens all that." Bailey stood and went to the bed, sitting down beside her. "I enjoyed making love to you," she said quietly, her gaze lowering to Marty's exposed breasts. "And I'd very much like to do it again."

Marty leaned closer, her lips brushing across Bailey's lightly. "Maybe we should start earlier than two a.m. then."

Bailey smiled against her lips. "I'll keep that in mind."

* * *

Marty stirred the mushrooms into the pan, mixing them with the onions. She had nixed her plan for omelets, instead deciding on scrambled eggs with the vegetables mixed in. She wasn't focused enough to make omelets. At least, not focused on food.

She glanced up, watching as Kris slowly paced in front of the bed. Kris was working on a plan, she'd said. She didn't want to take a chance going back out like they'd done last night, which was a great relief to Marty. She didn't have any faith that they would ever find the Scorpion, much less take him down, but she would follow Kris's direction.

She lowered her gaze, staring down into the pan, amazed at how different she felt this morning. She felt *normal*. She felt like she was now a functioning sexual being, something she'd never been. She didn't have the words to describe how it felt to have Kris touch her, kiss her, make love to her...and the wonderful, euphoric response of her body to those touches.

And yes, she wanted to experience it again. And again. But more than that, she wanted to experience making love *to* someone—to Kris—and know what her touch was doing to *her*. The handful of times she'd had sex, or attempted to have sex, she couldn't relate to what her partner was feeling. There was nothing emotionally or physically satisfying about it.

With Kris, though, she had felt all those things she'd only imagined people felt when they made love—the excitement, the stimulation, the desire. She could finally relate. And she wanted to touch Kris that way, knowing that her touch would make Kris feel what she'd felt last night. She wanted to know all of Kris. She wanted to feel Kris, be inside her when she climaxed. She wanted to make love to her with her mouth, like Kris had done. She wanted—

She jumped when a hand touched hers, moving the pan she'd forgotten about.

"It's starting to burn," Kris said.

"I...I was—" She met Kris's gaze head-on. "I was thinking about making love to you," she said. "And what I wanted to do to you." She turned the stove off, feeling bold. "And I don't want to wait."

Kris stood there, a slow smile forming, but she said nothing. Marty took this to mean Kris was allowing her to take the lead. So she did, moving closer, sliding her hands up Kris's arms, pulling her near. "Can we?" she whispered as her lips met Kris's.

All the heat, all the intensity she'd felt the first time came back, making her lightheaded, making her ache for something she'd never had before. Her tongue explored Kris's mouth at will, feeling nearly giddy at the moan she elicited from Kris. She pulled back, breathing hard, hearing Kris doing the same. She didn't pause for instructions. She lowered her hands, cupping Kris's breasts, her eyes closing when she found no bra to hinder her advances. "Can we?" she asked again as Kris's nipples hardened against her palm.

"I think we already are," Kris murmured, her mouth opening to Marty's questing tongue.

Kris's cell phone rang, breaking the silence and short-circuiting Marty's euphoria.

"Oh, *God*," she said as Kris pulled out of her arms. "*Now?*"

"It's Rico. I asked him to get some banking info for me," Kris said as she hurried to the phone. She paused before answering. "I'm sorry."

Marty waved her apology away. "Answer it."

She stared at the pan of vegetables, deciding it was not worth saving. She laughed a quiet laugh as the situation hit her. Here they were, in the middle of drug deals and money deals and guns, and she was bemoaning the fact that their attempted lovemaking had been interrupted. True, she wished they could forget the outside world, but the reality was, it wasn't going to forget them. No, they had to take care of business first. Her suddenly overactive libido would have to wait.

CHAPTER THIRTY-NINE

Bailey stared out the window, absently watching unnamed birds forage in the junipers outside their cabin. She was still processing the information Rico had given her. Lieutenant Marsh and Captain Diaz both had had several large deposits made into their bank accounts in the last five years. That was as far back as Rico could go. Vargas, the cop who worked Carlos Romero's case with Ortiz, also had had deposits made. Her partner, Marcos, had none. She'd given Rico about fifteen names. Only three had been clean.

She took a deep breath. Still didn't mean she could trust anyone. Still didn't mean she could trust Marcos. But she no longer felt they could get close to the man known only as the Scorpion. Not on their own, anyway. So she would start with Marsh. She would play her cards, she would tell what she knew, she would threaten him with exposure—him and his whole department—if he didn't give her some answers.

She turned back to the room, listening to the shower. She smiled. Marty would be naked and dripping wet. Under any other circumstances, Bailey would be tempted to join her. And she knew Marty would welcome her. Yes, she would be ravenous, as Bailey had suspected she'd be. And why not? Marty had spent a lifetime without sexual activity. It only stood to reason she'd have some making up to do. Bailey was just afraid she wouldn't be able to keep up.

But it'll be fun trying.

She picked up the phone, chasing away her thoughts. *Focus.* Yes, time to get the ball rolling. She dialed a familiar number, hearing Marcos's voice after only two rings.

"It's me," she said.

"Bailey? Are you okay?"

"Yes. Fine."

"Where are you?"

"Hiding, Marcos, that's where I am."

"You should come in. It'll be safer."

"Safer? Do I need safer, Marcos?"

He paused. Then, "We've heard things. There's been a woman on the streets. A woman with a gun."

"And you think it's me?"

"The description is not you, no. But…are you back in the Valley?"

"Let me talk to Marsh."

"The lieutenant?"

"Is that a problem?"

"No, no, Bailey. Maybe he can talk some sense into you. You need to come in before you get yourself killed."

"I'll take that into consideration."

She waited an eternity for Marsh to pick up. No doubt Marcos had to fill him in on what he knew or at least what he suspected he knew.

"Bailey, where the hell are you?"

"I'll be asking the questions, not you," she said quickly. "Let's

242

start with the ambush in Gulfport."

"What the hell are you talking about?"

"It was obviously a setup. You wanted me and the reporter out of the way."

"Don't be ridiculous, Bailey. I'm a goddamn cop, for Christ's sake."

"Come on, Marsh. The game's over. She wasn't expecting me. She hadn't been in contact with you. She didn't turn up new evidence. And she had no plans to return to Brownsville to open the case again. All just bullshit you fed me to get me up there."

"I don't know what she's told you, but she's lying. You think we'd just make that shit up?"

Bailey laughed. "Of course. Because you're just a puppet. You just do what you're ordered to do." She paused, glancing at the bathroom as Marty stepped out. "*El Scorpion*," she said, smiling at Marty. She covered the phone. "Marsh," she said quietly, getting a nod in return.

"You don't know what you're talking about, Bailey."

"The hell I don't." She turned to look out the window again. "I assume you found Fabio Perez's body. Along with that other nice gentleman. But I suppose that case never got worked either. Was that one deemed 'gang-related' as well? I saw the scorpion idol that was left on the body. Another unsolved case? Or did you haul in some innocent and pin it on him?"

"You're talking out of your head."

"Yeah. Maybe so. Maybe I dreamed it. Maybe I just *think* I have three hundred thousand dollars in drug money." She smiled. "Looks real enough, though."

"Listen, Bailey, you're going to get your ass killed if you're not careful. These gangs are ruthless. You should come in. I can protect you."

Bailey laughed. "Give me a break. Gangs? There's no gang, Lieutenant. There's just *el Scorpion* giving you the orders. But at least he pays you well."

"What are you talking about?"

"I'm talking about all those unexplained deposits in your bank account." She pulled up the report Rico had e-mailed. "Wow. Ten thousand bucks on April 24th. Wonder what that was for? Couldn't have been for a job well done. After all, we're still alive."

She tilted her head, listening to the silence on the phone. "No response?"

"What are you doing, Bailey? What do you hope to accomplish?"

"I want to know what the hell is going on. I want to know why you set me up. And I want to know who the Scorpion is."

Again, there was silence, then he cleared his throat. "Look, you're way out of your league here, Bailey. You want to stay alive, you need to just walk away."

"I know you never considered me a *real* cop, Marsh, but I'm not incompetent and I'm not out of my league. I know about the corruption on the force. I know about cases that were not worked because there was a scorpion idol left at the scene. And I know you, Diaz, and many, many others take payoffs instead of doing your goddamn jobs." She turned, pacing as she held the phone. "And so when this reporter stumbled upon your cold case and found the scorpion idol in the evidence box, you panicked. You tried to have her killed. When that didn't work, you sent me as bait, intending to kill both of us."

"You got it wrong, Bailey."

"Then tell me."

"I can't."

"Why do you protect him? Do you think I'm not going to the authorities with this? You're going to have investigators crawling all over the place. They're going to look at all your files. You're going to take the fall, Marsh. Not him."

"You can't do that, Bailey."

"The hell I can't."

"He won't let you."

"How's he going to stop me?"

"Look, let's talk about this."

"I thought we were."

"Not on the phone. Meet me tonight."

She glanced at Marty. "Okay. Where?" She saw Marty's brow draw together.

"How about on campus? There's a park next to the intramural fields."

"I know the place."

"Good. After dark. About nine. Near the tropical gardens."

Bailey laid the phone on the table, wondering if this was a mistake. She doubted Marsh would come alone. But still, she couldn't see him trying to take her out himself. That's not something a police lieutenant did. No, that's something one of his mysterious "gangs" would handle. More than likely, he would simply use this opportunity to try to find where she was hiding or, at the very least, attempt to follow her.

"Well?"

"I'm meeting Lieutenant Marsh tonight."

Marty shook her head. "Are you crazy?"

"Probably. But I'm hoping I can get some information from him."

"Why would he talk?"

Bailey went to her and took her hands. "Because sometimes, when you're being controlled and manipulated and you're scared for your life, then you want to talk. You want to unburden yourself of all that crap you've been carrying around. He's a cop. Yet, he's not being a cop. He's forced to compromise his sworn duty by giving in to the demands of this man we call the Scorpion. So I think he'll talk. I think he *wants* to talk."

"He tried to kill us," Marty reminded her.

"No. He tried to *have* us killed. He wasn't doing it. He's not going to pull a gun on me, Marty. That's not to say he'll be alone."

"I don't like this. It's too dangerous."

"It's at a public park on campus. I should be fine." Bailey squeezed her hands. "Now, how about a break?"

Marty raised her eyebrows.

"Let me take you to lunch."

"Oh? Like a date?"

"Yes, like a date."

"So I guess that means you're afraid to be alone with me here?" She laughed. "Afraid I'll drag you to bed?"

Bailey felt a blush creep up her face. "Hardly. But if you drag me to bed, I'll be in no shape to face Marsh tonight. The next time we're in bed together, I don't plan on letting you fall asleep on me."

Marty came closer, her hands sliding up Bailey's arms. "You know what I find fascinating?"

Bailey shook her head as her eyes dropped to Marty's lips.

"That you can face the barrel of a gun, you can face three thugs in an alley, yet at the briefest mention of sex, you blush like a schoolgirl." She leaned closer, brushing her lips against Bailey's. "I really like that about you. And I have no intention of falling asleep on you."

Bailey returned her kiss, then pulled away before she yielded to the temptation to do more. As much as she'd love to spend the afternoon in bed, she'd be wiped out for her encounter with Marsh. And she had a good suspicion she'd need to be sharp.

CHAPTER FORTY

As many times as they'd been out together—the first time she was in Brownsville and now this week—she thought she should be used to it by now. The danger. But she had a nagging feeling that tonight something critical wouldn't go their way.

"Quit worrying," Kris said as she drove them down the now-familiar International Boulevard.

"Oh, so now you think you can read my mind?"

Kris quickly glanced at her before turning her attention back to the road. "We're taking a bit of a chance, yes. But after last night, it's too dangerous to try to make contact with him on the streets. So we'll find out how much Marsh is willing to talk."

"Did you ever think that maybe Marsh is the Scorpion?"

"It's crossed my mind, yes. Captain Diaz is officially his boss, yet Diaz always defers to Marsh. At least he has as long as I've been here."

"But?"

Kris shrugged. "I don't know. Something tells me he's not the Scorpion. It just doesn't feel right. Besides, how do we explain the deposits into his bank account?"

"True." Marty absently watched the buildings flash by, her mind a jumbled mess as she tried to reconcile the fact that Kris was going out alone—and would be exposed—to meet a man neither of them trusted. Kris turned the car again, taking them to an area called Fort Davis. She could tell immediately that they were on a college campus as the buildings took on the same look and color. Suddenly, she gripped Kris's arm. "Oh, my God."

"What?"

"Look at the sign."

Kris looked where she pointed, a billboard congratulating the baseball team on making the playoffs. She laughed, grinning at Marty. "Pretty funny, huh?"

"I'll say." Apparently, the teams at The University of Texas at Brownsville were known as the Scorpions. "What's the name of the park where we're meeting him? Scorpion Park? Is it on Scorpion Drive?" She attempted to laugh, but her voice was laced with fear.

"Marty, it's just a coincidence, that's all. It's not like it's a warning or anything."

"Well, it's a terribly ironic coincidence."

Kris slowed as they approached the park, thankfully not called Scorpion Park. Palm trees lined the edges, and the interior was a mixture of open spaces and picnic tables landscaped with thick shrubs and flowering trees.

"Where are you meeting him?"

"On the other side, across from the intramural fields. There's a tropical garden there. Very lush."

"With places for him to hide?"

Kris ignored her question. "Put your headset on. We'll do the same as before."

"No satellite?"

"Not this time. I don't want anything to call attention to you."

"But—"

"Marty, I'll be fine. You've got to trust me."

"I do trust you. It's Marsh I don't trust."

Kris glanced at her watch and Marty did the same. It was nearly nine. She killed the lights and parked along the curb. "It's around the corner, on the other side, but I don't want you too close."

"Kris—"

"Don't argue with me. There's no time. Put your headset on. Lock the doors. Keep the engine running." Kris put the microphone clip on her watch. "Again, I'll be fine. But if anything happens, you call Rico."

"I know the drill." She didn't *like* the drill, but she knew it. She plugged her headset into her laptop, preparing to record the conversation. Kris's fingers wrapped around her wrist, and she turned, meeting Kris's eyes in the darkness.

"It'll be fine," she said again.

Marty nodded. "Okay." What else could she say? She didn't for a minute think it would be fine.

With another light squeeze of her fingers, Kris let go, slipping quietly from the car. Marty watched her go, jogging off into the park.

"Testing. You copy?"

"Yes, loud and clear," Marty said. She maneuvered across the console, getting behind the wheel. She locked the doors as she had been told to do, then waited, hearing nothing but Kris's breathing as she went to meet Marsh.

* * *

Bailey hid in the trees just outside of the tropical garden. Spring classes had already ended so there wasn't much foot traffic in the garden, especially at this hour. She spotted only a handful of people milling about. She finally saw Marsh, coming from the opposite direction. He paused near the fountain, looking around, then continuing forward. She stayed in the shadows, watching him.

"That's far enough, Lieutenant."

He stopped. "Bailey?"

"I'm here," she said, staying behind the foliage. "Let me see your hands."

"Good grief, Bailey, you think I'm going to shoot you?"

"I've been shot at *El Pirata del Parque*. The back window of my car was shot out in an alleged carjacking. And there was the ambush in Gulfport. So yeah, I think you might shoot me."

"Look, I was told to warn you and the reporter off. It didn't work."

"So you tried to have her killed at Captain Diaz's beach house?"

"Again, not my call."

"So when that failed, what?"

"Nothing. She left town. All was well. But you kept asking questions, nosing around. He wanted you out of the picture. Both of you."

"Who is *he*?"

"I don't know. I get phone calls. The voice is distorted. Sounds like a computer voice."

"And you just follow instructions without question? For what? *Money?*"

"Look, I've been on the force a long time. I know what goes down, what's been going down for years. He always picks someone to be the contact. You don't want to be that person, trust me."

"Why go along with it?"

"Why the hell do you think, Bailey? I've got a wife. I have kids. I used to have a dog. That was the warning. He killed our dog, then sent pictures of my kids that he'd taken while they were walking home from school. He sent pictures of my wife while she was out shopping." He raised his hands. "I have no doubt he'd kill them. I've been around, Bailey. I've been called to

250

the scene where a cop's been shot. And there's always a goddamn scorpion with him. If he'd kill a cop, he sure as hell would kill my kids, my wife."

"Then why hasn't someone put a stop to it? Christ, Marsh, you're a goddamn police officer. You run a corrupt office because you're threatened? Have investigators come in. Clean house."

"Yeah. Captain Diaz tried that very thing. He'd had enough. He told the voice on the phone as much, told him he was going to the authorities. And when he got home, he found his wife butchered. And the voice called again."

"Jesus," Bailey whispered.

"Diaz was worthless after that. He couldn't function. Now the voice calls me. We all know what happened. And we all know it could happen to us."

"Who the fuck is he?"

"I don't know. But he watches us. He knows everything."

"The phones are bugged?" Bailey guessed.

"Not the phones, no. But he must have someone on the inside."

"This has got to stop, Marsh. It's got to stop right now."

"I told you, he'll kill my family. I can't do anything."

"Well, I can."

"How? He's a ghost."

"No. He just wants you to think he's a ghost." Bailey stepped out of the shadows. "How does it work? When does he call you?"

"Bailey, I can't. I shouldn't even be here talking to you. I just wanted to warn you. He'll find you. You're targeted. You've got his money, and you killed one of his men."

"I shot him in self defense." She smiled. "But yeah, I took the money. Now tell me what goes down? He calls you. Then what? He has a job for you?"

"I can't." He backed up. "I can't tell you anything. I—"

But his words died as he fell to the ground, the unmistakable sound of a sniper rifle putting an end to anything he might have said.

"Oh, my God, no," she said, ducking back behind cover.

"What's going on?" Marty said urgently in her ear.

Marsh clutched his belly, the blood oozing through his fingers. Bailey was indecisive. Her police training told her to go to him, but her natural instinct told her to stay in the shadows.

"Marty, you copy?"

"Yes. What's wrong?"

"Marsh has been shot."

"What? I didn't hear—"

"Silencer on a sniper rifle. Sit tight."

"Oh, my God. Kris—"

"Sit tight," she repeated. She crept closer to Marsh, staying low. "Lieutenant? Hang on," she said as she fumbled with her phone, her hands shaking as she tried to dial 911.

He struggled to breathe. "Warehouse," he said hoarsely. "Tomorrow night. Old Baker's Ware—" His head was blown away before he could say more. The next two shots hit the dirt where Bailey had been before she rolled into the bushes a second earlier.

"Marty," she yelled, crawling away. "Bring the car. *Now.*"

"I'm coming, I'm coming," she said. "Where are you?"

"Just drive," she gasped, not daring to stand up, fearing he'd find her in the scope of his rifle. "Go around to the fields." She jumped as she saw the dirt kick up behind her. Where the hell was he? How was he seeing her? She stayed low, practically crawling along the ground, hiding where she could. She got to the edge of the garden, finally feeling safe as she stood behind a huge palm tree. She spotted Marty as she pulled to a quick stop along the curb by the intramural fields. She was in the open.

"I'm here."

"I see you. You're wide open."

"What should I do?"

"Back up. I'll come to you."

"Kris, what about Marsh?"

"He's dead." Bailey pushed off the tree, running fast in a

zigzag motion, hoping he could no longer see her. She paused at the street, looking around, then darted to the car, practically diving inside. "Go. *Fast*," she said, fearing they'd be shot as they sped away. Two blocks later, she touched Marty's arm. "Ease back. We're clear now."

"What happened?"

"He must have followed Marsh. Or tracked him. High-powered rifle with a silencer."

"Are you hurt?"

"No."

"I heard—"

"I know. He shot three times at me." Bailey watched as Marty's hands tightened on the steering wheel. She knew she'd been asking a lot of Marty. Marty wasn't trained for this, she wasn't mentally prepared for shooting and killing...and death. "I'm sorry I got you into this," she said.

Marty shot her a quick glance. "I think I started things by opening up the cold case in the first place. It's certainly not your fault."

"I'll understand if you want to bail on me. I can't expect you to—"

"Let's don't talk about it now, Kris. I can't even *think* right now. And as much as I disliked Marsh, I wouldn't have wished him dead. It's different when they're strangers, when you don't know them. But I had met this man."

Bailey kept quiet, seeing the misting of tears in Marty's eyes. No, she knew she wasn't crying for Marsh. It was just the events, the situation, the fact that Bailey herself had been shot at. It was getting to be all too much for Marty.

Bailey wasn't stupid. The sniper's rifle had been aimed at her too. She could have ended up just like Marsh, with her head blown open. Marty knew that as well. Bailey leaned back in the seat and closed her eyes. Was it fair to drag Marty through this? Maybe she should send her to Rico's. Better yet, maybe she should send her home, back to Atlanta. Bailey intended on going to the warehouse tomorrow night. She didn't know what she'd find there, didn't know if the Scorpion would show himself or not, but she would be there. As much as Marsh had made her professional life hell the last two years, she didn't want his death to be in vain. She didn't want him to just be another cop who succumbed to *el Scorpion*. She was ready to put an end to it. She was ready to get her life back.

CHAPTER FORTY-ONE

Marty went straight to the drawers, pulling out clean clothes. Without looking at Kris, she said, "I need to shower. I need to—"

"I understand."

Marty turned around. "I'm sorry. I just...I'm just having a hard time with all this."

"I know."

Marty escaped into the bathroom, closing the door behind her. She hated feeling this way...feeling weak, feeling frightened. Feeling alone again. It could have been Kris whom the sniper killed, not Marsh. And then she would be on her own, racing back to Corpus Christi, seeking shelter with Rico, a man she barely knew. Seeking comfort from him while she grieved, seeking answers, seeking closure that she knew somehow she would never get.

Kris had said it was a dangerous game, but it had proved far more dangerous than Marty had anticipated. She thought they'd left the worst behind after surviving the hit on her rented beach house. And as much as Kris wanted to believe they were the ones doing the hunting, it felt very much like they were the ones being hunted. She'd heard Marsh's last words, his *dying* words, she'd heard him tell Kris about the warehouse. She knew without a doubt Kris was already making her plans, trying to figure out how to get inside the warehouse. And Kris would need her to help.

She met her eyes in the mirror as she stripped naked. She would do what Kris asked, of course. There was no question about that. But she was plenty scared. Scared for both their lives. Scared that this time, Kris wouldn't be able to dodge the bullets. Scared that this time, when Kris reminded her to get to Rico should something go wrong, she'd actually have to do that.

She stepped into the shower, turning it to nearly scalding hot as she scrubbed her skin, trying to wash away the events of the night…and wash away her fears. But when she stepped out and wrapped a towel around her body, nothing had changed. The fears she had still haunted her, making her chest feel tight.

She found Kris sitting at the small table, her hands wrapped around a glass, the bottle of cognac sitting beside her. Across the room by the door, she saw the weapons and the rest of the equipment they kept in the false trunk. She raised her eyebrows.

"I moved the car," Kris said. "A couple of blocks away. Rico is sending someone to pick it up. A chop shop."

"That means we're getting another one?"

"Yes. He should be here by dawn."

"Just like that? He just has cars at his disposal?"

Kris smiled. "Let's just say he knows a lot of, well, car dealers." She poured a small amount of cognac into another glass. "You want to talk?"

Marty pulled out the other chair and sat down, taking the drink. "I want to run away," she admitted. "I want us to just leave here."

"And do what? You want to be Patty Stone the rest of your

life?" Kris shrugged. "I kinda like being Kristen Bailey. And I think you want to be Marty Edwards. If we run, we can't be those women ever again. Because they'll find us. Somewhere, someday, they will."

Marty leaned closer. "We can't find this man, Kris. I mean, if our own government can't stop drug cartels, how do we think we can?"

"You're right. But I don't think that's what we're dealing with." She stood up, pacing slowly in the small space of the kitchen. "I think this guy is a local. Small potatoes. He operates here." She turned to Marty. "Think about it. A drug cartel, a drug lord, they have a small army. They don't operate on the streets in dark alleys. They sell massive amounts of drugs to equally massive dealers. It's all very organized. They don't own police departments. They don't have to. They're worth billions of dollars."

"And this guy?"

"No. He's concerned about the three hundred thousand I took. He plays the cops and he *pays* the cops. That's the only way he can operate here. A drug cartel isn't going to pay bribes to cops. They don't have to."

"Okay, I follow your thinking. Our guy pays the police off to let him do his business. And he kills to keep the fear up."

Kris nodded. "Right. I think our original assumption is correct. This may have started years and years ago, passed off time and again. The current *el Scorpion* is dangerous. He thinks he has the power. He thinks we can't get to him. He took out his contact, Marsh, to keep it that way. Which gives us a little advantage. He doesn't have a voice in the police department right now."

"What about Diaz? Marsh said Diaz used to be the contact. Maybe he'll go back to that."

"Maybe." She paced again. "But something's still not right. Is a large drug cartel going to let some local operate here? The drug lords, the cartels, they're like giant gangs. They all have their own territories, on both sides of the border. Are they going

257

to let someone get a piece of their pie?"

"So maybe he does work for them?" Marty's head was spinning with all this speculation. It was just a guessing game.

"I don't think so. He has too much power here to be working for them. He controls too much of this city. It's something else. Something we're not seeing."

"But you're planning for us to go to the warehouse anyway," Marty said.

Kris sat down again. "About that. In the morning, I want you to leave with Rico. I think—"

"No." Marty's gaze was unflinching as she met Kris's. "No. No. I won't leave you."

"Marty, this is best. It's too dangerous—"

"Exactly," she said, standing. It was now her turn to pace. "I won't let you go there alone. Don't ask me to." When Kris started to speak, Marty held up her hand. "No. There's no discussion, Kris."

"You're not trained for this. *Mentally*, you're not prepared. I don't want to put you through this."

"It's not your decision to make."

"Yes, it is."

Marty spun around. "The *hell* it is. I'm not leaving. We're in this together."

Kris's gaze was steady and she stood too, coming closer. "I could never forgive myself if something happened to you. Please. Go with Rico."

"No, I won't."

"Marty, please don't argue about this. You know it's the logical thing to do."

Marty took a step back, shaking her head. "Logical? There's nothing *logical* about this situation." She pointed to the weapons on the floor. "There's nothing logical about that. There's nothing logical about having three hundred thousand dollars of drug money in our possession. No. And don't *you* argue with me about this." She spun around then, heading to the door. She needed some air. She needed to think. She opened the door, slamming it loudly as she stepped outside. She took deep breaths of air, trying to clear her head. So Kris wanted her to leave, wanted her out of harm's way, wanted her to logically think about the situation. She looked overhead, the stars obscured by the lights of the city.

"No. I won't go," she whispered.

* * *

Bailey flinched as the door slammed. Well, what had she expected? That Marty would easily agree to this? No, Bailey knew she wouldn't. But she thought perhaps she could persuade her, perhaps they could talk rationally about it. But no, they were too emotionally involved to be rational. If the tables were reversed, she would have reacted the same way.

She got up, feeling the grime from the night on her skin. She wanted a nice hot shower and a nice warm bed. And she wanted the comfort of Marty beside her. She got up, gathering her things for her shower. She didn't worry about Marty being outside. She knew Marty wouldn't go far or stay out long. She had just needed some space, some time alone to reconcile everything. Bailey couldn't blame her for that.

She hurried through her shower, not bothering to brush her wet hair when she finished, leaving the short blond strands to fall where they may. She had gotten used to the short hair, though not necessarily the blond color. She looked closer, seeing her dark roots beginning to show. Hopefully, this would be over soon and she wouldn't be forced to color her hair again.

When she stepped out of the bathroom, the lights were off. She glanced at the bed, seeing Marty with the covers pulled to her shoulders. Her silent breathing told her Marty wasn't asleep.

"I'm sorry," Bailey said softly.

"I'm not leaving."

"Okay."

She pulled the covers back, crawling in beside Marty. Bailey felt the heat of her and she was drawn to it. It was only then that she realized Marty wasn't wearing the flannel pajama bottoms she was so fond of. She moved her hand, expecting to feel a T-shirt blocking her path. Instead, she felt only warm skin. Marty's sharp intake of breath made her own breathing increase. Marty was naked. So Bailey sat up, pulling her shirt over her head. She was startled to feel Marty's hands tugging at her panties, peeling them off.

No words were spoken as Marty came to her, her soft hands touching everywhere, finally lingering at her breasts as their mouths met. Bailey moaned as Marty's tongue invaded her mouth, letting her know who was in charge. She lay back, opening her legs, giving Marty room as she settled between them.

Marty pulled her mouth away, moving it to Bailey's breasts instead. There was nothing hesitant about her touch as she ravished Bailey, her lips and teeth teasing her nipples, making Bailey squirm as she arched her hips, seeking relief. Her breath came in short gasps as she felt Marty's hand move lower. She opened her legs even wider, inviting Marty inside.

"Tell me what you want," Marty whispered as her mouth returned to Bailey's.

Bailey wanted so many things. She wanted Marty's fingers deep inside her, she wanted Marty's mouth on her, she wanted *her*. She took Marty's hand, sliding it between her legs, feeling her wetness. "Go inside me," she murmured as she released Marty's hand. She moaned loudly as she felt Marty filling her. Her own hand moved, searching for Marty, finding her wet and ready. She entered her, feeling Marty's hips jerk as she took Bailey inside.

"Oh, *God*," Marty breathed, her hips moving, starting a rhythm as her hand continued to pump in and out of Bailey, their pace slow and steady, their moans mingling. "So good. Feels so good."

Bailey used her other hand to grasp Marty's hips, urging her on, increasing the rhythm they'd set, their hips moving in unison now, their breathing labored as they slammed together, each thrust driving their fingers deeper within. Marty was close to orgasm—Bailey could feel it. So she let herself go, losing herself in Marty's touch, feeling the fingers inside her, the pressure building, threatening to explode.

Marty screamed out, one final thrust of her hips bringing her over the edge. Marty's orgasm thrilled Bailey, her hand soaking as Marty's hips stilled. She arched one last time, following Marty into the land of oblivion, nearly embarrassed by the sounds of pleasure she was making, groaning loudly as she felt her body pulse with life, her inside walls holding Marty tight within her. It had been so long, she'd nearly forgotten the immense gratification of lovemaking.

Marty collapsed on top of her, her breathing coming as fast as Bailey's was. Bailey's fingers slipped from Marty, and she gathered her close, placing light kisses across her face. She relaxed, releasing Marty's fingers, and she felt Marty pull out, felt her wet hand move across her skin.

"Is it always like this?" Marty whispered against her mouth.

Bailey smiled as she rolled them over, her thigh urging Marty's legs apart. "There's a difference between sex and making love," she murmured as her lips nibbled at the hollow of Marty's throat. She loved the deep moan she heard as Marty turned her head, offering more of herself to Bailey's seeking lips.

"I love how you make my body feel," Marty whispered, her hands moving freely on Bailey's backside. "I never thought it would be possible. Not for me."

Bailey slipped lower to her breasts, capturing a nipple, teasing it with her tongue. She felt the tremble of Marty's body, felt the subtle arch as her hips moved against Bailey's thigh. Bailey moaned, feeling the wet arousal coat her skin. She pulled her mouth away, finding Marty's lips again. But she paused when Marty's arms tightened around her.

"What is it?"

"You're not going to make me fall for you and then just disappear from my life when this is all over, are you?"

Bailey brushed the hair off of Marty's face, leaning closer to whisper into Marty's ear. "I've got no place to disappear *to*, sweetheart."

"I just don't want this to be about the 'mission,' you know. I want it to be about *us*."

Bailey leaned on her elbow, her hand lazily moving across Marty's nipple, still hard and aroused. "I haven't been with anyone in over two years," she said. "I certainly wouldn't have picked this situation to become involved with someone." She ducked her head, swiping her tongue across the nipple her fingers had been teasing, hearing Marty's sharp intake of breath. "Truth be told, I was attracted to you from the moment I laid eyes on you."

"You were?"

Bailey rolled them over again, settling Marty on top of her, cupping her hips and fitting her between her thighs. "Yes. And when you told me your 'secret,' I was crushed," she said with a smile.

"After I left here the first time, I thought about you a lot. I kept hoping you'd call, just to check on me, if nothing else."

"And I was waiting on you to call me." Bailey pulled Marty closer, her kiss slow, lingering. She felt Marty press hard between her thighs. Then Marty moved, resting her weight on her hands, her lips brushing Bailey's skin. She found the scar on Bailey's shoulder, and she paused there, her lips stilling. Was she thinking about the old wound? Bailey wondered. Or was she thinking of perhaps a new wound that could take its place?

"I don't want you to get hurt," Marty whispered.

"That makes two of us." Bailey lifted her hand, touching Marty's face. "I want this to be over with. I want us to have some time together. Some real time together." Her thumb moved, rubbing Marty's lips, feeling their softness. "Do you want that too?"

Marty turned her face, kissing Bailey's palm, then moving to her lips. "Yes. I'm falling in love for the first time in my life," she said, her voice soft and quiet. "I want to know what that feels like." She ducked lower, her mouth settling over Bailey's breast. Bailey closed her eyes, loving the slow, languid pace of Marty's lovemaking. She was surprised when Marty moved lower. "I also want to know what *this* feels like," she murmured as her mouth moved across Kris's belly, leaving wet kisses behind.

Bailey's legs parted, giving Marty room. She realized she was nearly trembling as Marty's hands spread her thighs. It had been too many years since a woman had touched her, and she relished it now, feeling Marty's breath against her skin. She moaned loudly at the first touch of Marty's mouth, her tongue tentative, hesitant, then attacking with a fervor that made Bailey arch her hips, her eagerness making Bailey writhe beneath her as Marty feasted.

"God, yes." Bailey's fists pulled at the sheets as the wet suckling sounds invaded her senses, her clit pulsing with life as Marty's lips surrounded it, her tongue flicking hard against it. The thrill of Marty's passion overtook her, and she succumbed to it, surrendering finally as her orgasm erupted with one last tug from Marty's mouth. Her pleasure was pulled from her throat, her guttural scream sounding loud in the quiet room.

She lay still, trying to catch her breath. She felt Marty's mouth leave her, felt her crawl up beside her, but Bailey's eyes refused to open.

"I've never felt so close to someone before," Marty whispered, her mouth close to Bailey's ear.

Bailey turned, forcing her eyes opened. "That was fantastic."

Marty leaned closer, her lips against Bailey's skin. "Yes, it was."

CHAPTER FORTY-TWO

Marty couldn't keep the giddy smile off her face, even while they tidied up the cabin, waiting for Rico's arrival. Never in her life had she felt so satisfied, both physically and emotionally. Their night of lovemaking, of giving and receiving, was something she'd never forget. For the first time in her life, she made love with someone, giving herself freely, taking what Kris offered and letting Kris take her places she'd never been. And the more they loved, the more she wanted, her appetite voracious and surprising. Sheer exhaustion had forced sleep upon them. But this morning, she had done something she'd never even considered before. The shower stall was small, with barely room for the two of them, but they'd managed quite well, their passion surfacing again, the light of day not dampening their desires.

She was pulled from her thoughts by the slamming of a car door outside their cabin. Kris hurried to the window, looking out.

"It's Rico," she said.

She had the door opened before he could knock. Marty smiled as they embraced, Rico ruffling Kris's hair much like a brother would do.

"Thanks for coming," Kris said.

"Anything for you, Bailey." He held up a bag. "I brought breakfast."

"Good. We didn't have dinner." Kris snatched the bag from him, going into the tiny kitchen.

He turned, bowing slightly in Marty's direction. "You are looking as lovely as ever. In fact, lovelier. Hanging with Bailey seems to be good for you."

Marty grinned, going to him. "She hasn't killed me yet. Or me her," she said, giving him a quick hug. "Good to see you again."

He studied her, a knowing smile coming to his face. "She is special. Do not break her heart," he said quietly, glancing at Kris as she unwrapped the tacos.

"I wouldn't dream of it," Marty said.

He nodded, then turned to Kris. "So, Bailey, you two have gotten into quite a bit of trouble in a very short time. You're on your third vehicle. Perhaps I should leave a fleet with you."

"Very funny," she said. "I'm just being cautious. Besides, a bright red sports car? What were you thinking?"

"I was thinking perhaps you'd put the top down and take Marty here for a drive on the beach." He took a plate from Kris and handed it to Marty, before taking another for himself. "But we're back to an SUV," he said. "Dark green. Same setup."

"Good."

"I've noticed you haven't used your credit cards much."

"Just for the rooms and food," Kris said, holding up a taco. "These are great. Where'd you get them?"

"In a part of town you have no business going to," he said. "So, your lieutenant was mixed up in it, as you suspected. Now what?"

"Now we continue on."

He put his taco down. "Do you really still think you can get to this guy?"

"Yes."

He glanced at Marty, eyebrows raised. She said nothing, not knowing how much Kris wanted him to know.

"Look, Rico, I know what I'm doing."

"Perhaps. But this lovely partner of yours is not trained for this."

"No, I'm not," Marty said. "But she hasn't put me in danger. I've been hanging back, doing surveillance."

He looked back to Kris. "I could stay. I could help."

"No way. You've got a wife, kids. I won't take that chance," Kris said. "Besides, you don't want to get mixed up in this. You have your business to protect."

"You're not a one-man army, Bailey."

"I don't need an army."

He sighed. "Well, as stubborn as ever, I see."

"Stubborn, yes. But not careless. I want this guy, but not at any cost." She glanced at Marty. "There's too much to live for. I won't take unnecessary chances."

CHAPTER FORTY-THREE

Bailey was nervous and she couldn't put her finger on why. Maybe it was just the fact that she felt like this was it. Tonight, it would all be over with, one way or another. Or maybe it was because Marty would be going inside with her, a decision she hoped she wasn't going to live to regret. She glanced at Marty, sitting beside her in the SUV. She was staring out the window, waiting for darkness, her fingers lightly tapping her black jeans.

They had driven by the warehouse earlier in the day. It appeared closed and shuttered, dark and dusty. She'd hoped they could find a place where Marty could hide with the satellite, but the warehouse, while still in the old district, was at the edge of the city. An open field adjacent to it separated the warehouse from an old, shabby street where houses stood decrepit and in shambles. She knew better than to suggest Marty stay at the cabin. The only other alternative was to take Marty with her, inside. At least that way, she could keep an eye on her.

"You're worried, aren't you?"

Bailey nodded. "This isn't one of my better plans."

"Actually, I think it is," Marty said. "I feel safer knowing I'll be with you. Sitting in the car alone isn't really appealing."

Bailey took a deep breath. "Okay, let's go over it again."

Marty smiled. "You don't think four times is enough?"

"Humor me."

"Okay. At full dark, we come up from the back of the warehouse. We check for sentries or surveillance cameras. We then use the old fire escape stairs to climb to the second-floor window."

Bailey nodded. "We get inside, using the catwalk to maneuver."

"We survey the scene, hoping there isn't an army of men inside. If there is, we get the hell out."

"If there's not, we proceed. If it appears empty, we hide and wait."

"If things go bad," Marty said, pausing.

"Finish it," Bailey said.

"If things go bad, I leave you and get out. And call Rico."

"Good." Bailey reached out, taking Marty's hand. "It'll be fine." Of course, the fact that they'd packed up their things from the cabin had convinced Marty that things wouldn't be fine. But Bailey didn't want to take any chances. If she went down, she didn't want Marty to have the delay of going back to the cabin. She just wanted her to be able to get the hell out of town.

"If something happens to you, it won't be fine, Kris."

Bailey leaned back in the seat, ignoring her statement. "So where do you want to go when this is over with?"

Marty squeezed her hand tight. "Anywhere with you."

"Yeah? A beach? The mountains?"

"A beach."

Bailey rolled her head to the side, meeting her eyes. "A beach it is, then." She answered the smile Marty forced to her face with one of her own. "I promise."

They sat quietly for a few moments, their eyes meeting often as darkness settled around them. Finally, Bailey stirred, knowing it was time. She opened the small case and pulled out a tiny microphone clip and earpiece, handing them to Marty. She then took one of each for herself, slipping the earpiece tight into her ear and clipping the microphone on her watchband. Marty did the same, mimicking Bailey.

"Test, one, two," Bailey said, her voice nearly a whisper.

"Copy," Marty responded, pushing the earpiece down a little farther.

"Stay behind me. Follow my direction."

Marty nodded, hesitating only slightly before opening the door. Bailey slipped on the black vest, its Velcro pockets already filled with extra clips for her gun, a knife, a silencer and anything else she thought she might need.

She was thankful for the low clouds that obscured the moon, adding to the shadows as they headed off. The SUV was parked a good four blocks away from their destination. They ducked behind the first warehouse, walking quickly and silently. Bailey slipped into the alley and pulled Marty with her.

"Surveillance," she whispered, holding up the small pair of night vision glasses. "Stay here."

Bailey went to the corner of the next building, looking for movement. She saw none. It was dark and quiet. She lifted her wrist to her mouth. "Clear."

Marty joined her and they continued, hugging the dark shadow of the building as they made their way to Old Baker's Warehouse. Bailey saw movement and quickly stopped, moving Marty behind her.

"Don't move," she said. She watched the man as he retraced his steps slowly, much as a sentry would do. She slowly lifted the glasses, searching, but saw no one else. She assumed there would be at least two guards, maybe more. She turned to Marty. "He's walking back and forth. There's most likely another guy on the other side of the warehouse."

"That's near the fire escape that we were going to use," Marty

269

said. "What'll we do?"

Bailey looked away. "We'll have to take him out." It went against all of her training as a police officer. But she had long since stopped being a cop. She'd broken too many rules—laws—for that. She wondered if Marty could ever forgive her for what she was about to do.

As if reading her mind, Marty grabbed her arm as she turned away. Bailey stopped, looking back at her.

"I know this is hard for you," Marty said. "I trust you to do the right thing. Whatever it is."

Bailey pulled her close, whispering in her ear, "I don't want you to think less of me." She moved, kissing her hard. "I hate what I'm about to do."

Marty gripped her arm tightly, holding her. "These aren't innocent people, Kristen. Let's don't lose sight of that."

Bailey nodded, knowing it was the truth. That didn't necessarily make it any easier. She released her weapon from its holster, attaching the silencer as she walked. When they reached the corner, she took cover behind a stack of wooden pallets. She brought her finger to her lips, telling Marty to keep quiet. She heard the light footsteps of the guard as he approached. She took a deep breath, then stepped out. He turned to her, and she fired twice, hitting her target, watching as he fell to the ground.

"Clear," she said quietly. "Help me move him."

Marty's face was grim as they slid him behind the pallets. He was one of the three guys who had followed Bailey that night on Ridgley. Marty looked away as Bailey searched his pockets. She found nothing that would help them, not even a radio.

"Are there security cameras?" Marty asked.

"Earlier today when we did surveillance, I spotted only one at the front entrance," Bailey said. "Hard to say if it was functional." She scanned the building from the back now but saw no cameras anywhere. Old Baker's Warehouse had been vacant for years. She didn't expect security. "Let's move."

They hurried along the back of the warehouse, heading to

the side where the fire escape was. The clouds parted, and the full moon peeked out, exposing them. There was nothing to hide behind so Bailey kept her weapon held in the ready position. She glanced over her shoulder, behind Marty, making sure no one was following them.

At the corner, she paused, listening for footsteps. She heard none. She leaned forward, looking down the long alley. The guard she expected to find was at the other end, his back to her. She grabbed Marty's hand, pulling her quickly into the alley where old crates were stacked four high, giving them a place to hide. She eased Marty against the wall, motioning for her to squat down. Bailey bent down beside her.

"I take out the second guard, then we head to the fire escape." Marty nodded. She appeared relatively calm, but her eyes betrayed her nervousness. "You're doing great," Bailey said.

Marty flashed a quick grin. "I'm scared as hell."

Bailey squeezed her shoulder. "You'll do fine."

She scooted along the crates until she had a view of the alley. The guard was making his way back toward them. Her hand involuntarily tightened around her gun, but she kept her breathing even and steady, her eyes glued to the approaching form. When he was within a few steps of them, she stood, firing quickly, dropping him to the ground. As before, they moved the body, hiding it between the crates.

Bailey used the night vision glasses to scan the perimeter, but she saw no other movement. "It's clear," she said.

They left their hiding place, walking quickly to the fire escape. It was old and rusty. She pulled on the lowest rung, grimacing as metal parts rubbed together. She paused, then pulled again, more slowly, hoping the noise couldn't be heard from the inside. When it finally was extended, she turned to Marty.

"Stay close to me."

"Don't worry."

Bailey stood on the first rung, testing it with her weight. It creaked, emitting a low groaning noise, but it felt sturdy. She climbed, keeping a lookout behind them. Marty followed, right at her heels. They paused at the first landing, Bailey using the glasses to scan the alley below them. It was quiet. They resumed climbing, not stopping again until they came to the windows, two stories high. The windows weren't boarded, no. But they were locked. From her vest, she pulled out the kit Rico had given her. The long, slender blade slipped easily between the pane and ledge. Once inside, she clicked the button on top of the blade, much like a ballpoint pen, releasing the hook that she'd use to unlatch the window.

Except the latch wouldn't budge.

"What is it?" Marty asked.

"It's old and rusty," she said, using more force. She finally felt it give a little. She pushed harder, watching as the latch turned. After what seemed like precious minutes had passed, the latch gave way. She clicked the blade again, the hook recoiling inside. She pulled it out, then pushed lightly on the window. It opened easily. After putting away her tools and slipping the case back into her vest, she turned to Marty.

"You ready?"

Marty nodded, her eyes swimming in fear. Bailey had no reassuring words for her. They were about to go into the lion's den.

She opened the window fully, then tilted her head, listening for sounds from within the warehouse. She heard none. She slipped over the ledge, dropping silently to the catwalk. It was dark up here among the rafters, but a lone light shown down below, near the entrance. She turned to Marty, motioning her inside. She closed the window again, leaving it opened just a crack. She didn't want outside noise to filter in, alerting someone to their presence. She pointed to the light below, then brought a finger to her lips, again indicating silence.

She crept along the catwalk, circling the ground floor of the warehouse. She saw no movement, but something told her they weren't alone. As they neared the staircase that would take them down, she was able to make out what appeared to be twenty-five or thirty wooden crates, all rectangular in shape. They weren't something she imagined drugs to be stashed in.

She shrank back into the darkness when she saw movement. A man walked slowly into the light, his hand tapping a cell phone impatiently against his leg. Bailey pulled out the glasses, flipping off the night vision before bringing them to her face. Her eyes widened in disbelief as she saw him. She took a deep breath, then handed the glasses to Marty.

Marty pulled them away, her brow furrowed in a frown. Bailey nodded.

It was Marcos. But what the hell was he doing here? Had Marsh tipped him off? Or was he the mole in the department?

Her breath caught as his phone rang, the sound loud and shrill in the quiet warehouse. She listened intently as he answered.

"I have the package, yes." He paced again, then stopped. "What? You want proof? My word is not good enough?"

Bailey watched as he took a crowbar that was leaning against a crate and popped open one of the boxes. She took the binoculars from Marty, again surprised at what she saw. Not drugs. Weapons.

"I'll send the photo," Marcos said. "You have five minutes to call back. If not, I'll go to my second buyer."

Son of a bitch. Was Marcos the Scorpion? And dealing weapons, not drugs? Weapons were far worse.

She glanced at Marty, motioning to the stairs with her head. They would wait until he got his call back, then move while he was distracted. It didn't take long for his phone to ring. Bailey moved, her feet silent as she took the stairs down, glad they curved around to the back of the warehouse, which was still shrouded in darkness.

"Transfer the money to this account," he said. Bailey watched as he pulled a small notebook from his suit pocket. "S-H-1-9-0-0-4-0-2-7-2." He slipped the notebook back into his pocket, then clicked on a nearby laptop. "I'll wait."

Bailey moved again, nearly at the bottom now. The crates

obscured her line of vision, but at least they would have cover. She took Marty's hand, urging her along.

"Excellent. I see the transfer. Old Baker's Warehouse. You have thirty minutes."

Bailey crouched down, hiding in the shadows. Now what? Confront him? Wait for his buyers? No. His buyers would come armed. And there would be a lot of them. She needed to confront him now. She turned to Marty, pulling her close.

"You stay here," she whispered as quietly as she dared. Marty grabbed her arm, but Bailey shook her off, moving away. If there was gunfire, she didn't want Marty involved.

She crouched low, moving among the old boxes and crates, closer and closer to the center where the lone light hung. She rested her back against a stack of pallets, then, taking a deep breath, moved into the light. But the space was empty, no sign of Marcos.

She ducked back into the shadows, her heart stopping as Marty's scream echoed through her earpiece.

"Well, Bailey, I see Marsh was able to give you some information after all. Shocking, really. I didn't think he had the balls."

She slipped between two crates, moving toward his voice.

"And I should thank you for bringing your little friend with you. How nice."

Bailey brought her wrist to her mouth. "Hang tight, Marty," she whispered.

"That means that you took out my two very faithful guards." He laughed. "Good thing I believe in being thorough. Motion activated cameras come in very handy, Bailey. But you surprise me. I didn't think you'd come in from the top. I actually left a window unlocked down here, hoping to aid you."

She kept moving, finally getting a glimpse of him. He had his gun held to Marty's head, his other arm wrapped around her shoulder.

"Bailey? Come on. I can't hear you." He looked at Marty.

"And you, my dear, have been a hard one to eliminate. Like a cat with nine lives."

Bailey moved again, keeping them in front of her. Sharpshooter or not, she didn't dare take a shot at him. Not with Marty being held so close.

"Come on out, Bailey. You have no leverage here." His arm tightened around Marty. "I'm going to kill her, Bailey. Don't you want to watch?"

Bailey felt perspiration dampen her skin. This man was not Marcos, her mild-mannered partner. This man was *el Scorpion*. Or *el Diablo*, as Mrs. Romero had called him. Bailey didn't doubt that. She also didn't doubt that he'd kill Marty as he'd threatened.

Focus. Focus.

Her hands were shaking as she searched her vest for her phone. She leaned against one of the crates, going through her numbers, finding Marcos's cell that she'd programmed in earlier.

"Bailey? Come on. I don't have time for this. What do you say?"

She heard Marty's breathing, heard her moan when Marcos tightened his grip. Bailey brought her wrist to her mouth, speaking quietly. "I'm going to call his cell. When he moves to answer it, you drop to the floor."

"Come on, Bailey. I can't hear you."

Bailey pushed call on her phone, then waited for what seemed minutes instead of seconds. She held her weapon ready, keeping him in her sights. At the first ring, his arm loosened from around Marty. Marty jabbed him with a fierce elbow to his gut, then fell to the ground. Bailey fired, hitting his shoulder, sending his gun sliding across the concrete floor of the warehouse. Marty scrambled away, taking cover behind some wooden boxes.

Bailey stepped out from behind the crates, her gun fixed on him. "Can you hear me now?"

He laughed. "I can't believe you shot me, Bailey."

"Marty? Are you okay?"

"Yes."

"I want you to leave now."

"No way."

"Yes. Back the way we came. I'll meet you."

"No. I'm not leaving."

"Goddamnit," she said loudly. "Do it."

"Kris—"

"This is no time to argue. Now get the hell out of here," she said, her eyes never leaving Marcos.

She heard Marty's running footsteps, heard the stairs creak as she hurried up them. She finally relaxed, knowing Marty was safe. She took the microphone clip from her wrist and slipped it into her pocket. She didn't want Marty to hear what was about to happen. She also removed the earpiece. She wanted no distractions.

"So now what, Bailey? You gonna call the cops? That's a good idea. Why don't we call them right now?"

She shook her head. "There'll be no judge and jury for you, Marcos. You don't deserve that."

He pressed his hand against his injured shoulder. "What are you going to do? Kill me?" He laughed again. "I don't think so. You're a cop, Bailey. A good cop. You're not going to shoot me. It goes against your principles."

"I no longer have any principles, Marcos." She turned, walking back toward the crates. She lifted the lid on the one he'd taken a picture of. "Weapons? And here I thought it was all about drugs."

"My father moved drugs. But the cartels became too powerful."

"Your father?"

"It's a family business, Bailey. I still dabble in drugs some." He winced as he flexed his shoulder. "In fact, you have my money from a deal. I want it back."

Bailey ignored him. "*El Scorpion?* It started with your father?"

"Grandfather." He came closer. "What do you want, Bailey? You want a cut of the action?"

It was her turn to laugh. "*A cut*, Marcos?" She held the gun, pointing it at his head. "No. I don't want a cut."

"Stop pretending that you're going to use that thing. If you were going to kill me, you'd have done it with the first shot. Or did you miss your target and hit my shoulder instead?"

"Well, I'm a woman. You know we shouldn't be allowed to play with guns."

"That was Marsh's theory, not mine." He glanced at his watch. "My buyers will be here very soon, Bailey. Trust me, they will far outnumber you."

"So you think I should just leave? What purpose would that serve?"

"You can't beat me, Bailey. I own this city. I control the police. I have the power and the resources to do whatever I want." He smiled. "You are nothing. A woman holding a gun at me." He laughed. "You think I'm scared of you? I am *el Scorpion*. I fear no one."

Bailey lowered her gun. "Tell me one thing, Marcos. The kid, Carlos Romero. Why was he killed? What did he see?"

"Ten years ago? You think I remember?"

"Yes. I think you remember exactly what happened."

Marcos turned away from her. "He was nothing. Why was the reporter interested in him?"

"Because he was something to his mother, to his sister."

Marcos coughed, his hand still rubbing his shoulder, his suit jacket soaked with blood. "One of my men was skimming off the top. I had to take care of him, and I had to do it publicly. I needed the rest to see what would happen to them if they took my money." He lowered his hand. "The boy, unfortunately for him, chose that moment to walk into the alley. I had no choice."

"So you butchered him there on the street," she said.

"I had just killed one of my men in much the same manner, Bailey. It was no big deal."

The disgust that Bailey felt for him at that moment went far beyond anything she'd ever experienced. He was indeed the

277

Devil.

"Now, why don't we stop this little game, Bailey? My buyers will be here in ten minutes. If you want to live another day, you'll run along." He pointed at Bailey. "You and I, we can finish our business later."

She shook her head. "I don't think so, Marcos." She raised her gun again. "*El Scorpion is dead.*" She pulled the trigger. Her first shot hit him square in the chest, knocking him backward and to the ground. He stared at her in disbelief as she walked closer, his eyes pleading. "I have no mercy," she murmured, firing a final shot between his eyes.

She stared at his body, feeling no remorse for what she'd done. He had no doubt killed countless people, but the one thing that stuck in her mind was the man he'd sent to kill Marty. If Bailey had been a half-second slower, he'd have sliced her throat open, leaving her to die there as Bailey watched—helpless. No, she felt no remorse. Besides, there was no other way. She didn't trust the police. Marcos would never be arrested, never do jail time. Not here in Brownsville.

She went to him, pulling open his coat. She removed the tiny notebook she'd seen him stash there earlier. If there was someone waiting in the wings, someone to follow in his footsteps, she didn't plan to leave them with millions of dollars to operate. She'd make sure Rico handled that.

She turned back to the weapons, knowing she had to do something. And fast. Whoever his buyers were, they would be here soon to claim their purchase. There was only one way to destroy the weapons—fire. She searched the floor of the warehouse, looking for something, anything to use as an accelerant. She found cans of paint, but no paint thinner. She spotted what looked like a small jug of diesel fuel, but it was empty. There were a few old offices tucked along one wall. She ran to them, quickly searching each, finding nothing. She was about to give up when she spotted an old oil lamp, the globe dusty and filled with cobwebs. But the base? It appeared to be filled—with kerosene she hoped. She ripped the globe off and unscrewed the wick, sniffing the liquid inside.

"Oh, yeah," she said, screwing the top back on. In the first office she'd searched, she'd seen a stack of old newspapers. She grabbed a handful and hurried back to the crates. Using Marcos's crowbar, she popped the tops on as many crates as she could get to, stuffing the newspapers inside. To her surprise, she found a smaller crate containing grenades, making her wonder who the buyers were. The grenades appeared to be armed. She carefully grabbed a handful, placing them in with the weapons, then taking two for herself, just in case. She doused the crates with the kerosene just as she saw headlights flash across the windows in the front. She had no more time. She used the last remaining liquid to make a small trail, then eyed the stairs. She would never make it before the fire started.

She whipped her head around at the knocking on the door, spying Marcos's laptop in the process. She grabbed it, tucking it under one arm with one hand while with the other hand she searched for the matches in her vest pocket. Finding them, she struck one, held it for a second, then tossed it into the trail of kerosene, which caught quickly. As she darted for the stairs, the fire whooshed toward the crates, eager to consume the old warehouse.

The window in the front door shattered, and a hand reached through it to unlock the door. As she ran up the stairs, five men rushed inside and began swinging wildly, hoping to stop the blaze before it devoured the weapons they had just purchased. She had just reached the top of the catwalk when the first grenade exploded, its force tossing her around like a rag doll and slamming her shoulder against the wall. Screams from down below were masked as more explosions rocked the warehouse.

Flames and smoke crept higher as she made her way to the window. Marty had left it open for her. Then her eyes widened. *Oh, God.*

"Marty," she whispered, fumbling in the pocket for her

microphone clip. She found the earpiece, but not the microphone. She shoved it in her ear, immediately hearing Marty's frantic voice.

"Goddamnit, Kris, answer me," she screamed.

"Oh, baby, I'm sorry," Kris said, still searching her pockets for the microphone.

"Don't you do this to me."

"I know, I know. I'm sorry."

Kris tumbled out the window and onto the fire escape. She heard sirens in the distance. The fire department would be on the scene soon. Fire and police.

"Hang on, Marty. I'm coming." She had a moment of panic, fearing Marty would think the worst and leave her, running to Rico as Bailey had instructed her to do.

"Oh, God, Kris, please answer me," Marty pleaded in her ear.

Kris froze on the fire escape. Two men were down below in the alley, talking animatedly into cell phones.

She closed her eyes. *Don't leave me, Marty.*

She slowly pulled her weapon from behind her back. They spotted her before she could get a shot off.

* * *

Marty stood by the SUV, her eyes glued to the warehouse, now engulfed in flames. Silent tears streamed down her cheeks. She heard the sirens. She knew if she wanted to get out before the place was crawling with police, she had to do it now.

"I can't leave her," she whispered. "I can't."

Yes, she knew the drill. Yes, she knew she was supposed to call Rico. Yes, Kris had pounded it into her head to leave, to get to safety.

She had seen Kris take the microphone and earpiece off, had seen her shove them into her pocket. She knew what that meant. Kris didn't want her to have to witness another killing, to have to hear as she shot Marcos. Marty wanted to tell her it didn't matter. It would make her think no less of Kris. They'd never talked about it, but they both knew it was the only way to put an end to the Scorpion.

Something must have gone terribly wrong. Kris had no doubt started the fire. Surely she had. But why hadn't she gotten out? Why hadn't she used the microphone to let Marty know she was okay?

She brought her wrist to her mouth, her eyes staring at the microphone as if it were a lifeline.

"Kris, please…come back to me." She paused, glancing at the fire, the night sky glowing a bright orange as the flames danced. "I love you. Don't leave me like this."

* * *

Bailey's heart skipped a beat as she heard the whispered words. She ran back the way they'd come, keeping to the shadows. The sirens were loud now, only a few blocks away. She had to hurry.

"I'm coming, sweetheart," she murmured as she ducked into the last alley before she'd have to make a run for the SUV.

She waited, hearing the roar of fire trucks speeding by. She pressed close to the building, pausing to catch her breath. She held her arm, feeling the blood seeping from her wound. The men had gotten off two shots before she could return fire. They missed. She didn't, even though one of their shots had ricocheted off the metal fire escape, slicing through her arm. She hadn't had the time or strength to hide their bodies. The firefighters would spot them very soon, and then the hunt would be on.

She pushed on, hoping Marty was still waiting. Nearing the SUV, she spotted her lover leaning against it, arms wrapped around herself protectively. Bailey watched her for a second, wondering what was going through Marty's mind. Was she fearing the worst? She shook her head to clear it. Now wasn't the time for reflection. They needed to be on the move.

"Wasn't the plan for you to find Rico if things got crazy?"

Marty whipped her head around, relief flooding her face. She ran, nearly knocking Bailey over as she flung herself into her arms.

"Oh, my God. I was so scared."

"I'm sorry." Bailey pulled her close in a tight hug.

"Why the *hell* didn't you answer me?"

"I kinda lost my microphone." She stepped away, pointing at her arm. "You drive. We need to go."

"You're hurt? What happened?"

"Come on. We'll talk on the way. As soon as they find the bodies, this place will be crawling with police." Marty didn't ask what bodies or how many, and for that, Bailey was thankful. "Leave the lights off until we're a block or so away," she instructed.

The glow from the fire brightened the night sky, and Bailey watched it fade from view as she leaned her head against the glass, viewing the reflection in the side mirror. She slowly turned her head.

"Thank you for not leaving me."

Marty smiled. "I only agreed to your plan to humor you. I never had any intention of leaving without you." Marty glanced at her arm. "Do you need a doctor? There's a lot of blood."

Bailey shook her head. "Can't. Gunshot wounds have to be reported to the police."

"My God. What happened?"

"Wasn't a direct hit. Two guys were in the alley when I was leaving the warehouse. They got a couple of shots off. A ricochet got me."

"What happened inside?"

"Doesn't matter. It's taken care of."

"Kris—"

"No. Please, Marty, I don't want to talk about it." Maybe later, she'd tell Marty what happened, but not now. Yes, it had to be done. But still, she was a cop, she wasn't supposed to kill. But that was a lie, wasn't it? She was no longer a cop. She had long ago crossed that line. The events of the night just cemented that deal. She took a deep breath. "I killed him," she said quietly. "It was the only way to end this."

"I know. I also know the kind of person you are. I know this is going to haunt you." Marty paused, reaching over and touching Bailey's face. "I know you sent me away so that I wouldn't have to witness that. I want you to know—it wouldn't have made me think any less of you."

"He killed Carlos because he came into the alley. He saw Marcos kill a man, a man who worked for him. He was stealing money so Marcos was making an example of him. Carlos saw. So Carlos got the same fate as the man—butchered on the street."

"And our assumptions that the Scorpion was just a name?"

"It started with his grandfather, then his father. A drug business, apparently. Marcos moved it to weapons."

"So the whole time he was a cop, he was dirty?"

"Yes. He's been on the force over twenty years. He was his own mole." She pointed to a strip center with a 24-hour pharmacy. "Pull in here."

Marty did as she instructed, parking away from the door.

"Get some bandages, something to stop the bleeding."

"Let me see it."

Bailey pulled her sleeve up, revealing her mangled skin. There was only a dull throbbing now, but blood still seeped from the wound.

"You need a doctor," Marty said.

"I know. But not here. We'll cross the border in the morning."

Marty smiled. "So I get to play nurse tonight?"

"Yes. You can play nurse. I'll be a good patient," Bailey said with a wink.

Marty leaned over, brushing her lips across Bailey's cheek. "I'm really, really glad this is over with."

"Me too."

Bailey watched her hurry into the store. She leaned her head back on the seat. She was extremely tired, but there was still unfinished business. She pulled out her phone, not bothering to note the time. Rico answered on the second ring.

"Bailey? Are you okay?"

"Yes, fine. It's done."

"You found him?"

"Yes." She paused. "I need a favor."

He laughed. "Anything for you, Bailey. Need another car?"

"No. I think we can make do with this one." She opened up the small notebook she'd taken from Marcos. She ignored the blood that was smeared on the front. "If I gave you bank account numbers and passwords, could you move the money?"

"Of course. What are we looking at?"

"I'm not sure. He was dealing weapons, not drugs. I heard him give them an account number. He watched on his laptop for the transaction to go through. I have a notebook with about ten or fifteen account numbers. In case there are others to carry on the business, I want to take their assets."

"Okay. I'll take a look and see what's out there. Can you e-mail me the info?"

"Yes. I'll have Marty do it. I've also got his laptop. We'll take a look and see if there's anything useful on it. It might have some of his contacts or something. I'll want to get that to the authorities, but I haven't decided how to go about that yet. I want this mess cleaned up down here, but I don't want us dragged into it, you know." She leaned her head back against the seat and sighed. "And Rico, I need another favor."

"Name it."

"We need a safe place to hang out for a while. Across the border. I think we're going to have to stay under a little longer." She turned as Marty came out of the pharmacy. "I promised her a beach somewhere. Private."

"I can help you with that, yes. So tell me, Bailey. Have you lost your heart to this one yet?"

She smiled. "Afraid so, Rico."

"Wonderful. I like her. She's good for you."

"Yes, she is," Bailey said, her eyes on Marty as she got back

284

inside. "Thanks, Rico. I'll be in touch."

Marty's eyebrows rose. "Everything okay?"

"Yes. A few loose ends." She held up the notebook. "We're going to send Rico these account numbers. Marcos never talked about having a son, but if there's a brother or a cousin waiting in the wings, I don't want them to have the resources to continue in the business."

"Good. And we'll cross the border in the morning?"

"Yes. He'll find us a safe place to stay."

Marty started the engine, then glanced at Bailey. "Tonight?"

"We still have to stay under, Marty. For awhile longer, at least. I'm sorry. No hotel with room service."

Marty smiled. "So, a cheap motel it is. I'm getting used to those."

CHAPTER FORTY-FOUR

The sun beat down on them, but the constant breeze off the ocean cooled their skin. Bailey rolled her head, her eyes lighting on Marty's sleeping form as she rested on the chaise lounge, only four or five feet from the lapping waves. Four months in the sun had turned both their skins a golden brown, evidence of the lazy days they'd enjoyed. The blond hair Marty used to pay good money for had been replaced by her natural color, a light brown that Bailey had grown fond of. While they had both taken to keeping their hair short, she was particularly happy when her bleached hair had lost its color.

She got up quietly, not wanting to disturb Marty. She took their glasses, the ice in them long ago melted. She followed the path they'd made back to the main cottage, pausing to look over the dilapidated remains of the other cottages.

After Rico had secured the millions of dollars from Marcos's accounts, the most recent transaction—two million—deposited on the night of the warehouse fire, he'd found them this rundown resort. What might have been a promising endeavor years and years ago had failed when the previous owners couldn't provide the amenities necessary to remain in business. The place was nearly two hours from the nearest town of any size. Electricity had been provided by generators, water hauled in weekly. It had been vacant for at least five years, if not longer.

When Rico had first presented the idea to them, she'd balked. After the cheap motels and fishing cabins they'd stayed in, she assumed Marty would want nothing to do with it. But Marty fell in love with the place, the beach, the ocean—the privacy. So, they'd spent the first month making one of the cottages livable. They'd replaced the old generator with solar power and spent a small fortune putting in a well. Every other week they made the two-hour drive to town for supplies. Other than that, they spent their days in the sun, talking, getting to know each other, planning for the future.

Marty wanted to write. She thought the adventure they'd just been on would make for wonderful fiction. But so far, she'd been content with lazy days, only occasionally pulling out her laptop.

Bailey's future plans included tearing down the old cottages and building a home for them. She'd come to embrace the beach life, loving their morning and evening swims in the ocean, the solitude this private beach afforded them and the freedom they had to just be themselves.

Their contact with the outside world was limited, and Marty didn't seem to mind. Bailey certainly didn't. She'd asked Marty if she wanted to make a trip to Atlanta to get some of her things. Marty had declined. There wasn't anything there she couldn't live without, she had said. Her only request was that Kesara Romero be contacted. Rico took care of that.

Bailey regretted not being able to make it to Houston to say her final goodbyes to her mother, but she didn't want to chance it yet. The personal things she held dearest, mementos of her family, old photos, were still safe in the storage room in Port

Isabel. Rico would collect it for her later.

And after all that had transpired in Brownsville, Rico had convinced them to remain under. Bailey agreed. Even though everything they'd supplied to the authorities was done anonymously—Marcos's laptop included—Bailey wasn't naïve enough to think that they wouldn't eventually connect her, and possibly Marty, to Marcos's death. She also assumed they would make some attempt to find them. So despite her earlier declaration that she wanted her identity back, this place wasn't owned by Kristen Bailey and Marty Edwards. No, it belonged to Amanda Raines and Erica Jones. And Amanda and Erica were very wealthy women, thanks to Marcos's little notebook.

Bailey didn't care who the outside world thought they were. Here, they were simply two people learning to live—and love. For the time being, that was acceptable to both of them.

She finally moved on, going into the small cottage, which was kept cool by the breeze and the ceiling fans. She rinsed out their glasses, then filled them with ice and the last of the margaritas they'd made earlier. She stuck a lime wedge on each glass, then made her way back to Marty.

"I wondered where you'd gone off to."

Bailey's eyes lingered. Marty had removed her top, as she often did. Bailey pulled her eyes from Marty's breasts, blushing slightly for staring. Marty laughed at her.

"It still amazes me, sweetheart, that you can blush like a schoolgirl sometimes." She took a sip of the drink Bailey handed her. "I can't believe you got me hooked on margaritas."

"I do not blush like a schoolgirl," Bailey said. "I blush like a teenaged boy who got caught staring," she said. "And I do believe it was you who started the margarita ritual in the afternoons."

"So it was." Marty reached across the sand to take Bailey's hand. "Have I told you lately how much I've enjoyed being out here?"

Bailey smiled. "Not since this morning."

"Would it surprise you if I said this place feels like home?"

"No. The place we call home is the place we're comfortable in, the place we love in, the place we share with family."

"Yes, I suppose so. I'm certainly comfortable here." She grinned as she looked at her naked torso. "And we've certainly loved here." She stared out at the water, watching the endless waves crash on shore. "And we are each other's family. I like that." She turned, meeting Bailey's eyes. "I've never really felt like I had a home before. You make it a home, Kris."

Bailey brought their joined hands to her mouth, gently kissing Marty's. "I've had a home before, but I realize I've never really loved before. Not until you. When I tell you 'I love you,' I mean it from the depth of my soul."

She was no longer surprised by the misting of tears in Marty's eyes. It was something that occurred nearly every time Bailey told her she loved her. She had to remind herself that Marty had spent a lifetime without love. She knew Marty would never take this for granted.

Marty smiled and looked back to the ocean, blinking several times to keep her tears away. She squeezed Bailey's hand tightly.

"I love you."

The breeze carried the words away, but they were etched in Bailey's heart.

Forever.

Publications from
Bella Books, Inc.
The best in contemporary lesbian fiction

P.O. Box 10543, Tallahassee, FL 32302
Phone: 800-729-4992
www.bellabooks.com

WARMING TREND by Karin Kallmaker. Everybody was convinced she had committed a shocking academic theft, so Anidyr Bycall ran a long, long way. Going back to her beloved Alaskan home, and the coldness in Eve Cambra's eyes isn't going to be easy.
978-1-59493-146-8 $14.95

WRONG TURNS by Jackie Calhoun. Callie Callahan's latest wrong turn turns out well. She meets Vicki Brownwell. Sparks would fly if only Meg Klein would leave them alone!
978-1-59493-148-2 $14.95

SMALL PACKAGES by KG MacGregor. With Lily away from home, Anna Kaklis is alone with her worst nightmare: a toddler. Book Three of the Shaken Series.
978-1-59493-149-9 $14.95

FAMILY AFFAIR by Saxon Bennett. An oops at the gynecologist has Chase Banter finally trying to grow up. She has nine whole months to pull it off.
978-1-59493-150-5 $14.95

DELUSIONAL by Terri Breneman. In her search for a killer, Toni Barston discovers that sometimes everything is exactly the way it seems, and then it gets worse.
978-1-59493-151-2 $14.95

COMFORTABLE DISTANCE by Kenna White. Summer on Puget Sound ought to be relaxing for Dana Robbins, but Dr. Jamie Hughes is far too close for comfort.
978-1-59493-152-9 $14.95

ROOT OF PASSION by Ann Roberts. Grace Owens knows a fake when she sees it, and the potion her best friend promises will fix her love life is a fake. But what if she wishes it weren't?
978-1-59493-155-0 $14.95

KEILE'S CHANCE by Dillon Watson. A routine day in the park turns into the chance of a lifetime, if Keile Griffen can find the courage to risk it all for a pair of big brown eyes.
978-1-59493-156-7 $14.95

SEA LEGS by KG MacGregor. Kelly is happy to help Natalie make Didi jealous, sure, it's all pretend. Maybe. Even the captain doesn't know where this comic cruse will end.
978-1-59493-158-1 $14.95

TOASTED by Josie Gordon. Mayhem erupts when a culinary road show stops in tiny Middelburg, and for some reason everyone thinks Lonnie Squires ought to fix it. Follow-up to Lammy mystery winner Whacked.
978-1-59493-157-4 $14.95

NO RULES OF ENGAGEMENT by Tracey Richardson. A war zone attraction is of no use to Major Logan Sharp. She can't wait for Jillian Knight to go back to the other side of the world.
978-1-59493-159-8 $14.95

A SMALL SACRIFICE by Ellen Hart. A harmless reunion of friends is anything but, and Cordelia Thorn calls friend Jane Lawless with a desperate plea for help. Lammy winner for Best Mystery. #5 in this award-winning series.
978-1-59493-165-9 $14.95

FAINT PRAISE by Ellen Hart. When a famous TV personality leaps to his death, Jane Lawless agrees to help a friend with inquiries, drawing the attention of a ruthless killer. #6 in this award-winning series.
978-1-59493-164-2 $14.95

STEPPING STONE by Karin Kallmaker. Selena Ryan's heart was shredded by an actress, and she swears she will never, ever be involved with one again.
978-1-59493-160-4 $14.95

THE SCORPION by Gerri Hill. Cold cases are what make reporter Marty Edwards tick. When her latest proves to be far from cold, she still doesn't want Detective Kristen Bailey babysitting her, not even when she has to run for her life.
978-1-59493-162-8 $14.95

YOURS FOR THE ASKING by Kenna White. Lauren Roberts is tired of being the steady, reliable one. When Gaylin Hart blows into her life, she decides to act, only to find once again that her younger sister wants the same woman.
978-1-59493-163-5 $14.95

SONGS WITHOUT WORDS by Robbi McCoy. Harper Sheridan runaway niece turns up in the one place least expected and Harper confronts the woman from the summer that has shaped her entire life since.
978-1-59493-166-6 $14.95

PHOTOGRAPHS OF CLAUDIA by KG MacGregor. To photographer Leo Wescott models are light and shadow realized on film. Until Claudia.
978-1-59493-168-0 $14.95

MILES TO GO by Amy Dawson Robertson. Rennie Vogel has finally earned a spot at CT3. All too soon she finds herself abandoned behind enemy lines, miles from safety and forced to do the one thing she never has before: trust another woman.
978-1-59493-174-1 $14.95

TWO WEEKS IN AUGUST by Nat Burns. Her return to Chincoteague Island is a delight to Nina Christie until she gets her dose of Hazy Duncan's renown ill-humor. She's not going to let it bother her, though…
978-1-59493-173-4 $14.95